LAST WISH

Passage of Promise

LAST WISH

Passage of Promise

A NOVEL

TOM ROULSTONE

Covenant Communications, Inc.

Top cover image: *Sunlight* by Frank Benson, courtesty of *120 Great Impressionist Paintings*, Dover Publications, Inc., New York.

Bottom cover image: Tsar Nicolas II rowing with his family at Cowes during a royal visit, 1909 © MARY EVANS/MARY EVANS ILN PICTURES.

Cover design copyrighted 2008 by Covenant Communications, Inc.

Published by Covenant Communications, Inc.
American Fork, Utah

This is a work of fiction. The characters, names, incidents, places, and dialogue are products of the author's imagination, and are not to be construed as real.

Printed in Canada
First Printing: June 2008

14 13 12 11 10 09 08   10 9 8 7 6 5 4 3 2 1

ISBN 13: 978-1-59811-546-8
ISBN 10: 1-59811-546-4

To Diane and Larry

Acknowledgments

My thanks to all the good folks at Covenant, especially Angela Eschler, Noelle Perner, and the several anonymous evaluators, whose suggestions have greatly enhanced the original story. Much appreciation to Serenity for being my sounding board, in-home editor, and gentle critic.

Chapter 1

Dressed in a hunter-green travel suit with a small, feathered hat perched on her jet-black hair, Nell Keene looked every bit the London actress. With her delicate facial features and petite frame, she could pass for twenty. Actually, she had just marked her thirtieth birthday. Her lips formed a slight smile as she leaned back onto the plush head-rest, closed her eyes, and thought about her upcoming reunion with Ken and Karen Sanderson, both of whom Nell had befriended in England five years earlier.

"Tell me again why you're performing in Salt Lake City," Nell's manager and fiancé, Sir Lionel Freeport, said with ill-concealed disdain.

Sir Lionel was staring vacantly out the train window as the high prairie of southwestern Wyoming glided by. A big, handsome man with muttonchop whiskers, Sir Lionel wore a very English three-piece tweed suit and fashionable fedora. Nell shook her head impatiently, and her large, hazel eyes took on an uncommon firmness.

"Lionel, you *know* why," she said resolutely. "I made a promise to Mr. Sanderson, and I always keep my promises."

"Mmm," he harrumphed. "This one you could well have broken."

Sir Lionel continued staring out the window at the dotted tufts of sagebrush showing through a thin blanket of snow. Suddenly, his eyes flickered with interest on seeing a prong-horned antelope silhouetted against the blue sky. He focused on the animal's shoulder and knew just where he would place a bullet.

Nell let her memory pull her back five years. The first time she met Ken Sanderson was at the massive front door of Stephen Langton's shooting lodge on an island in Loch Lomond, Scotland. Langton, a man of dubious character, had lured Nell to the island under false pretenses, and she had been desperate to escape. Ken had an open, honest face, and Nell had no fear of asking him to take her from the island in his small, rented rowboat. Nell recalled with a shudder the icy water that had poured into the small boat and the horrific realization that Langton had sabotaged the craft. Nell and Ken had barely escaped drowning.

She wound her fingers tightly through the lace trimming on the seat cushion as she remembered the depth of hate she had seen in Langton's black eyes the day he had been sentenced to ten years in Newgate Prison. Langton had vowed not to rest until he had exacted vengeance on those whose testimonies had convicted him.

Nell slowly released the breath she had been unconsciously holding. It had been five years since that fearsome day. The memories had vividly resurfaced, however, in light of the news she had received days earlier. Langton had escaped from prison. *Would he carry out his threats?* Her knuckles blanched as she gripped the armrest. Glancing past Sir Lionel, she gazed out the window at the semibarren wastes, and her grip relaxed. *Stephen Langton can't touch me here in America.*

With some effort, Nell shrugged thoughts of Stephen Langton aside and turned her mind back to the Sandersons. She fondly remembered Ken's wife, the former Karen Gage. Nell and her late husband, Lord Darnley, had been dining in Karen's home, the ramshackle Gage Hall, in Somerset, England, when Karen, eyes sparkling with love, had announced her engagement to Ken. Nell smiled, thinking of Karen's shy but bright smile and Ken's expression of utter happiness. Nell applauded the union of the slim, handsome American and the pretty, strawberry-blonde English girl.

Nell felt all the more endeared to the Sandersons as she knew she had played a role in their engagement. She and Lord Darnley had helped Karen free herself of debt, paving the way for the Sandersons' marriage. Seeing the unfettered happiness of Ken and Karen had also strengthened Nell's sometimes-faltering belief in the reality of true love.

"Maybe I'll go hunting in Utah," Sir Lionel said, breaking into Nell's thoughts again. "Then our stop won't be a complete waste of time."

"You do that, Lionel," Nell said. "And I'll hold you to your word that you'll be courteous to my friends in Utah Territory." She stood up, and with a quick motion of her small, well-shaped hands, smoothed the front of her skirt. "I think I'll go check on the others."

* * *

"She should be here soon if the train got in on time," Ken Sanderson said to his wife, Karen, as he entered the parlor of their modest Salt Lake City home.

Karen stuck a dusting cloth into the top drawer of a sideboard, glanced around the room, and sighed. "I think the house is clean."

"It's been clean for days," Ken said wryly, "and still you've been dusting all morning."

Karen smiled at her husband's teasing. After five years of marriage, her heart still beat fast when she heard his footsteps coming up the walk. And when he came through the door, she still hurried to kiss his kindly face.

"Perhaps you should have gone to the station to meet them," Karen said.

"And leave you alone in your delicate condition? No chance." He smiled. "You'd think the queen of England was coming to visit. Nell may be from England, but she's only an actress."

Karen stared into the mirror behind the sideboard, pushing a blonde wisp from her brow and touching her plump cheek with her fingers. She sighed again. "A slim, beautiful actress, and me big as a house." She laid her hand on her protruding stomach and winced. "I wonder if she's changed in five years—her looks, I mean. I certainly have."

"As have I," he said with a smile, slumping his five-foot-ten frame and patting his barely rounded stomach. You feed me too well. As for you, dear, you've never looked more beautiful. You have a glow about you when you're with child."

She looked at him askance. "Fibber!" Then her face softened into a smile. "But a nice fib—I never tire of hearing it. By the way, what should I call her? Nell, Miss Keene, Lady Darnley? You know her better than I do."

"Shortly after I met her in Scotland, she insisted I call her Nell. But maybe we should use 'Miss Keene' in public."

Karen nodded thoughtfully. "I'm surprised she's really stopping here to perform. Salt Lake isn't exactly Boston or New York. I know she said she'd like to visit us someday, but those one meets abroad often say they'll visit, though they seldom do."

"True," Ken said. "But I believed her when she said if she ever did an American tour, she'd make Salt Lake one of her stops. Besides, Maggie is with her. After all the years Maggie looked after you and Mother, she wouldn't set foot in America without visiting you. Nell performing in *Sweet Lavender* is a bonus."

Karen smiled. "It will be wonderful seeing Maggie and Jack again. And this visit will give us a chance to truly show our appreciation to Nell for all she did for us."

Ken nodded. "Yes. If it hadn't been for her and Lord Darnley's generosity, you might still be saddled with the burden of that white elephant Gage Hall, and we might never have married."

He kissed her softly on the cheek as the noise of wheels on gravel reached them. "That's probably them now."

Hand in hand, the two walked out onto the covered porch just as a carriage drew up in front. "Wait here, my love," Ken said. "I'll bring them to you."

Ken gently helped Karen onto a bench and turned toward the carriage. As she watched her husband walk away, Karen caught her breath at the sharp pain of her stomach contracting. Ken was halfway to the carriage when her cry called him back.

"Ken, it's time," she gasped.

Hurrying back to his wife's side, Ken tried to steady himself. "Don't panic," he said, on the edge of panic himself despite the fact that this was their third child.

Ignoring the guests, he helped Karen into the house and onto a daybed in the parlor. Uncertain what to do next, he looked to his wife for guidance, anxiety mixed with adoration written across his face.

Karen smiled through her pain. "Perhaps you should get the midwife—your mother," she reminded gently.

"Of course! I'll get mother."

"You do that, Mr. Ken," an English voice called from behind them. Ken turned to see Karen's former maid—plump, middle-aged Maggie Tolley.

"Maggie!" Ken exclaimed. "You couldn't have come at a better time. Karen's having a baby."

"I've known that for months," Maggie said with a grin.

"No. I mean she's having it right now! I'm off to get my mother."

"So be off with you," Maggie said, giving Ken a light pat on the shoulder and briskly stepping toward Karen. Maggie was followed closely by Nell Keene and her long-serving maid, Marian Treadwell, a small, mousy spinster who had been a ladies' maid since she was fifteen.

"Don't you worry now. We'll take care o' things here," Maggie said.

"Thanks, Maggie," Ken replied. He acknowledged the other two women with a quick nod. On the porch he ran into Maggie's husband, Jack, and a gentleman with whom he was not acquainted. "Welcome to Utah, Jack, and . . ."

"Sir Lionel Freeport," the stranger said in a clipped, English accent. "Miss Keene's manager."

"Welcome, Sir Lionel," Ken said hurriedly. "I'm sorry, but I must run. Please, go inside—I'll return shortly."

Jack and Sir Lionel stared after Ken, surprised by his brusque greeting and hasty departure.

Inside, Nell, who had never had a child or much experience with childbirth, stayed out of Maggie and Marian's way as they bustled about, preparing Karen for the arrival of the midwife, Elisabeth Sanderson. Amidst the activity, Karen caught Nell's eye and mouthed hello, wincing as another contraction came. Nell smiled, and the years melted away.

* * *

"All'll be well," Jack said in his thick cockney accent. He sat in the hall watching Ken pace back and forth. A former British sailor, Jack propped his peg leg on a footrest to get more comfortable. "Ye should be used to it, lad," he chided gently. "Yer third, ain't it?"

Ken stopped pacing and sat across from Jack. He tried hard to concentrate on the conversation, but the knot in his stomach made it difficult. His eyes dropped to the floor, and his brow furrowed. Shaking his head, he heaved a sigh and looked at Jack. "I don't think I'll ever get used to it. But, yes, we do have two other children. Ainsley is four, and Gage is two."

He inhaled deeply and exhaled with another sigh. "This time something feels different, though. It's taking a lot out of Karen, and I'm worried. My mother and Dr. Shipp have been in there a long time. With all Mother's medical education and midwifery experience, she's never had to call Dr. Shipp before. And the way Karen cried out on the porch . . ." Ken left the sentence unfinished.

Jack's seaworn face took on a sober expression, and he didn't reply for a moment. Searching for a way to divert Ken's attention, he finally asked, "Did you hear about yer man Langton escapin' Newgate?"

Ken grimaced inwardly. Now, of all times, he wanted the dark memory far from his mind. But Stephen Langton's contorted, hate-filled face was indelibly etched into Ken's mind. Over the years Ken had tried to forget Langton's treachery and threats of revenge, but a slim shadow of foreboding had always remained—a foreboding that had grown stronger since Ken and Karen had received the news of Langton's escape. However, as much as Ken wished that Jack had not spoken of Langton, Ken was curious whether Jack had any more information about the escape.

"Yes," Ken said. "Maggie wrote us about it. Is his henchman, Jacob Gandy, still locked up?"

"Naw. They let 'im out a while back. 'Twas in all the papers afore we left 'ome."

Jack went on to tell Ken that when Chief Inspector Soames of Scotland Yard had learned of Gandy's release, he had assigned a plain-clothes policeman to follow Gandy in the hope that Gandy would lead him to Langton. However, Gandy "gave 'im the slip." When the policeman eventually picked up Gandy's trail, it had ended abruptly at the docks in Liverpool. A ship bound for Halifax, Canada, had just left with the morning's tide.

The possibility of Gandy and Langton being in North America tied a new knot in Ken's stomach. Although he felt little concern for his own safety, icy fingers gripped his heart as he thought of Karen, the children, and Nell.

"So, Gandy could be somewhere in Canada?" Ken asked Jack tentatively.

"Aye, lad. That's what the papers say. It's a good bet 'e's linked up w' Langton by now. Who knows where they might be headed," Jack replied grimly.

Ken knew that he could no longer dismiss his worries about Langton. Langton would have no scruples when it came to dealing with those on whom he had vowed revenge, and what was worse, the man was slippery when it came to the law. Not only had Langton attempted to murder Ken and Nell, he had killed a man in a knife fight—and gotten away with it. He had great wealth and would stop at nothing to get his way. Had he come to America to carry out his threats against Ken and Nell?

"Who knows, indeed," Ken repeated dolefully.

Seeing the concern etched across Ken's face, Jack regretted bringing up Langton and Gandy. With a dismissive wave of his hand, he tried to change the subject.

"Did ye know Nell and Sir Lionel are to be wed?" Jack asked.

"No, I didn't know that," Ken said absently.

"Aye, they's waitin' to get to Australia afore they make it public, like."

Seeing Ken's preoccupied expression, Jack tried again.

"Where are the little nippers?" he asked.

"Over at the Kimballs'," Ken said as he stood and began pacing again. He stopped in front of Jack. "You remember Jonathan Kimball. He taught Karen the gospel in London and confirmed her a member of the Church."

"Aye, the missionary chap. 'Ave you 'n' the missus got a name for the wee'un yet?"

"Karen if it's a girl; Kenny if it's a boy." Ken paused and smiled thoughtfully, and then Jack saw his face cloud over again.

"Aye, Mr. Ken, all will be well," Jack said quietly.

"There's something Karen said just after we were engaged, something that's haunted me for years," Ken said. "She had a feeling that we'd be separated for a season. I've felt . . ." Ken trailed off and again stood to pace the floor. "Never mind. I'm sure you're right. All is well."

Even as Ken said these last words, the knot in his stomach tightened and he suspected that all was not well.

Suddenly, a baby's cry came from the parlor.

"There," Jack said with a knowing nod, "Didn't I tell ye?" He removed his pocket watch and added, "Born at ten minutes o' ten in the mornin' o' Feb'ry eighth, in the year o' our Lord eighteen hun'red and ninety-one."

Ken breathed a relieved sigh. "Thanks, Jack. I'll note the time. Karen will want to know. I'm feeling better already."

Later, however, as Ken gazed on his wife's pallid face, his fears returned. Taking her hand to comfort himself as much as her, he sat beside the bed. He craved her assurance that, despite her faltering grip on his hand, her health would soon return.

"How are you, sweetheart?" he asked softly.

Karen had never seen her husband so worried. His brown eyes searched hers for assurance, and his brow was knit in concern. Not wanting to add to his sorrow, she squeezed his hand and said, "I'm sure I'll be fine, but this one's taken the strength out of me. How is she?"

Ken smiled encouragingly. "She's beautiful, like you. And she's in good hands. Mother, Maggie, Nell, and Miss Treadwell are all fussing over her."

"I'm glad." A sad smile played on Karen's pale lips and then disappeared. "Ken, if I . . . if I don't come through this—" She paused, staring straight ahead, as if trying to peer into the future.

The knot in Ken's stomach tightened.

"Of course you'll come through this," he said quickly, trying to keep the anxiety out of his voice. "Let's have no such talk."

She gazed up at him. As steadily as she was able, she said, "But what if I don't? I've been lying here thinking of what life would be like for you and the children if the worst were to happen."

Ken's body felt weak as the full weight of reality settled upon him and he considered the possibility of losing his beloved Karen. He could feel the blood draining from his face. But for Karen's sake, he held his composure.

Screwing up his courage, he spoke tenderly but firmly. "Karen, please don't. Don't talk of such things. I love you with all my heart and soul. You're going to get well. Let's not talk about such things. Please try and get some sleep."

Karen lay still, searching her husband's face. As much as she didn't want to distress Ken more than necessary, she felt a deep desire to discuss this somber possibility with him.

Drawing his hand to her lips, she kissed it and said, "I know you love me, dear. But please, we must be sensible. I saw the concern in Mother's eyes and in Dr. Shipp's. And more than that, I know my body. I never felt like this with Ainsley and Gage." She winced in pain, inhaled, and slowly exhaled before continuing. "Something's awfully wrong." She hesitated a moment, then said, "But you're right. I need to rest. We'll talk more later."

To Ken's relief, Karen did not broach the dreaded subject the next day. He hoped it had only been a temporary depression that had prompted the conversation the day before. However, on the morning of the third day after the baby's birth, Karen softly asked him, "Do you remember reciting Robbie Burns's poem 'Red, Red Rose' to me in the garden at Gage Hall?"

Rivers of ice flowed through Ken's veins. "I . . . I remember," he said.

"Please let me hear the last verse again."

Ken wanted with all his heart to refuse, but the expectancy in Karen's eyes and his desire to please her forced him to comply. Haltingly, he quoted:

> *And fare thee weel, my only love,*
> *And fare thee weel a while!*
> *And I will come again, my love,*
> *Tho' it were ten thousand mile.*

His voice caught as he finished, and tears ran down his cheeks unabated. Karen's eyes too were wet with tears. For a long moment, neither of them spoke. Ken wiped his eyes with his handkerchief and, taking a clean handkerchief from the drawer of the bedside table, dabbed his wife's face.

"When you first recited those lines in England," Karen finally whispered, "I had the impression that we'd be parted for a time." Her voice cracked, and it took several seconds before she could continue. "I think perhaps the season is here." Fixing Ken with her eyes, she added as firmly as her pain-wracked body would allow, "If I don't come through this, I would want you to marry again. The children would need a mother, and you would need a wife—a faithful, kind woman whose greatest joy will be in creating a happy home."

Ken wiped his eyes again. He desperately wanted to exude confidence, but his voice still shook as he spoke. "Don't fret, my love. If you were to pass on—and I don't for a minute believe you will—with Mother and Aunt Becky and everyone, the children would be well cared for. As for me, I don't know how I'd live without you . . . I know we'd be together again, but I don't know how I'd go on in this life."

"All the same," she said tenaciously, "I would want you to marry again. There are a great many good, single women in the valley—"

Ken kissed her on the lips to stop her from going on. But the stratagem didn't work. As soon as he withdrew from the kiss, she took a ragged breath and continued. "I only want you to know that you have my permission. I wouldn't want you to feel guilty in any way about taking a new wife." Pain tightened her lips as she tried to find a more comfortable position. "I've heard of wives suggesting whom their husbands should marry should they pass on. I won't presume to . . . to do that."

"Thank you for that, love. Now, can we please talk of something else? Or better still, let's not talk at all. You're worn out."

In the afternoon of the next day, Ken was reading the Book of Mormon at Karen's bedside when a light knock sounded at the door. Ainsley and Gage played quietly in the corner of the room, and Karen was asleep. Ken went to the door.

"Ah, Miss Keene," he said in a hushed tone, "how are you today?"

Nell smiled and, keeping her voice low, said, "Very well. Is Karen awake?"

Ken glanced back at his wife. "No" he said. "She has finally fallen back asleep."

"Good. In that case I'll not bother her. And may we go back to first names as before?"

Ken nodded sheepishly. "Karen and I were wondering what you would prefer to be called. Nell it is—at least in private."

Her lips formed the smile made famous on a thousand theater playbills.

"How are your accommodations?" he asked.

"The hotel is grand," she whispered. "And everyone is treating me royally. I have some time before I have to go to the theater tonight, so I thought I'd see how Karen is doing. Also, I have this little gift for the children." She held up a brown paper package. "But perhaps I'll stop by another—"

"Mine!" Gage cried out, yanking a well-worn rag doll from his sister.

"'Tis not," Ainsley said, grabbing the doll for herself. A tug-of-war ensued, neither child willing to give up the prize.

Karen stirred and moaned pitifully as her body woke to pain. Nell quickly crossed the room and knelt down beside the children. She took Gage, whose blond curls had been mussed in the tug-of-war, on her lap and returned the doll to Ainsley. She soon had the children playing quietly again.

Karen glanced at Nell and smiled appreciatively through her pain. "Thank you, Miss Keene," she whispered.

"My pleasure," Nell said. "But please, call me Nell. May I take the children to the parlor?"

"You needn't bother," Ken said. "I can ask Maggie to mind them."

"Oh, it's no bother at all," Nell said, pulling the children's surprise from the paper bag. "I'd like to show them how Jacob's ladder works."

When it was time for her to leave for the theater, Nell reluctantly turned the children over to Maggie's care.

"Thank you for letting me play with the children, Karen," Nell said before leaving. "They were fascinated with their new toy. We had a grand time."

"Thank you," Karen said. "I hope they behaved themselves."

"They were angels." And with an impish smile and a flick of her raven hair, she added, "My audience awaits. Cheerio for now."

Karen glanced at Nell and smiled. Despite her discomfort, peace filled her heart as she drifted back to sleep.

The next evening Ken brought Karen milk and English biscuits, her favorite snack. He tried to ignore the lack of color in her face and her weak manner. He wanted to viciously kick the bowl of damp, dark rags peeking out from under the bed. The bowl seemed to fill faster than it was emptied, and each hour Karen seemed to slip further away. But Ken forced a smile as he placed the tray before her.

"I'm sorry, dear," Karen said. "I just can't eat a thing. Please put them aside and sit by me." She took his hand and was comforted by its warmth.

"Nell came to see me this morning while you were out with the children," she said. "We had a nice talk. She's so kind." She paused, staring up at the ceiling, and whispered, "She laughs and plays with the children. She even sings with them. Maggie says she read them a story the other night and listened to their prayers before hurrying to the theater."

Karen's voice caught. She turned her head away and stared at the wall a moment to gather her emotions. Ken softly squeezed her hand. Facing him again, she continued resolutely with all the strength she could muster. "And besides everything else, I know she . . . she likes you."

Ken's brow furrowed. *Surely she isn't suggesting . . . No, it's absurd.*

"She likes us both," he said evenly.

Karen made a slight nod and went on. "When she and I talked at Gage Hall all those years ago, I sensed she had . . . well, a certain kinship with you. I was even a little jealous. But I knew you loved me, and I knew that she was devoted to her husband."

Ken didn't like where the conversation was going and quickly tried to steer it in another direction.

"Nell is a wonderful person," he said. "Perhaps if she comes back this way again, you and she could spend more time together—or maybe someday we could take a trip to England to visit her."

He stood up, walked to the window, and looked out. "Did she mention that she and Sir Lionel Freeport have an understanding? Jack told me when we were waiting for baby Karen to make her appearance."

Karen slowly turned her head from side to side, an indiscernible look crossing her pale face. "No. She didn't mention it." She paused. "They may have an understanding, but she doesn't love him."

Ken turned from the window and stared at her, his eyebrows coming together in a confused expression. "How could you possibly know that? You hardly know Sir Lionel."

Karen smiled weakly. "Yes. But despite our brief acquaintance, I think I know Nell."

Ken didn't question Karen but instead took another angle. "Apparently, they're to be married in Australia. It should be a good match, both of them being in the theater and all—a famous actress and a theatrical agent and manager. They live in a very different world from us, hobnobbing with the cream of English society as they do."

Karen sighed, tilted her head, and raised her eyebrows. "Is England so different from here? We have theaters, too."

He shook his head. "Theaters, yes, but not English society."

Karen slowly nodded. Her meager reservoir of energy depleted, she suddenly felt very tired. "Will you please give me another priest-hood blessing?" she asked in a voice so quiet he could barely hear. "I feel the need of it."

"Of course, dear. Rest now, and I'll fetch Jonathan to assist."

Chapter 2

"You should have gone to see Nell perform tonight," Karen whispered to Ken the next evening. "She came all the way from England. You should have gone."

Ken shook his head, leaned forward in his chair, and took Karen's hands in his. Even in her weakened condition, she was still beautiful to him.

"There's no place else I'd rather be than here with you, especially on the eve of St. Valentine's Day." Swallowing a lump in his throat, he continued. "And you're looking better. Soon you'll be up, and things will be back to normal."

Karen smiled ruefully. "What does it say in the Book of Mormon about liars?" In an attempt to hide the tears pricking his eyes, he bent his head and kissed her hand. She stroked his head gently. "Have you thought more on what we spoke of earlier?"

"No," Ken replied with resolve. "The mere idea appalls me. Please, sweetheart, mention it no more."

Karen sighed as the tears pricked her eyes as well. "I'm sorry, love, but since I may not be able to raise our children . . ."

Now the tears flowed freely, preventing her from going on. Ken gently took her in his arms and held her.

"Oh, Karen," he said. "Please don't distress yourself. The Lord will take care of us, whatever happens."

"I know," she said when she could speak again. "I know He will. And I have no fear of death, but I think of Ainsley, Gage, and baby Karen. That's why I want you to promise that you'll marry again . . ."

someone kind. I need to know that the children have a kindhearted mother to raise them in the gospel."

"I promise," he said at last, gently stroking her hair. "If you were to pass on, and I were to marry again, it would be to someone kind and sweet like you."

The sound of muted voices in the hallway drew their eyes to the door.

"Thank you, my love," Karen said softly. "I will speak of this no more."

At that moment a soft knock sounded at the door. "Come in," Ken called.

"We're sorry for visiting so late," Nell said as she and Maggie entered the room. "We were on our way home from the theater and wanted to pop in. I hope we're not disturbing you."

"Not at all," Karen said. "I've slept most of the day."

"And it's done you a world of good," Maggie said kindly. "You're looking much better. Isn't she, Nell?"

Nell smiled and nodded noncommittally.

Karen smiled at Ken. "So my husband tells me," she said. "But I certainly don't feel any better. How was the performance tonight?"

"Brilliant!" Maggie gushed. "It's a pity you wasn't there. Nell sparkled like a diamonite as Lavender. Surely, Salt Lake City has never seen the likes."

Nell blushed. "Hush, Maggie," she said. "I merely did an adequate job—neither a diamonite nor a diamond. What truly surprised me were the local players. Of course, they knew for months that we'd be doing *Sweet Lavender*. They had had plenty of time to prepare, but even so, they were marvelous—as good or better than those on the London stage. I felt honored to be part of the company. I wish I could stay longer."

Karen's brow creased. "Must you leave so soon?" she asked.

Nell sighed. "First thing Monday morning—several weeks in Los Angeles, the same in San Francisco, and then off to Australia." She knelt beside the bed. "I hate to leave you like this, Karen. I was hoping you and Ken could show me the sights and spend more time catching up."

"I would have liked that," Karen said reflectively and turned to her husband. "But there's no reason Ken can't show you around . . . you, Sir Lionel, and Miss Treadwell, I mean. Perhaps Ken's aunt Becky could go along too. She's been eager to meet you."

Nell shook her head firmly. "I wouldn't think of imposing. Ken's place is here with you."

For a moment, no one spoke. Then Ken added, "Aunt Becky's a great choice, Nell. She would jump at the chance to show you the valley. She's an amateur actress herself, actually, and as Karen said, she's very—" he paused and smiled, "*keen* to meet you." He ignored the groans at his pun and continued. "She's Jonathan's mother. You remember Jonathan, don't you?"

"Of course," Nell said, "Elder Kimball. How is he?"

"Just fine," Ken said. "His wife, Doris, gave birth to a fine boy only two weeks ago."

* * *

"It's magnificent," Nell said to Becky Kimball, a well-preserved, middle-aged woman with a kindly face. Nell, Becky, Sir Lionel, and Marian Treadwell stood at the mouth of Emigration Canyon, gazing down on the valley of the Great Salt Lake.

"It surely is," Becky agreed. "It's been a long time since I've been up here. Of course, it's much nicer in the spring."

Nell looked off to the west, relishing the feeling of the breeze blowing through her hair. "I like the snowcapped mountains very much," she said and then added reflectively, "I don't think I'd mind living in this beautiful place."

"In this bleak place!" Sir Lionel exclaimed, his forehead wrinkled in disbelief. "You can't be serious, Nell. It's . . . it's so disgustingly arid. Why people would settle in such a place is beyond me."

Nell, used to her manager's strong opinions, made a little clucking sound and shook her head. "Now, Lionel," she said, "restrain yourself. After all, we're guests here. It's true, the climate is rather arid, but the city has such beautiful, tree-lined streets. I really do believe I could be happy here. And I wouldn't even have to give up the stage. I'd be proud to associate with the Salt Lake City actors and actresses."

Becky smiled inwardly, tickled that such a renowned actress and widow of an English peer would look on her valley with such admiration. She wondered, however, if Nell were mostly being polite.

"Wouldn't you miss all the excitement of London, Miss Keene?" Becky asked.

"Of course she would," Sir Lionel interjected, indignantly attempting to disentangle a stubborn sticker weed from his bootlaces. Without looking up, he added, "Despite what you say, Nell, you're part and parcel of London's social life. A few months here and you'd be bored beyond belief. You'd be crying to go back to England."

Nell slowly shook her head. "No. I don't think I would. With Lord Darnley's passing, there's nothing to hold me there. I have no children, and I could easily dispose of my town house." Nell suppressed a smile as she watched her fiancé struggle with his bootlaces.

"Nothing to hold you there?" Sir Lionel said with dismay, finally dislodging the sticker weed. "I guess I don't count." He stalked toward the trail in a huff.

"Don't mind Sir Lionel," Nell said to Becky. "He'll cool down in a few minutes. He really is a good man. He's my late husband's nephew. Ever since Lord Darnley died, he's become much more than my business manager." Nell was silent for a moment. Then she sighed. "Perhaps he's right, though. He could never live here and—what do you think, Marian?"

The maid, who had been standing silent through the conversation, smiled wryly. "A body could live anyplace with the right man," she said.

"And is Sir Lionel the right man for me?"

Marian pushed a graying wisp of hair from her forehead and sidestepped the question. "It's not for me to say, is it?"

Nell glanced at Becky, who seemed ill at ease, looking like she'd been eavesdropping on a private conversation.

"I'm sorry, Mrs. Kimball," Nell said. "I fear we've been airing our linens in public. Let me explain. Although we won't make an official announcement until after I meet his family in Australia, Sir Lionel and I plan to be married by his brother Francis, the archbishop of

New South Wales. We're going there after my theater engagement in San Francisco."

Becky acknowledged Nell's words with a nod and a small smile but didn't comment. Marian turned to Nell as if about to say something but returned her gaze to the scenery. For the next few minutes, the three women surveyed the valley of the Great Salt Lake in silence.

"Have you seen enough, Nell?" Sir Lionel asked, returning to the trio. He had cooled down considerably and offered a warm smile. "I'm going hunting tomorrow and want to get back to the hotel and prepare my gear."

Nell nodded and turned to Becky.

"Yes. I must be getting back too," Becky said. "Would you like me to drop you off at the hotel?"

"Yes, please," Sir Lionel said. "Nell?"

"I think I'll go to the Sandersons'," Nell said. "I'm worried about Karen."

"We all are," Becky agreed solemnly. "She's in good hands, though, with Elisabeth and Dr. Shipp."

"And Maggie Tolley," Nell said. "She and her husband have agreed to stay here in the valley and help look after things. Karen needs Maggie more than I do. I have Marian, and we can hire women to help with wardrobe in Los Angeles and San Francisco."

As they rode back to the city, Nell still wished that she could stay longer. She had seen such goodness here. But her audiences were waiting in Los Angeles and San Francisco. And promises must be kept.

Chapter 3

Three days after Nell left for California, Ken awoke early in the morning. Since Karen's illness, he had been sleeping on a narrow cot alongside the double bed he and Karen shared. He glanced over at Karen. She was still asleep, but her breathing was irregular.

As he watched his wife's labored breathing, Ken was suddenly overcome by a feeling he could not brush aside. He knew with a sudden surety what Karen had been telling him for days: she was not going to recover. In a strange way, the realization was a relief. Denial had not permitted him to prepare himself and the children for Karen's death. Now he knew what he must do.

Slipping out of the cot, he knelt down and prayed for the courage and wisdom to do what was necessary. As he looked up from prayer, his eyes met Karen's.

She smiled weakly, reading the emotion in his eyes. "You feel it too."

He had become so accustomed to denial that he fervently wanted to maintain that she was wrong, but he could not. He hesitated, and his hesitation confirmed to Karen that he too knew the end was near.

"Over the last few days," she whispered, "I have said good-bye to friends and family. Today, I wish to bid farewell to you and the children. Will you please fetch the children after breakfast?"

He sorely wanted to say something profound and comforting to the woman he loved more than life, but no words came. He simply nodded and said, "Yes, dear."

Karen reached out her hand, gently stroking his hair, and together they wept.

Later, with Ken by her side, Karen held her baby daughter for the last time. Then Gage cuddled next to his mother. After a few moments, he reluctantly allowed himself to be placed in Maggie's arms. Ainsley was next. She crawled onto the bed, and Karen took her in her arms.

"Ainsley, my love," Karen whispered. "This will be hard for you to understand, but I must go away to a place called paradise, and you will not see me for a very long time. You're a big girl, and I want you to help Papa and Auntie Maggie look after Gage. And Auntie Doris will need your help with baby Karen. Will you do that?"

"I don't want you to go, Mama," Ainsley whimpered, tears streaming down her face. "Please don't go."

Karen tried to whisper words of comfort to her little daughter, but they caught in her throat. For many moments she simply held Ainsley tight. Ken leaned over and wiped the tears from the wet faces of his wife and daughter.

After a while, Karen drew strength and continued in a wavering yet resolute voice. "Ainsley, someday Papa will marry again and you will have a new mama who will love you as I love you. Until then, please help your papa and always remember that we are an eternal family. Someday we will all be together again. Until that day, goodbye, my sweet love. Never forget that I love you very much and would not leave you if I could—"

Karen's strength was gone. Ken took Ainsley from Karen's arms and led her to the door. At the door, Ainsley suddenly swung around and ran back to her mother.

"I love you, Mama," she said, burying her face in Karen's shoulder.

"I know, dear," Karen whispered. "And I love you more than I can tell you. But it's time to go with Papa now."

Ken gently took Ainsley in his arms and carried her from the room. They found Maggie in a large rocking chair with Gage in her arms, stroking his blond curls. She held out an arm to Ainsley, who crawled onto her lap beside Gage. After watching his two beautiful children a moment more, Ken returned to Karen.

Ken eased onto the bed beside her and took her in his arms. He slowly stroked her cheek, and with great emotion whispered the things he had dared not say when he thought that there was a chance his beloved wife might live.

That evening, with Ken and Elisabeth Sanderson by her side, Karen slipped peacefully away.

* * *

"Are you coming, son?" Elisabeth asked, gently touching Ken's arm.

He slowly shook his head. "No, Mother. You go on with the others. I'd like to stay for a while."

It broke Elisabeth's heart to see the worry lines of a much older man on her son's face. She thought of the five wonderful years he and Karen had shared, and she prayed fervently that Heavenly Father would ease Ken's transition to being a widower.

"Of course," she said. "I'll see you back at our house. Your father and I want you and the children to stay with us tonight."

He did not know how long he stared down at the casket in the open grave, but all the while a gnawing in his stomach increased, a gnawing that had started when he had heard Karen's cry on the porch. Each morning he had woken with it, and each night it had kept him from sleep. *How can the children and I live without you, Karen? I do know we'll be together again, but the thought of this long separation frightens me more than I can say. How will the children and I survive the years that lie ahead?*

His mind took him back to the bliss of their courtship. They had gone boating on the River Barle in Somerset, England, the day after they'd met. It felt like only a moment ago. He could see her sitting in the stern of the rowboat, dressed in a yellow frock with a pale green sash and matching bonnet. Her gloved hand slowly twirled a paisley parasol. *I've loved you since that day, my love, and I always will. No woman could ever take your place. I'll work hard to raise our children well. With Mother, Maggie, Jack, and everyone, Ainsley and Gage will be well looked after. Doris is wet-nursing baby Karen, along with her own new babe, and all will be well.*

Ken drew his eyes from the grave and stared up at the gray outline of the Wasatch Mountains etched into a cerulean sky. The mountains had always given him a sense of security, of permanence. But with Karen's death, even they seemed insubstantial. Next to the Savior, Karen had been his sure foundation, his rock. Now he felt adrift, anchorless on the sea of life.

A cold wind blew down the canyon, and he buttoned his coat against the chill. Bowing his head, he prayed for strength. The Spirit led his mind back to all he had learned about the Mormon pioneers, many of whom had lost loved ones. He thought of the persecution they had faced in the East, the hardships they had endured in crossing the plains, and the struggle they had endured to tame this inhospitable land. The Lord had sustained them in their trials—and he knew in his heart that the Lord would sustain him as well. The assurance did not relieve the pain, but he felt an unmistakable strength.

* * *

In the following weeks, Ken went numbly about his business as a reporter for the *Deseret Evening News.* His father, Gren, who was a senior editor at the *News,* kept a concerned eye on his son and did his best to lift his spirits. Charles Penrose, Ken's supervisor at the newspaper, suggested that Ken take some time off, but he refused. At least work kept his mind occupied.

Ken was grateful for the love and concern of friends and family. He had plenty of help with everyday chores—the fact was, he had too much help. He was left with long stretches of time to fill, time where he hardly knew what to do with himself. Before Karen's death, much of his time had been spent with her. Now he often spent his hours at home wandering the house, trying to keep his grief at bay.

Daytime was not as bad as the evenings. He soon established a new routine with the children. In the mornings, he had breakfast with Ainsley and Gage before walking to work. Maggie looked after the children during the day, and in the afternoon, she took them over to the Kimball home, where they spent some time with baby Karen. After work, Ken would walk to the Kimballs', and he and his three children would spend time together. Often, Doris Kimball invited Ken to stay for supper, giving Maggie some time alone with Jack.

The nights were brutal. After reading to Ainsley and Gage and seeing them safely tucked in bed, the hours stretched before Ken like a prison sentence. He had tried retiring early, but when he did, he woke in the small hours of the morning and lay awake thinking of Karen and his barren existence without her. Their love had made them one. Now he felt like only half a person. Although his faith in Christ and the restored gospel helped him continue on, he felt hollow inside and wondered if he'd ever be whole again.

One warm day in early spring, Ken took Ainsley and Gage down to City Creek to catch pollywogs. They were having a wonderful time. Ken was pleased that the children seemed to be doing so well. The three of them were sitting on the riverbank, dangling their toes in the clear water and eating a lunch Maggie had prepared, when Gage suddenly cried out, "Where Mama? I want Mama!"

Ken felt at a loss. How did one explain death to a two-year-old? But it was Ainsley who answered. She took her little brother in her arms, and, with her earnest blue eyes, she looked at him and said, "Mama's in paradise with Heavenly Father. We won't see her for a long time. But she promised us a new mama."

Ainsley turned her petite face toward her father. "Didn't she, Papa?"

Tears sprang to Ken's eyes. "Yes, dear, she did," he said, and he wrapped both children in his arms.

To Ken's surprise, Ainsley's words satisfied Gage, and his attention was soon taken with the tadpoles wriggling in the jam jar.

Ken savored these little triumphs. But they did not take away the agonizing void Karen had left. One evening as he was writing some notes for a newspaper article, the tip of his pencil broke. As he stared at the broken lead, he recalled a quote he had read during happier days: "Life is like a broken pencil—pointless." He rolled the lead back and forth until his fingers were blackened. In earlier days, the witticism had struck him as amusing; now it seemed profound.

Chapter 4

"Here I go again," Nell said to Marian as the two stood in the wings of the Orpheum Theater in San Francisco. Since leaving Salt Lake City in February, Nell had completed a successful, five-week run of *Sweet Lavender* at the Opera House in Los Angeles and another three-week run in San Francisco. She was now at the end of the second week of a two-week extension. Soon, she and Marian would be off to Australia.

Nell felt a pang of regret as she thought of the friends she would be leaving behind in America. She had wept when she received the news of Karen passing. She thought of Ken and his children and was deeply sorry for Ken's loss and wished she were there to offer words of comfort, however meager they might be.

"One more performance to end the week," Marian said, breaking into Nell's thoughts as she peeked out at the expectant audience. The hall was beautiful, with crushed velvet seats under an ornate, gold-leaf trimmed ceiling and bright crystal chandeliers. She closed the crack in the curtain and smiled encouragingly at Nell. "You'll win their hearts tonight just as you always do. But I wish you'd take it a bit easier. You'll ruin your health. You hardly took a break in Los Angeles. It was work, work, and more work! Instead of agreeing to these extra performances here, you should be relaxing on your way to Australia. I can only imagine how angry Sir Lionel will be when he gets your letter telling him you postponed your voyage."

"Don't fuss, Marian," Nell replied. "Sir Lionel will no doubt be cross at first, but he is my business manager and bookings are his business. Besides, working takes my mind off other things."

"Like your upcoming wedding?" Marian said. Nell ignored the question, and Marian quickly added, "Well, you only have next week's performances left, and then you're through. At least you'll have tomorrow to rest. I'm glad we'll have next Saturday and Sunday to prepare for our journey to Australia." She paused before adding, "As ever, I'll have a nice cup of tea waiting for you when you're done this evening."

"Thanks, dear," Nell said. "But about next weekend. I've been meaning to tell you that I've agreed to do a charity matinee on Saturday and attend a dinner at the British embassy that evening."

Marian's mouth fell open. "Why did you agree to such things? You need your rest. Besides, I planned on us having all day Saturday to pack. You know we have to have our baggage to the ship that day." She heaved a miffed sigh. "I guess I'll have to do it myself."

Nell wished she had consulted with Marian before agreeing to the matinee and dinner, but it was too late to do anything about it now. Her audience waited. She resolved to make it up to Marian.

"Thanks, Marian," Nell said. "I can always count on you. I must go now."

She swept onto the stage to great applause.

"She's quite a gal," Mr. Wylie, the elderly theater caretaker, said from behind Marian. He cleared his throat and said proudly, "I've been learnin' her American."

Marian's lips pursed. "*Teaching* her American," she said and stalked off to Nell's dressing room.

After the last curtain call, Nell went to her dressing room and found a still-miffed Marian poring over Nell's schedule for the following Saturday.

"I'm sorry, dear," Nell said soothingly as she began to remove her stage makeup. She touched a sponge to the exaggerated blush in the hollow of her cheek. "I just couldn't say no. The money raised from the matinee will go to the new Boys and Girls Clubs of San Francisco."

"Couldn't you at least get out of the dinner?" Marian asked, handing Nell another sponge. "What's it all about anyway?"

Nell paused and sighed. "I've no idea, but how could I refuse the British ambassador?" She paused in thought. "If we're not ready to go on Monday, I suppose we could postpone the trip until the next sailing."

Marian cocked her head to one side and studied her friend closely. "You're having second thoughts about your marriage, aren't you?"

Nell shrugged and averted her thickly lashed eyes. "What bride doesn't have second thoughts about marriage?" she asked quietly.

Marian's thin lips pursed. "I wouldn't. I'd jump at a proposal—if the right man asked me." Her last words, heavy with meaning, cried out for comment. But Nell didn't take the bait, and Marian added with a sigh, "But let's not postpone the sailing again. I'll take the bull by the horns, as they say, and get things all packed up by Saturday evening. You can rest on Sunday. On Monday we'll be off to the land Down Under."

"Thanks, Marian. How could I get along without you?" Nell closed her makeup case and stared into the mirror. She watched Marian leave the room in the mirror's reflection. Then she stared at her own solemn face looking back at her and quietly mouthed the words *Mrs. Nell Keene Freeport.* She sighed and shut her eyes, closing out the unsettled feelings that fluttered in her stomach.

* * *

On Sunday, Nell and Marian had breakfast in the dining room of the opulent Palace Hotel, where they were staying. An older man and his young companion entered the room. A waiter seated them near Nell and Marian.

"Handsome man," Marian said.

Nell glanced in the newcomers' direction. "They're both handsome," she said, "although they could do with some tonsorial attention."

"Tons . . . what?" Marian said, screwing up her slim face.

Nell smiled. "Haircuts," she said, smiling, twisting a lock of her own dark hair around her finger. "And their choice of clothing does leave something to be desired. They're about twenty years behind the times."

Marian nodded in agreement. "They seem a little awkward too—as if they're not used to dining in public. I wonder who they are."

Nell raised her eyebrows. "Should we invite them over and ask them?"

"Heavens, no," Marian said, hunching her shoulders to make herself less conspicuous, while at the same time surreptitiously glancing back over at the men. Suddenly, her hand went to her mouth and her head snapped forward. "Oh, my, I think they've noticed us spying on them."

Nell had no such inhibitions. She boldly smiled at the men. The older man acknowledged her smile with a nod. The younger man also smiled but quickly averted his eyes and gazed down at his plate.

"You bold thing," Marian said, chastising her employer. "Don't encourage them or they'll be over here after an autograph—or more."

But the men didn't approach them, and Nell and Marian finished their breakfast in peace. At Marian's insistence, Nell slept the rest of Sunday in an attempt to recover her strength. Room service provided their meals. At lunch the next day, however, the women again saw the odd pair in the restaurant.

"Oh, no!" Marian said. "The older one's coming this way."

"Good day, ladies," the man said as he approached their table. His words had a decided New England accent to them. "Please excuse my intrusion and permit me to introduce myself. Mr. Abraham B. Hawkins, at your service." He accompanied the introduction with a pronounced bow, which caused a shock of white hair to fall across his forehead. He swept the lock back in place as he straightened. Nodding toward the younger man, he added, "And that young fellow is Benjamin Franklin Hawkins, my son."

The younger Hawkins glanced at the ladies, nodded, and shyly averted his eyes.

"Good day, Mr. Hawkins," Nell said with a smile. "I'm—"

"No need, Miss Keene," he interjected with a wave of his hand. "We attended your performance on Saturday night, and I must say, you were superb as Sweet Lavender. I'll have you know that Benjamin is your greatest admirer." Nell glanced over at the younger Hawkins, whose cheeks were tinted with a blush. "We have tickets for the remaining five performances."

Nell smiled wryly. "You and your son must be gluttons for punishment, Mr. Hawkins," she said. "Actually, I've agreed to extend the run for one more day, a matinee on Saturday afternoon."

"We may even attend that one too," Mr. Hawkins said. "We're not heading for home until late that evening." Turning to Marian, he nodded and said, "And this must be Miss Treadwell, your faithful companion for many years. We've read nothing but good about you in the papers, Miss Treadwell."

Now it was Marian's turn to blush. "Thank you, Mr. Hawkins," she said, modestly lowering her eyes.

"But I'm intruding on your repast," Mr. Hawkins said. "Let me leave you to your meal. Expect a missive from me and my son anon."

"A missive?" Marian said curiously when Mr. Hawkins had returned to his own table. "What do you suppose he meant by that?"

Nell shrugged her slim shoulders. "Who knows? Perhaps they're going to invite us to dine with them."

Marian stole another glance in the men's direction and studied the older man's rugged, chiseled face. "I wouldn't refuse if Mr. Hawkins asked me to dine with him," she said with a sigh, her pale face crimsoning.

"Now who's being a bold thing?" Nell said with a grin.

That evening Nell and Marian returned to the hotel from the theater to find the promised "missive."

"What does it say?" Marian asked impatiently as Nell, sitting on her bed, broke the seal.

Nell read it silently, and her eyes became wide. "It's a proposal of marriage!"

"Marriage? Mr. Hawkins has asked you to marry him?" Marian exclaimed.

Nell slowly shook her head, "No. He's asked me to marry his son, Benjamin. Here, read it," she said, leaning back against the bed.

Marian took the sheet of hotel stationery and read aloud:

Dear Miss Keene,

Recently, when we deemed it was time for Benjamin to marry, he saw your image in a newspaper. He was so

taken with you; we saw it as a sign. On his behalf, there-
fore, I am requesting your hand in marriage.

I am a man of no small substance, the owner of Hawkins
Haven, a fine estate set in three hundred and twenty
acres of pristine land. Upon my death, all will be settled
on my son, who is an upstanding, God-fearing lad. He
will treat you well, Miss Keene, and you will want for
nothing.

You will, of course, need time to weigh your answer; hence
I invite you and Miss Treadwell to visit our estate and
take the time to acquaint yourself with Benjamin. We
eagerly await your reply.

Your servant,
Abraham B. Hawkins

"I wonder if his middle initial stands for 'bold'?" Nell asked.

Marian smiled wryly and facetiously asked, "Well, are you going to accept?" Marian caught the pillow Nell threw at her and added, "I mean their offer to visit their estate."

"Of course not," Nell said dismissively. "But it's sweet of them to make the offer. Benjamin appears to be a sensitive boy. I'll have to be careful in my reply. I don't want to hurt his feelings more than necessary."

For the next hour, Nell worked on her letter of rejection. Finally, she heaved a sigh, rewrote her scribblings on the bottom of Mr. Hawkins's proposal, refolded it, and sealed it with her personal seal.

"Well, Marian," she said. "That is the best I can do. It's late. I'll have a bellboy deliver it in the morning." Marian looked at Nell. It seemed to Nell she wanted to add something, but she remained silent. Nell caught the look and smiled. "Out with it, Marian. What have you to say?"

Marian lowered her eyes. "May I deliver it myself in the morning?" she asked shyly.

Nell cocked her head and curiously observed Marian for a moment before saying, "As you wish." Nell smiled, feeling all the more endeared to her loyal friend as Marian carefully tucked the letter inside her jacket for safekeeping and patted the pocket.

Nell lay in bed listening to the faint sounds of the city and Marian's snoring from the next room. She thought of Mr. Hawkins's proposal and smiled. *I wonder how many proposals I've had since going on the stage?* Inevitably, her mind turned to Sir Lionel's proposal, which wasn't really a proposal at all. "Lord Darnley spoke to me before he died," Sir Lionel had said, "and promised me your hand. We should wed in Australia. My brother can perform the ceremony after you meet my mother. Agreed?" Numb with the loss of her husband, Nell had nodded her head, and the die had been cast. Now she sighed at the memory. *I imagine I could do worse. Despite his gruff manner, I think Lionel does love me.*

The next morning Nell awoke to the sound of Marian walking into the suite.

"So early in the morning and all dressed up?" Nell teased playfully.

A blush started at Marian's neck and flushed her pale cheeks.

"I just delivered your note. Mr. Hawkins is a very nice gentleman. He invited me in to wait while he read your note. He was very disappointed when he read it, but he wasn't discouraged. Not one bit! He said if you only knew what a fine young man Ben is and how wonderful Hawkins Haven is, you'd reconsider. Then he went on to describe the estate. It's up in the mountains and sounds beautiful. The upshot is he's reinvited us. I'm for it. It would do you good to get away for a few days."

"Get away, Marian? I'm surprised at you. We're off to Australia on Monday. You're the one who said we must not postpone our voyage again."

Marian tilted her head and fixed her small brown eyes on Nell. "And you're the one who said we *could* postpone the trip until the next sailing. It takes such a long time to get there. A few more days wouldn't matter."

Part of Nell wanted to accede to Marian's wishes, but she knew she had delayed long enough.

"I'm sorry, Marian, but it's out of the question. I must go to Australia and face . . . and meet Lionel's family. Besides, we hardly know this Mr. Hawkins and son. They could be American Jack the

Rippers for all we know." She paused before adding, "I hope you didn't encourage them."

Marian seemed not to hear the question.

"I don't think Mr. Hawkins will give up easily," Marian said with conviction. "He's a very single-minded man."

"Single-minded or not, we are not going to visit his estate and I'm certainly not going to marry Mr. Benjamin Franklin Hawkins."

For a moment neither of them spoke. Then Marian, a little miffed, said, "Well, if we're not going to visit the Hawkinses' estate, at least it would be nice to have a change of scene. All we've done since arriving here is eat, work, and sleep. The food downstairs is excellent, but it would be nice to dine somewhere else for a change."

Nell knew that Marian was right and felt guilty about forcing her to follow such a rigid schedule, a schedule that kept even Nell too busy to think much about her upcoming wedding.

"We can do that," Nell said in a conciliatory tone. "Any suggestions?"

Marian didn't hesitate. "Mr. Wylie mentioned the Cliff House," she said. "It's supposed to be the best restaurant in the area."

"All right, Marian. We'll go there soon. I promise."

The next day, just before noon, Nell and Marian entered the Palace Hotel Restaurant and observed a third man sitting at the Hawkinses' table.

"Isn't that our hackney driver, Mr. Starkey?" Nell said. "The one who drives us to the theater? I wonder what he's doing with the Hawkinses?"

Marian shrugged. "Probably being pumped for more information about you. I told you, Hawkins is a very determined man."

Later that day, Nell was in her bedroom preparing to leave for the theater when a knock sounded at the suite door. "Please get that, Marian," she called.

"It's the hackney driver," Marian said. "He asks if Mr. Benjamin Hawkins could ride to the theater with us. His father is indisposed and won't be going tonight. Benjamin will ride up front with the driver."

Nell sighed and fixed a last curl in place. "I suppose. But I hope this isn't some scheme concocted by his father."

Benjamin Hawkins was already sitting beside the empty driver's seat when Mr. Starkey held open the carriage door for Nell and Marian. Ben nodded shyly at Nell, who gave him a tight smile.

"Young Ben is a likely lad. Thanks for letting him ride shotgun," the driver said as he closed the door and folded up the carriage steps.

Nell glanced at Marian and raised her eyebrows at the curious expression.

* * *

"I'm plumb tuckered out," Nell said with a grin as she entered her dressing room after her performance and plopped down on a sofa, landing in a sea of petticoats.

"'Plumb tuckered out,'" Marian repeated. "What language are you speaking?"

Nell smiled. "American. I got it from Mr. Wylie." Suddenly, her eyes lit up as she glanced at the dresser. "Red roses! My favorite." She got up, went to the flowers, and searched for a card. "Who are they from?"

"Your greatest admirer," Marian said. "Benjamin Hawkins. I discovered them when I came back here to make your tea. There was no card, but Mr. Wylie said the Hawkins boy left them."

Nell sighed and fingered a delicate crimson petal. "They're lovely, but I must put a stop to that young man's infatuation. Would you please have Mr. Starkey come see me?"

Marian fetched the driver, who had been waiting in his carriage to drive the ladies home to the Palace Hotel.

"Yes, ma'am?" Mr. Starkey asked apprehensively. "Have I done somethin' amiss?"

"No, Mr. Starkey," Nell said. "It's just that I think Mr. Benjamin Hawkins should find his own way to the theater from now on. He's . . . he's rather infatuated with me, and I don't want to encourage him. Do you understand?"

"I do, ma'am," the driver said. "I'll tell him right away. Is it all right if he rides back with us tonight? He's already on the seat."

"That would be fine, Mr. Starkey," Nell said, "as long as he realizes it's the last time." Nell slipped the man a coin. "Thank you, Mr.

Starkey, I'm sure I can count on you." Nell closed the door behind the man and turned to Marian. "All taken care of."

Marian raised her eyebrows. "If you say so, Nell. But I have my doubts."

Chapter 5

The next evening when Nell and Marian entered the carriage for the theater, the seat beside the driver was empty.

"Well, it appears that Mr. Starkey did his job," Nell said. "Benjamin is no longer—what did Mr. Starkey say—'riding shotgun'?"

Marian smiled. "He may not be riding shotgun any longer, but I doubt you've seen the last of him or of Mr. Hawkins."

Marian was right. That evening another bouquet of red roses appeared in Nell's dressing room.

Upon seeing them, Nell sighed. "It seems I must be firmer," she said to Marian. "Tomorrow I'll put an end to it."

The next morning in the hotel restaurant, Nell left Marian sitting at the breakfast table and confronted the two admirers.

"Thank you for the lovely flowers, gentlemen," she said. "But I really must insist that you cease your attentions. As I mentioned in my note, I am very flattered, but, I reiterate, all further expressions of your interest must end." Although she felt a bit unladylike speaking with such boldness, Nell knew that if she was not firm, the men might think she was simply being coy.

Mr. Hawkins, who, with his son, had stood up when Nell approached them, bowed his head contritely. "Our apologies, Miss Keene, if we have been too forward," he said. "But a man gets nowhere in this life if he gives up at the first rebuff—or the second for that matter. However, we will respect your wishes—no more flowers. As I mentioned when we first met, we are returning to our home tomorrow and would consider it a great honor if you and Miss Treadwell would dine with us this evening."

Nell was taken aback by the man's tenacity, and her first inclination was to decline; but Ben's hopeful expression melted her resolve. She also recalled her promise to Marian to dine at the Cliff House and knew that she would be making both Marian and the Hawkinses happy. Besides, she thought, what ill could come of dining in a public restaurant?

"Well," Nell said, "since you are leaving tomorrow, I imagine it would be all right. May I select the restaurant?"

"By all means," Mr. Hawkins said with a smile.

"In that case, I'll choose the Cliff House. Miss Treadwell mentioned it the other day."

"Capital!" Mr. Hawkins said. "We'll collect you in a carriage after your performance. Would that be acceptable?"

"No, but thank you all the same," Nell replied. "We'll have Mr. Starkey, our usual driver, transport us. We should arrive at about nine thirty."

"As you wish," Mr. Hawkins said. "Nine thirty, then."

"Well?" Marian asked when Nell returned to their table. "Have you put an end to it?"

Nell smiled sheepishly. "Not exactly. They've asked us to dine with them tonight, and I agreed." A broad smile crossed Marian's face, revealing her seldom-seen dimples. "And you'll be happy to know that we're going to the Cliff House Restaurant. Father and son are leaving San Francisco tomorrow, so that will be an end to it."

Marian continued smiling. "You really do have a soft heart, Nell."

"A soft head, more like," Nell said, self-deprecatingly.

That evening after her performance, Nell removed her stage makeup, changed into her street clothes, and was soon ready to go to the Cliff House. Marian took an uncharacteristically long time getting ready, and Nell, in a reversal of roles, ended up doing her maid's hair. It was after nine thirty when they met the Hawkinses at the restaurant.

Before seating them, the waiter ushered them out onto a deck where they enjoyed a magnificent view of the Pacific Ocean by moonlight. Eventually, they dragged themselves from the view and were seated. They all agreed on seafood, and soon a huge platter of scallops, crab legs, oysters, clams, salmon, swordfish, lobster, mussels, prawns, and squid was placed before them. While they ate they talked.

"Please tell us more about your estate, Mr. Hawkins," Marian asked.

For the next twenty minutes, Mr. Hawkins spoke expansively and proudly about his estate near Placerville in the Sierra Nevada mountains. Several times during his oration, Nell glanced across at Ben, who hung on every word his father spoke. Marian also seemed fascinated by what the senior Hawkins had to say.

When Mr. Hawkins had fulfilled Marian's request, he looked across the table at Nell and said, "Well, Miss Keene, has my description intrigued you enough to accept our offer for you and Miss Treadwell to pay us a visit? We're catching the late train tomorrow evening, so you have until then to change your mind."

Nell smiled. "It does sound intriguing, Mr. Hawkins, but I'm afraid I must decline. You see, Miss Treadwell and I are scheduled to leave for Australia on Monday. We are already almost a month late and my . . . my friend who is waiting for us will be much displeased if we tarry longer here."

"Your friend?" Mr. Hawkins asked.

A sheepish look spread across Nell's face. "Sir Lionel Freeport, my fiancé."

Mr. Hawkins's face fell. "Fiancé?" he said. "You said nothing in your note about being betrothed."

Nell bit her lip, feeling like she'd been caught in a lie. She sighed. "Actually, we're not officially betrothed. I must first meet his family."

"I see," Mr. Hawkins said. He shrugged. "Well, no matter. It has been wonderful dining with both of you. Living so far from people has its benefits, but it's nice to come to the city once in a while. Your company has made this trip special. Don't you agree, Benjamin?"

Ben nodded. "Yes. It has been very agreeable." He turned his eyes to Nell. Nell smiled inwardly as she watched the young man struggle to maintain eye contact. "Miss Keene, I . . . I never for a moment thought you'd be interested in me as a husband, although I was much taken with your picture. When my father suggested we go to San Francisco and see you, I was thrilled to go along. Thank you for being so gracious."

Nell was impressed by Ben's kind words. "Thank you, Benjamin," she said. "Tell us a little more about yourself; what are your interests?"

He thought about the question for a moment and shyly said, "Nature."

"And what can you tell us of nature, young man?" Marian asked.

Hesitant at first, Ben soon forgot his anxiety and, over the next half hour, described in detail the flora and fauna of northern California.

By the time the meal ended, with tea for the ladies, coffee for the men, and pastries for all, Nell felt a kinship with Mr. Hawkins and Ben and almost wished that she and Marian did have the time to visit Hawkins Haven.

"Are you sure you won't change your mind about going to the Hawkinses' estate for a few days?" Marian asked when she and Nell were back in their suite at the Palace Hotel.

Nell smiled. "Mr. Hawkins did make it sound wonderful," she said. "But I'm afraid I've dillydallied long enough. My duty is to go to Australia and bite the bullet."

Marian shook her head. "It sounds like you're going to a firing squad, not a marriage." She paused. "On the other hand, I imagine it would only encourage young Benjamin if we did go there. Despite what he said, he's still smitten with you."

And you, Marian, with Mr. Hawkins, Nell thought.

Chapter 6

"Are you sure you don't mind waiting for me, Mr. Starkey?" Nell asked as she descended from the cab in front of the British embassy. She wore a fashionable lavender silk frock and matching silk wrap. A small, sequined clutch purse completed her outfit.

"Not in the least, miss," the driver said. "I'll be here puffing on my pipe when you're ready to go back to the hotel. Enjoy yourself."

A burly, liveried doorman raised his hat to Nell as she entered the elegant building, and a butler took her wrap, handing it to the girl in the cloakroom. The girl gave the butler a chit, which he gave to Nell. She deposited the ticket in her purse. Following other well-dressed guests, she climbed a broad staircase to the second floor, passed several side hallways, and entered a magnificent dining room. All eyes were upon her as she was seated in a place of honor next to the ambassador's wife. On the other side of the ambassador sat a distinguished-looking man with a full, black beard. Before the meal began, the ambassador, Sir Stanley Arnold, welcomed the guests and especially the guest of honor, Miss Nell Keene. The host paused and smiled at Nell's expression of absolute surprise. He then introduced the man at his side as Sir Reginald Cripps, the proprietor of several diamond mines in South Africa, who was on a world tour.

"Sir Reginald," the ambassador said, "is a great admirer of Miss Keene, and he is, so to speak, the author of this feast. Sir Reginald, we would be honored if you would take the floor."

The man from South Africa rose and, leaning forward slightly, bowed at the guest of honor. For some reason, when he glanced in her direction, a feeling of alarm shot through Nell, but she brushed the feeling aside and smiled graciously at the man.

"I first saw Miss Keene perform in London several years ago," Sir Reginald said, stroking his beard. "And I must say, I have yet to see a better performance. When I learned that she was performing here in San Francisco, I made it a point to attend. During the performance, I felt moved to honor her with this dinner. I thank Sir Stanley for his kindness in hosting this affair and Miss Keene for gracing us with her presence. Please raise your glasses with me and toast our guest of honor. Miss Nell Keene, thespian extraordinaire."

As she listened to Sir Reginald's speech, Nell could not dispel the growing sense of alarm she felt. From her seat next to Lady Arnold, she could not get a good look at Sir Reginald, but there was something about his voice that triggered a fearful memory. The waiters had just begun to serve the second course, French onion soup, when she realized with shock who Sir Reginald Cripps actually was. He was none other than Stephen Langton, the man who had hired London toughs to assault Ken Sanderson; the man who had tried to drown her and Ken in the depths of Loch Lomond; the man who had vowed vengeance against her for testifying against him and who blamed her for his ten-year prison sentence; the man who had escaped from Newgate Prison after five years and was now at large. This dinner in her honor was a sham, she realized, a ruse put together to allow Langton to take his vengeance. Nell tried to think clearly, weighing her options and trying to quell the hammering of her heart.

As the waiter leaned over to place a bowl of soup in front of her, she joggled his arm, and the soup splashed onto her lap. She leapt up with a cry. The waiter turned white, and Lady Arnold turned red, both of them apologizing profusely.

"Please don't distress yourselves," Nell said. "It was my fault entirely." Turning to the waiter she added firmly, "Please show me to the powder room."

Behind the closed door of the powder room, Nell quickly sponged off her frock and then peeked into the corridor.

Seeing no one, she started toward the stairs. A feeling of relief engulfed her as she saw the exit door at the end of the hall. However, as she passed a side hallway, a man suddenly leapt from the shadows, yanking her off her feet and into the hallway. With an arm around her waist and a hand clasped firmly over her mouth, he hissed in her ear, "If you want to see your maid alive, don't make a sound. Gandy's got her, and he'll slit her throat if you don't cooperate. Now, I'm going to take my hand from your mouth, and we're going to walk out the front door together. If you scream, I'll break your neck, and you'll seal your maid's fate."

Shaking with rage and fright, Nell's first thought was to bite the man's hand and scream for help. But if what he said were true, she'd be endangering Marian. She decided to cooperate—at least for the time being—for her friend's sake. Slowly, the hand came away from her mouth, and she turned to face her attacker, a man of medium height, slender build, and piercing black eyes. A black beard obscured his face.

"Langton," she said through her teeth. "I knew it was you behind that phony beard."

Langton tilted his head slightly, and his lips formed a mirthless smile. "I should have known I couldn't fool an actress," he said. "No matter. I have you anyway." His lips curled into a sneer. "I swore retribution, and I'll have it; first on you and then on Sanderson. Act naturally or you and your maid will suffer the severest of consequences."

Nell's mind raced as Langton held her firmly, his fingers digging into her arm. She winced in pain as he further tightened his grip and marched her into the main corridor and toward the stairs.

Marian couldn't be in his power, she thought as they started down the stairs. *I left her dining with Mr. Hawkins and Ben. He's bluffing!* A chill swept through her. *But what if I'm wrong?*

When the doorman, who had been chatting with the coat girl, saw Nell and Langton approaching them, he speedily returned to his post.

"Leaving early, Miss Keene?" the coat girl sang out as Nell and Langton passed the cloakroom. "You're forgetting your wrap."

"So I am," Nell said lightly.

"Miss Keene has taken ill," Langton said quickly.

"Let me find my ticket," Nell said. "Oh, silly me, I've left it at the table. Sir Reginald, would you get it for me, please?"

Langton hesitated for only a split second. "Of course, Miss Keene," he said. "But first, let me escort you to your carriage."

"Oh, you don't need your ticket," the girl said to Nell. "I know right where I put your wrap."

The girl disappeared into the cloakroom. Langton held Nell fast by the arm and glanced nervously up the stairs. As the seconds ticked by, Nell's heart pounded against her rib cage, and her mind searched frantically for a way to extricate herself from Langton's clutches.

"What a pretty wrap," the girl said, handing it to Nell. "May I say how much I enjoyed you as Lavender? You were simply—"

"Come, Miss Keene," Langton interjected, subtly pushing Nell forward. "We must go."

Nell resisted and smiled pleasantly. "Please," she said handing Langton the wrap and indicating by a slight shrug of her shoulders that she wished him to put it on her. Under the gaze of the cloakroom girl and doorman, he had no choice but to release his hold, take the wrap in both hands and drape it around her shoulders. In a flash, Nell spun around, grabbed his phony beard with both hands and yanked as hard as she could.

Langton roared an oath, his hands clutching his searing face. Nell darted for the door, dragging her wrap with one hand and holding up her long skirt with the other.

"That man's an imposter," she yelled as she slipped past the astonished doorman. "He's Stephen Langton, a murderer and escaped convict."

Outside, she sprinted to the waiting cab.

"Quick, Mr. Starkey," she yelled, bounding up the folding steps, swinging the cab door open and jumping in. "To the Palace at all speed."

Wide eyed, the driver stuck his still-lit pipe in his pocket, folded up the steps, and leapt onto his seat. As the cab rattled away, Nell glanced back and saw the brawny doorman blocking Langton's way. She hung on as the carriage careened up and down San Francisco's hilly streets. As the adrenaline of her experience began to wear off, Nell shook with relief and fear. *Marian and I must flee the city immediately. But where to, and how?*

As the vehicle approached the hotel, Nell was overjoyed to see Marian chatting pleasantly with Mr. Hawkins and Ben beside another cab. An idea suddenly popped into her head. Leaping from the cab, she called, "Mr. Hawkins, does your invitation to visit your home still stand?"

The old man's face showed astonishment and then lit up. "Of course," he said. "But we must be off immediately or we'll miss our ferry to Oakland and our train."

"All the better," Nell said. Turning to her dumbfounded cab driver, who was still staring at her, she asked, "May I settle up with you later, Mr. Starkey?" The man nodded with surprise. With a quick motion of her hand, Nell waved her maid into the other cab. "Come, Marian."

Marian's mystified look turned to one of pleasure as she preceded Nell into the vehicle. Mr. Hawkins and Ben quickly joined them.

"Let's go," Nell said as she pulled down the window curtain closest to her. "Please close the window and draw the curtain, Ben."

Mr. Hawkins thumped the head of his cane on the ceiling, signaling the driver to go. As Ben started to close the window, he noticed smoke coming from Mr. Starkey's coat pocket.

"Mr. Starkey, you're on fire!" he yelled through the open window. Mr. Starkey, whose eyes were still fixed on the retreating coach, came to at once.

As the cab lumbered away, all eyes were fixed on Nell for an explanation of her erratic behavior.

She took a deep breath before saying, "I'm sorry for this intrusion, Mr. Hawkins, but Marian and I must get out of the city posthaste. A very dangerous man from our past has returned and means to do us harm. He—" She stopped talking and listened as a vehicle rattled past them going the other way. "That could be him now, heading for the Palace Hotel."

By the time they reached the ferry, Nell had related the story of Stephen Langton's crimes.

"Surely we should go to the police, Miss Keene," Mr. Hawkins said.

Nell shook her head. "No need," she said. "The British ambassador will call the police when the doorman tells him Sir Reginald's true identity. In the meantime, I'm sure Langton will go back into hiding. I doubt very much he'll follow us to your place."

At the ferry dock, a deckhand hustled the foursome aboard. Mr. Hawkins, Marian, and Ben, carrying two large suitcases, went into the passengers' lounge, but Nell remained on the deck. She pulled her wrap tighter around her and watched with relief as the deckhand winched up the hinged apron to a vertical position. It was at a forty-five degree angle when a black carriage rattled onto the dock. Nell's hand went to her mouth. The deckhand glanced up to the captain on the bridge for guidance. Nell's eyes likewise darted to the bridge, her heart racing. A sigh of relief escaped her lips when the captain signaled to continue raising the apron and get the ferry under way.

As the boat began to move away from the dock, Nell looked back to see a man get out of the black carriage and stare after the departing ferry. In the dim light, Nell couldn't make out the man's features, or those of the driver, but she knew in her heart it was Langton and his henchman, Jacob Gandy. As the black water between the ferry and the dock widened, Nell heaved another thankful sigh and joined the others in the lounge.

Later, on the train, Marian glanced at Nell and said, "I did manage to get the trunks packed and off to the ship, but I didn't get our suitcases packed. I can't imagine what the chambermaid will think of us when she takes a look at our rooms all at sixes and sevens, a jumble of clothes everywhere. I was hoping to finish up after supper, but—"

Nell smiled. "Don't fuss, Marian," she said. "We've just escaped the clutches of Stephen Langton. A messy suite is the least of our worries."

Marian nodded. "I suppose you're right." She glanced over at Mr. Hawkins, and a new worry line crinkled her brow. "Are you not well, Mr. Hawkins?" she asked.

Mr. Hawkins was wiping his shiny brow with a large handkerchief.

"It's probably nothing," he said. "But since I've been in the city, I've been getting bouts of perspiration and dizziness. That's why Ben attended the theater alone the other day." He shook his head dismissively, angry with himself for being ill. "I haven't been sick in many a year. I'm sure it will pass."

But it didn't pass. By the time they disembarked from the train at the village of Latrobe, Mr. Hawkins had to be helped to the waiting room. Nell and Marian attended him there until Ben returned from the livery stable with the Hawkinses' wagon, which would take them the rest of the way to Hawkins Haven in the Rubicon Valley.

With some difficulty, they managed to get Mr. Hawkins into the back of the wagon. Nobody seemed to know what to do next. Then Marian withdrew a handkerchief from her purse. "Does the bucket attached to the outside of the wagon have water in it?" she asked Ben.

"Yes, ma'am," he said.

"Please bring it here. I'll stay in the back and attend your father while you drive him to a doctor."

Mr. Hawkins's eyes blinked open. "No doctor," he rasped. "Don't believe in them. Get me home, Benjamin."

Ben looked to Marian for guidance.

"What should I do?" he asked her. "Pa knows more than most doctors. He has all kinds of natural remedies at home. We'd planned on traveling through the night, but we didn't figure on having you ladies with us. What should we do?"

"It's late," Marian said. "Is there a hotel in town?"

"Yes, the Latrobe Inn," Ben said.

Marian glanced at Nell, who nodded. "Then let's go there," Marian said. "We'll see how things are in the morning."

The next morning, Mr. Hawkins was no better, but he stubbornly refused to see a doctor. Ben and the ladies decided to take him home. After hitching the horses to the wagon, Ben picked up some food for the journey at the Latrobe Mercantile.

"So this is a covered wagon," Nell said later as she sat up front with Ben, a horse blanket around her silk-clad shoulders. Marian was in the back attending to Mr. Hawkins. "I've read about them and seen pictures, but this is the first time I've ridden in one. I guess you Americans would say I'm riding shotgun?"

Ben glanced sideways at Nell in her silk dress and wrap, both covered by the rough blanket. "And most appropriately dressed for the occasion," he said with a grin.

Nell laughed. "I hope you have some clothes at your place I can change into."

"We have," he said. "You know, I helped my father build this wagon. There is little he can't do with his hands."

Nell stared up the rutted, tree-lined trail and then at a range of purple mountains framed against the blue sky. She breathed deeply of the bracing, fir-scented air and pulled the blanket a tighter around her.

"The Sierra Nevada mountains?" she asked.

"Yes," Ben said. "Home."

"So you live out here in the wilderness."

Ben nodded. "I guess you could say that. Our closest neighbor is Mr. Watkins at the Sequoia Trading Post—over a day's journey from us by bridle trail."

"Could you get help for your father at this trading post if he needs it?"

"Not really. Mr. Watkins knows little about doctoring."

"How long have you lived in these mountains?"

"All my life. My parents are from Boston originally. They removed here over twenty-five years ago. It's been a wonderful life, but my father's not been the same since my mother died three years ago."

Nell gave Ben a compassionate look. "And you?" she asked. "How have you been getting along without your mother?"

Ben shrugged but didn't answer. For the next few minutes, they traveled in silence.

To lighten the mood, Nell said, "So you saw my picture in a newspaper and decided to come to San Francisco and woo me. Did you realize that I am somewhat older than you?"

Ben grinned. "No. You looked younger in the picture."

Nell smiled. "The power of stage makeup. By the way, how would you get a newspaper out here?"

Ben told of seeing Nell's picture in a copy of a newspaper someone had left at the Sequoia Trading Post. He had told his father he would like to marry someone like Nell, and his father, a self-made, single-minded man, had determined to get Nell for his son. When Ben suggested that Nell might not want to marry him, Mr. Hawkins had waved the objection aside. He maintained that any woman could be won with the right inducements. And wonders, he maintained, could be brought about with a positive attitude.

"At least we didn't try to kidnap you," Ben said with a grin, "like the Romans did the Sabine women."

"The Sabine women?"

"I read the story in Plutarch's *Parallel Lives,* one of the books in my father's library. Apparently, it was mainly men who founded Rome, and in order to build the population, they needed women. So they appealed to the surrounding tribes but were constantly rebuffed. Try as they would, they couldn't get wives. So they decided on a stratagem. They put on a huge religious festival and invited the local tribes, especially the Sabines. The Romans did such a wonderful job of advertising the festival, the whole Sabine nation came and were treated royally. However, on a prearranged signal, the youth of Rome suddenly grabbed the girls they had previously picked out and ran off with them. The parents had no choice but to go back home without their daughters."

"The poor mothers," Nell said. "They must have been heart-broken."

"Yes. And the fathers were so enraged, they declared war on Rome. But by the time the war began, many of the Sabine daughters had reconciled themselves to their lot, and some had even given birth. When the two armies faced off, the daughters threw themselves between the combatants and pleaded for their husbands' lives. Their request was successful, and the Sabines and Romans eventually became one people."

"An interesting story," Nell said. "Today it's called kidnapping, and there's a law against it."

As she spoke the word *kidnapping,* the vivid image of Stephen Langton entered Nell's mind, and a shiver went through her.

"Are you cold?" Ben asked, concern on his face. "Is that blanket not warm enough?"

"No. I'm fine. I just thought of Stephen Langton and the plans he could have for revenge on Mr. Sanderson and me. I shudder to think what he has in mind for us if we do fall into his clutches."

"I think you'll be safe here," Ben reassured her.

Nell nodded and took the conversation in another direction. "Anyway, you're right. You didn't resort to kidnapping Marian and me, but your father was very persistent."

"My father is a very determined man. He doesn't give up until he's exhausted all possibilities. He even wrote to a minister in Placerville asking him if he'd come to our home to perform the wedding." Nell laughed and shook her head in amazement. "You must understand," Ben quickly added, "that our living up here makes it almost impossible for me to find a wife."

Nell disagreed. "It's not impossible. You could do what most civilized people do to find wives—go to town and meet people at social events, like dances and such. You're a handsome man. I'm sure it wouldn't take you long to attract a young woman."

Ben pushed a lock of black hair from his forehead and glumly said, "I tried that. They only laughed at me."

"Who laughed at you?"

"The people at the Placerville Saturday-night dance."

She turned in her seat and inspected him.

"Well," she said, "they probably judged you by your appearance. If you cut your hair and dressed in a more modern way, you'd be a real prize. You need a woman's touch. Speaking of which," Nell began cautiously. "How did your mother die, Ben?"

Ben's face clouded, and Nell regretted bringing up the subject.

After a moment, he said, "She fell from her horse and hit her head. There was nothing we could do for her. It almost killed Pa, too. They were as close as two people can be. She's the only woman I've ever really known."

Nell's voice softened. "I'm sorry. You must miss her terribly."

Ben nodded. "Every day."

"Tell me about your parents. How did they meet? How did they come to be out here in the wilderness?"

Ben concentrated on his driving for several minutes in order to coax the horses up a steep incline. When they were on the level again, he said, "Pa was a bachelor until he was in his forties. By then he'd built up a successful business supplying mechanical parts to the cotton mills in Massachusetts. He started out with a small workshop—as I said, he can make just about anything by hand—and ended up with five factories. Then he met my mother, and his whole life changed. Her father was Elisha Potts, one of the mill owners. When Pa met her, Mother was a spinster schoolteacher in her late thirties."

Nell's eyebrows lifted. "A spinster schoolteacher?" She smiled.

Ben returned the smile and continued. "Mother talked Father into selling his business and removing to a place where they could get closer to nature. For two years they roamed America, finally settling on the Rubicon Valley. They each filed a homestead claim and gained title to three hundred and twenty acres."

"Where you now live."

"Yes." Ben glanced nervously behind him. "Would you please see how my father is doing?"

Nell pushed aside the canvas flap. "How is he?" she asked Marian.

"Sleeping fitfully," Marian said. "We really have to get him home. How much farther?"

Nell looked at Ben.

"We'll have to travel into the night," Ben said. "But don't worry, I know this trail well, and so do the horses. There's some food in a basket back there if you get hungry."

"Why did your parents settle on such an out-of-the-way place?" Nell asked later as they bumped along the rutted trail.

"It had everything they were looking for. You'll see. They first built a log cabin and lived in it while they built a bigger house. I was born in the cabin." He smiled shyly. "I was a great surprise to them."

"Yes. I imagine your mother must have been on the edge of her childbearing years." Lost in their own thoughts for several minutes, neither of them spoke. Then Nell said, "You know, you're quite articulate for a young man growing up in the wilderness."

"You can thank my mother for that. She was a great teacher. As far back as I can remember, she kept me to a strict study regimen."

"I have another question," Nell said. "Staying in the Palace Hotel in San Francisco, attending the theater every night, and taking us to the Cliff House Restaurant must have cost your father a fortune. Is he very rich?"

"I guess you could say that. He sold his factories for a huge sum, all of which he still has at interest in a San Francisco bank."

"I must admit your father's a remarkable man," Nell said. "Even if he's a little . . . a little unconventional."

Ben smiled. "He would consider that a compliment. He's committed to memory Mr. Emerson's essay 'Self Reliance.' He often quotes from it." Lowering his voice, he said in the tone of an actor, 'A foolish consistency is the hobgoblin of little minds, adored by little statesmen and philosophers and divines.'"

Nell laughed and shook her head. "What have Marian and I gotten ourselves into?"

Chapter 7

It had been three months since Karen's death. Ken sat at his desk in the newspaper office staring idly out the window. A huge bluebottle fly buzzed angrily, bouncing itself off the window glass. Ken empathized with the insect's frustration. Without Karen, he felt boxed into a life of duty to his church, his family, and his employer without the commensurate joy of sharing these responsibilities with someone who was equally committed to the task. It wasn't that he couldn't meet his responsibilities; it was just that they no longer gave him the joy he had known with Karen by his side. *Truly, "It is not good that the man should be alone,"* he thought.

"Here's some shocking news, son," Gren Sanderson said, coming up behind Ken with a piece of paper in his hand. "I just got it off the wire."

Ken scanned the headline and sat bolt upright. "Miss Nell Keene kidnapped!" he exclaimed.

"Well, that's the headline to sell papers," Gren said. "The real story is that Miss Keene and her maid, Miss Treadwell, have gone missing. Apparently, Miss Keene abruptly left a dinner in her honor at the British embassy. She had a scuffle in the lobby with a man masquerading as a Sir Reginald Cripps, who Miss Keene identified as escaped convict Stephen Langton."

Worry creased Ken's brow. "So Langton has finally surfaced."

Gren nodded. "Miss Keene managed to get away from Langton and make it back to her hotel. Almost immediately, the two ladies left in a cab with two other guests and haven't been heard from since. No one knows where they went."

Ken took all this information in before saying, "I knew we hadn't seen the last of Langton." He rubbed his temples and took a breath. "Nell may have escaped from him at the embassy, but I feel certain that he had something to do with her disappearance. He vowed to get even with both of us for putting him in jail. That was five years ago, but according to Chief Inspector Soames, Langton has a long memory and a long history of maliciousness."

"It's hard to believe he'd go all the way to San Francisco to get even with Miss Keene. I remember all you told me about this Langton character, but the notion does seem rather far-fetched," Gren said.

Ken nodded. "It does, I admit. But it appears to be the case."

Ken told his father about the conversation he had with Jack Tolley, and about how Langton's henchman Jacob Gandy eluded the police and was thought to be in Canada.

"Langton certainly took a chance of getting caught by showing up in San Francisco, and especially at the British embassy," Ken said. "With his aristocratic accent and ways, he'd stick out like a sore thumb."

For a moment, the two men were silent. "You say he escaped to Canada," Gren said thoughtfully. "I know of a place not far from San Francisco where he wouldn't stick out. A place he would blend in beautifully."

Ken stared at his father quizzically. "Where?"

"Victoria. Up in British Columbia. Victoria is very English. It's filled with second sons, retirees, remittance men, and the like. Langton could have gone there, changed his name, and no one would be the wiser."

"But according to Jack, Gandy took a ship to Halifax, on the east coast of Canada. If he was heading for the west coast, wouldn't he take some other route?"

"In the old days, yes, around the Horn. But since the Canadians completed their transcontinental railroad a few years ago, landing in Halifax and then taking the railroad across the continent is the fastest way to get to British Columbia from England."

"How do you know so much about Victoria?"

Gren smiled. "The chief of police—or chief inspector as he's called in England and Canada—is a friend of mine. I met Laird Mackenzie in California years ago when we were both panning the rivers for gold."

Ken pulled an atlas down from a shelf and opened it to British Columbia. Father and son studied it for a few minutes in silence.

"By sea, Victoria's certainly not very far from San Francisco," Ken said. "A couple of days by boat, I figure. Do you suppose Langton might have read about Miss Keene coming to San Francisco and traveled there to kidnap her and Miss Treadwell?"

"It's . . . possible," Gren said thoughtfully. "Does Langton know much about boats?"

"He does. He had an extravagant launch at his hunting lodge on Loch Lomond and operated it himself." Ken studied the map for a moment and excitedly tapped his finger on the expanse of water between Vancouver Island and the mainland. "The Strait of Georgia's dotted with islands just like Loch Lomond. I'll wager Langton has bought himself another island and built a lodge on it. It all fits!"

Gren smiled at his son's enthusiasm. "In folly ripe, in reason rotten," he quoted. "It all fits in theory, but if Langton's hideout is in Canada, he could be anywhere. It's a big country."

Ken heaved a sigh. "I suppose you're right."

Gren regretted throwing a wet blanket on the first enthusiasm Ken had shown since Karen's death.

"I'll tell you what, Ken," he said. "Brother Penrose has offered you time off, and you've refused. So instead, how about doing a story on this alleged kidnapping? I'm sure there's enough interest among our readers since Miss Keene was just here a few months ago. Go to San Francisco and tell the police all you know about Langton. You could even go up to Victoria and check out your theory that Langton might be hiding out on one of the islands. I could wire Chief Inspector Mackenzie to let him know you're coming. At the very least you'd get to see some of the most beautiful country in the world—at least that's what Laird claims. You could even do a travel piece on Victoria and the islands. It could be a wild-goose chase, but—"

"Like my running off to Scotland to rescue Karen and her aunt?"

Gren smiled. "If you hadn't run off to Scotland, you never would have met Miss Keene or started the chain of events resulting in Karen's getting out of debt and you two getting married."

"True," Ken said. "I do owe Nell a lot. Perhaps I could help pay my debt to her by working with the police." A surge of adrenaline pumped through him. Then he thought of his motherless children, and his enthusiasm died. "I couldn't leave the children. Maybe I'll just wire the police in San Francisco and Victoria and tell them our theory about Langton."

Gren placed his hand on his son's shoulder. "Ken," he said, "the children are doing fine. It's you that your mother and I worry about. You've lost your enthusiasm for life, and, if you don't mind me saying it, you haven't been much use around here. Take the assignment, son; it's what you need right now. And if Langton has kidnapped Miss Keene, you'll be invaluable to the police."

* * *

"Why can't me and Gage go with you?" Ainsley whined, wiping her tear-stained face with the back of her hand.

Ken's heart went out to his daughter. He sat on the edge of her bed and took her in his arms, hugging her to him and stroking her soft blonde hair.

"I'm sorry, sweetheart," he said, releasing her. "It just wouldn't work. Aunt Maggie and Uncle Jack will take good care of you."

"Auntie Maggie talks funny. I can't understand her sometimes. And Uncle Jack walks funny with that wooded leg. Clump, clump, clump. Why can't we stay with Auntie Doris?"

"Auntie Doris has her hands full with two babies to look after. You'll get used to Auntie Maggie and Uncle Jack," he said. "Did you know that Auntie Maggie took care of Grandma and Mama over in England? Now she's taking care of you and Gage."

Ainsley would not be consoled.

"Why do you have to go away?" she asked.

Ken heaved a sigh and had second thoughts about leaving.

After a pause he said, "Miss Keene . . . needs my help. She helped Mama and me a long time ago in England, and I feel I should help her now. I won't be away long. You're older than Gage, so you must look after him. Will you do that?"

Ainsley was slow to respond, but she finally nodded, and for a long moment neither of them spoke.

Ainsley broke the silence. "What if you don't come back, Papa?" Tears formed in her blue eyes. "What if you go to paradise like Mama and don't come back?"

Tears stung Ken's eyes. He took his daughter in his arms again and squeezed her tightly. "I'll come back," he said. "As soon as Miss Keene is safe, I'll come back. You can depend on it."

Ken took a handkerchief from his pocket and dried his daughter's eyes. Again there was silence.

"I like her," Ainsley finally said.

"Who do you like?"

"Miss Keene. When Mama was sick, she played with me and Gage. Will she come back with you?"

Ken shook his head. "I'm afraid not. She's going all the way to Australia—a very faraway place. And then she's going home to England where Mama was born. Go to sleep, my darling. I'll be gone before you get up in the morning, but you'll be well looked after while I'm away. I promise to return home as soon as I can."

Chapter 8

"It certainly is a beautiful room," Nell said to Marian. "It catches the morning sun."

Marian nodded in agreement. They were both dressed in nightgowns and robes smelling strongly of mothballs. They had arrived at Hawkins Haven late the night before, and, after Ben had supplied them with nightclothes, they had fallen into bed exhausted. Nell was sitting on the bed and Marian on a velvet-covered wingback chair.

Nell got up and went to the window.

"Come look," she said, excitedly pointing to the blossom-filled orchard and well-cultivated surroundings.

Marian joined her.

"It's just as they described it," Marian said.

Nell returned to the hand-carved bed and studied the comforter.

"I thought so," she said. "It's a rendition of this place! There's the cabin, the orchard, the waterwheel, and all. It must have taken months to make."

"No doubt the work of the late Mrs. Hawkins. My room is equally pleasant. I was so happy to have clean sheets! For two bachelors, they keep the place up nicely." She glanced out the window again. "The whole valley is a showplace."

Nell smiled in agreement. "True. It will be nice staying here for a few days. Hopefully, Langton will give up looking for us and crawl back to wherever he came from."

"It may be more than a few days, Nell," Marian said without a trace of regret in her voice. "We can't very well leave a sick man.

Besides, you've finished your run of shows. We should stay until Mr. Hawkins is feeling better. Like I said, a few more days late to Australia won't matter, considering the long distance."

Nell sighed guiltily, thinking of how upset Sir Lionel would be to realize she had yet again delayed their journey. "I suppose you're right. But as soon as Mr. Hawkins is up to it, we must make arrangements to get back to San Francisco and off to Sydney. Despite the letter I sent him, Lionel will be furious. In the meantime, we should find some clothes to wear."

"Ben said to help ourselves," Marian said, opening the wardrobe door. She fingered the material of a black housedress. "It seems strange to be wearing the late Mrs. Hawkins's clothes."

"Oh, don't worry, my friend. You'll get used to it. As you well know, I wear many costumes, most of which have been worn by others."

The next day, Marian continued her care of Mr. Hawkins while Nell toured the property with Ben. Although shy when away from the environment he grew up in, Ben was an outgoing and pleasant companion at home.

* * *

"It certainly is a paradise here," Nell said to Marian in their room on the morning of the third day. "If one doesn't mind the isolation, one could be very happy here."

"My sentiments exactly," Marian said with a wistful smile. Her eyes took on a dreamy, faraway look until a pleasant aroma from downstairs brought her back to reality. "What is that wonderful smell?" she asked.

"Freshly baked bread, if I don't miss my guess," Nell said. "The Hawkinses are surely treating us royally. Before we are completely won over, however, I think it's time to say something to Mr. Hawkins about Ben and me. He probably thinks his positive attitude has won the day and that I've fallen in love with Ben and this place."

"Must you, Nell? Everything is going so well. I wouldn't want to spoil things."

"I'm afraid I must."

Within the hour, they were called downstairs for breakfast. Nell wore a gray riding habit and Marian the black housedress. Both costumes were a little large for them. The table sparkled with the finest cutlery and blue willowware china service on a field of white linen.

"Please take a seat, ladies," Mr. Hawkins said. His self-doctoring, aided by Marian's ministrations, seemed to be working as he was now able sit at the table, although his face was still very pale. "I hope you like bacon and eggs and fresh bread. Ben baked the bread this morning."

"It all looks and smells so wonderful," Nell said. "But when Ben showed me around, I didn't see any chickens or pigs."

Ben grinned at his father and then turned to Nell.

"Keeping chickens was the only thing Father and Mother ever disagreed about," he said. "When Mother died, that was the end for the chickens. We stuck them in the icehouse. As for pigs, we never did keep them. Now we get our chickens, eggs, and cured ham from Mr. Watkins at the trading post."

"Icehouse?" Marian asked.

"Yes. We have an excellent icehouse," Mr. Hawkins said. "Every winter, we saw blocks of ice and preserve them in sawdust. Keeps things cold right into the summer."

At this break in the conversation, Nell cleared her throat. "Mr. Hawkins, in spite of the fact that you and Ben have treated us extremely well, I must make it clear that he and I are not a match. Besides being older than he is, I am engaged, remember. I wouldn't want you to think we came here under false pretenses. So if you would like us to leave, we will go immediately."

On hearing Nell's last words, Mr. Hawkins fixed his gaze on Marian, who answered his look with a small smile and then dropped her eyes to her plate. He then faced Nell.

"Thank you for your honesty, Miss Keene," he said. "I've known for a while that you and Benjamin are 'not a match,' as you put it. However, I can't tell you how much I appreciate your visit—both of you." Again, he turned his eyes to Marian. "You may stay with us as long as you wish. Your mere presence is our reward, Benjamin's and—"

A fit of coughing cut off his words, and Marian leapt up to attend to him. She remained standing by him when he was composed. He wiped his mouth with a napkin and looked to Nell for a reply to his previous words.

"Thank you, Mr. Hawkins," Nell said. "I will discuss with Miss Treadwell as to when we should return to the city."

"Oh, I don't think Mr. Hawkins is ready to be left alone," Marian quickly volunteered. "We must stay till he's better."

Mr. Hawkins nodded at Marian. "Thank you, Miss Treadwell," he said. "You truly are my Florence Nightingale. And now, if you would be so kind as to help me to the parlor, there is something important we must discuss."

As Marian assisted Mr. Hawkins from the room, Nell and Ben looked on with quizzical expressions.

"What does your father want to discuss with Miss Treadwell?" Nell asked.

Ben shrugged. "I have no idea."

Chapter 9

"Come in, Mr. Sanderson," the San Francisco police chief Brian Doherty said, rising from his cluttered desk and towering over Ken. As Ken took the policeman's extended hand, he was surprised at its softness. Dark circles showed under the policeman's eyes in an otherwise ruddy complexion. "Have a seat. Sergeant Blunt says you know the actress Nell Keene and might have information on the fugitive Stephen Langton."

"Yes, sir. I do know Miss Keene, and I do have a theory about Langton."

Chief Doherty's face showed disappointment. "I guess a theory's better than nothing. We have precious little to go on regarding his whereabouts, and the British ambassador is threatening to make an international incident out of it. He's understandably embarrassed that Langton used him to get at Miss Keene."

"What do you know about Miss Keene's whereabouts?" Ken asked. "You must have some clues to her kidnapping."

The policeman shrugged. "First of all, we don't believe she's been kidnapped. She and her maid could well be on their way to Australia, for all we know. The press started that kidnapping rumor. As to clues, we know they went off with two men who befriended them at the Palace Hotel, a Mr. Hawkins and son. As far as we know, they went willingly. It's my theory that after the set-to with Langton at the embassy, Miss Keene sought the protection of Mr. Hawkins, who took care of the ladies until Monday morning when they presumably boarded the ship to Australia as scheduled. As far as I'm concerned, the case is closed, but the British ambassador is pressuring us to find them and bring Langton to justice. So the missing persons file on the ladies is still open. I guess we'll find out for sure if they went to Australia when the ship returns in about five weeks."

"What do you know about these men, Mr. Hawkins and his son?"

The policeman raised his hands, palms up. "From all we've learned, their characters are beyond reproach. They rarely come to town. When they do, they stay at the Palace, a very expensive hotel. Mr. Hawkins has a bank account in town, and although he wouldn't give me any details, the bank manager vouches for his financial stability. From what we know they're a strange pair—old-fashioned clothes, long hair, and so forth. Apparently, over a period of days, they befriended Miss Keene. On the night before the disappearance, she and her maid dined with them at the Cliff House, a fancy restaurant out on the coast. The next night, Miss Keene attended the dinner in her honor at the British embassy, but, as you probably know from press reports, she left suddenly, before the meal had hardly started. Langton accosted her in the embassy lobby, but she got away from him."

"I'm so glad she did," Ken said. "There's no telling what he would have done to her had she not escaped. He vowed to punish Miss Keene and me for putting him in jail five years ago."

"So you know him personally?"

"Too personally. He tried to murder me," Ken stated bluntly. "My theory is that he tried to kidnap Miss Keene and, had he been successful, he'd have come after me. Where did Miss Keene go after she got away from him?"

"That's what we'd all like to know. From the embassy, she went back to her hotel and, according to witnesses, left with the Hawkinses in a hackney cab."

"What happened to Langton?"

The policeman shook his head. "We don't know. After a tussle with the embassy doorman, he got away in a waiting carriage— rented, we learned later. We found it abandoned at the San Francisco docks. We figure he might have left the area by boat since we can't find hide nor hair of him."

Ken thought for a moment before asking, "Have Mr. Hawkins and his son disappeared also?"

"Well, not to our knowledge," the policeman said with chagrin. "From what we've learned, they live away up in the Sierra Nevada mountains, which, of course, is far beyond my jurisdiction. However, if I knew exactly where, I'd love to take my fishing rod and go up there to see them." He glanced at the papers cluttering his desk and heaved a sigh. "Or maybe not. I'm swamped with paperwork. And as I said, I really don't think the ladies have been kidnapped. If it weren't for the pressure the British ambassador is putting on me, I'd put the file aside and concentrate on real crime."

The chief's confidence that Nell and Marian were safe lightened Ken's mind.

"If Miss Keene and her maid dined with Hawkins and his son," Ken said, "they must have been on familiar terms. Perhaps you're right. Maybe they are on their way to Australia."

The policeman nodded. "That's my theory. There is one puzzling aspect, though. Their suite at the Palace was a bit of a mess, clothes all over the place. Also, it appears that they didn't take much, if anything, with them. According to the bellman, someone from the shipping company picked up their trunks late Saturday afternoon and put them aboard the ship. Their hand luggage, though, is still in the suite. If they'd planned to go with Hawkins and son, surely they'd have left the suite in better order and taken some luggage with them. But this problem can easily be solved. After fleeing Langton, Miss Keene went directly to her hotel and, according to the Palace doorman, put herself under the protection of Mr. Hawkins and immediately went into hiding. For fear of Langton, I figure, she didn't even return to her room. We know from the cab driver that Miss Keene, Miss Treadwell, and the Hawkinses took the ferry to Oakland and were dropped off at the train station there. After that, we don't know what happened to them. They could have taken the train somewhere—one left for the east that evening—or stayed in Oakland until Monday morning."

"Wouldn't there be a record if they purchased tickets on the train east?"

The policeman shook his head wearily. Apparently, he'd answered these questions before.

"No. The ticket office was closed at that time of night. Of course, they could have purchased tickets from the conductor on the train, who is back east somewhere. I've left word for him to get in touch with me when he returns."

Chief Doherty glanced at the stacks of paper on his desk. "I'm sorry, Mr. Sanderson, but I really must get back to work," he said. "Can you briefly tell me your theory about Langton? I've requested information from Scotland Yard about him, but it'll be some time before I get a reply."

"Basically, my theory is this," Ken said. "After Langton escaped from Newgate Prison, it was rumored he managed to get to Canada. My father suggested that he might be in Victoria, British Columbia, as there are many Englishmen there, and he would blend in. Furthermore, like Loch Lomond, Scotland, where Langton has a hunting lodge, there are many islands near Victoria. So I reasoned that he might have bought an island and built another hunting lodge. I'm booked to go to Victoria on the *Osprey* tomorrow morning to check this out."

"It's a bit of a long shot," Chief Doherty said, "but it's worth a try. In the meantime, I wouldn't worry about Miss Keene. I'm sure Mr. Hawkins saw her safely onboard the ship to Australia. If that weren't the case, he would have reported it to us. As far as Langton's concerned, he's probably hightailed it back to wherever he's been hiding, and Victoria is as good a guess as any. It goes without saying that you should contact the local police in Victoria and not go after Langton alone."

"Don't worry. I have that covered. I'll be working with Chief Inspector Laird Mackenzie, a friend of my father."

"Inspector Mackenzie. I've met him. Good man." The chief rose and again offered his hand to Ken. "I'll wire Mackenzie if anything comes up at this end. Good hunting."

Ken paused at the door. "If you do decide to find Hawkins and his son—and if I'm available—may I go with you?"

The chief nodded hesitantly. "Yes. But you might have to find your way back by yourself—unless you like fishing."

* * *

That night as Ken lay in bed, his mind filled with unanswered questions: *Are Nell and Miss Treadwell truly on their way to Australia? Am*

I on another wild goose chase? If Nell has gone to Australia, will she and Sir Lionel soon be married? This last thought was strangely unsettling, but he brushed it aside. *Strange that Chief Doherty didn't mention Sir Lionel. Surely he would have gone to the embassy dinner with Nell. Or maybe he went ahead to Australia.* Ken sighed and closed his eyes, grateful for sleep, which temporarily freed him from the dull throb of loneliness, his ever-present companion.

Chapter 10

Chief Inspector Laird Mackenzie wasn't exaggerating, Ken thought as the ship from San Francisco steamed into the Victoria Harbor late Sunday afternoon. *Victoria surely is a beautiful place.* The screeching of gulls filled the air, and the tangy aroma of the sea filled Ken's nostrils as the *Osprey* docked at the wharf. Chief Inspector Mackenzie was there to meet the boat.

"Welcome to Canada," Laird Mackenzie said with outstretched hand. He looked just like Ken's father had described him—short, squat, and of a ruddy complexion. His sandy hair was thinning on top, and his blond mustache showed a hint of red. "Your father wired me a while back to tell me you might be coming, and yesterday Chief Doherty wired me some of the facts about Stephen Langton and the Keene disappearance. He let me know that you were on the *Osprey*. How was your voyage?"

"Very agreeable," Ken said. "A little mist and drizzle to start with. But it cleared up after a while. The scenery is marvelous, especially through the San Juan Islands and into Victoria harbor."

Laird nodded, pleased at Ken's reply. "For years I've tried to get your father to visit, but so far he hasn't taken the bait. Maybe when you tell him the facts, he'll come."

"I'm sure he and my mother would enjoy it."

"Well, follow me. I have a cab waiting to take you to the Camosun Hotel. I, unfortunately, must run off on some police business. Can you come to my office first thing tomorrow morning? The police station is within walking distance from the Camosun."

"I'll be there. Do you know if there's a branch of my church in Victoria? I thought I might be able to attend an evening service."

Laird shook his head. "Anthony Stenhouse, a member of the legislative assembly, converted to your church a few years ago, but he resigned his seat and went to Cardston, Alberta. I've also heard of a Copley family up island at Shawnigan, but as far as I know there are no other Mormons here."

"Thanks anyway," Ken said. "See you in the morning."

After checking in at the hotel, Ken went for a stroll, marveling at the lush greenery that graced the town. Upon returning to his room, he read the scriptures for a while and turned in early. In the unfamiliar surroundings, it took him a long time to fall asleep. As always, his thoughts turned to Karen, and he wondered what she was doing in paradise and whether she was thinking of him at that very same moment. He relived their last days together. *Was she really suggesting that I consider marrying Nell?* He shook his head and thought of the impossibility of it. *First of all, she's a famous actress and wouldn't want to leave the stage to raise children. Second, how could a woman who rubs shoulders with English nobility, politicians, literary greats, and so forth be happy living in provincial Salt Lake City?* And third, of course, Nell was not a member of the Church. However, he knew that Karen had not been a member of the Church when he had first met her. Nell did meet Karen's standard of kindness, which she had fully shown to Karen and the children. Furthermore, Nell had once mentioned to Ken in England that she longed to have children of her own.

"This is ridiculous," he said with a good measure of self-reproach. "Nell is most likely on her way to Australia to be married to Sir Lionel. And here I am wasting my time and my employer's money."

To salve his conscience, he resolved to waste no more of either. *Tomorrow, I'll diligently gather as much information as I can about Victoria and Vancouver Island and write the best article I'm capable of.* He smiled and mentally corrected himself: *of which I am capable.*

* * *

The next morning Ken found himself sitting across from Laird Mackenzie in the latter's tidy office, which contrasted greatly with Chief Doherty's cluttered one.

"Your father mentioned the possibility of an English fugitive being in this area," Laird said. "What proof do you have?"

"No real proof," Ken said. "Only conjecture. It's rumored that after escaping from Newgate Prison, Stephen Langton fled to Canada. Since he recently surfaced in San Francisco, my father and I thought that he might be hiding up here where he wouldn't be so conspicuous, being English. Also, if Miss Keene and her maid have been kidnapped, Langton is undoubtedly behind it. As you may know, on the evening of Miss Keene's disappearance, he accosted her at the British embassy, but she got away from him. Later, his rented carriage was found abandoned on the San Francisco docks."

The policeman nodded with interest. "Any other reasons that he might be here?"

"Well, he likes boats, and he has a hunting lodge on an island in Loch Lomond. My father and I feel that he may have bought one of the many islands in the Strait of Georgia. He's very wealthy and can pretty well do as he pleases."

Laird nodded thoughtfully. "What's your connection with Langton and Miss Keene?"

"That's a long story. Are you familiar with the Saladin ring case at the Old Bailey back in '86?"

The policeman's face lit up. "Ah, I wondered why Langton's name seemed familiar. Wasn't he after the ring but lost it to someone else?"

"Exactly. And I'm that someone else—at least, my mother is."

"But didn't Langton go to jail for attempted murder?"

Ken nodded. "He did. And I'm the one he tried to murder—actually, Miss Keene and me. He put a hole in my rented rowboat."

"Why?"

"To keep me from testifying against him. Earlier, he'd hired three London thugs to persuade me to withdraw my mother's claim to Saladin's ring. They roughed me up and might have done worse had a bobby not happened along. Later, we tied Langton to one of the thugs, Jacob Gandy. I brought charges against Langton for conspiracy to inflict grievous bodily harm and won the case."

"What was Miss Keene doing in your boat?"

"Langton had lured her and her maid to his lodge under false pretenses. When I showed up, she asked me to row her ashore so she wouldn't have to ride on Langton's launch."

Chief Doherty's brow furrowed. "When you showed up? What were you doing in Scotland?"

Ken smiled sheepishly. "What indeed? I was on a wild goose chase. Let me back up. Before the ring trial actually took place, Langton and one of the other claimants, Miss Karen Gage—whom, incidentally, I later married—made a pact. Miss Gage promised to sell the ring to Langton at a set price if she won it. After this agreement, Langton began treating Miss Gage as if he owned her. When she balked, he threatened to ruin her financially. Shortly thereafter, I tried several times to contact Miss Gage at her aunt's home but had no luck. When I found out Langton had fled to Scotland with two women—a younger woman and an older one—under mysterious circumstances, I assumed he had kidnapped Karen and her aunt. Off I went to Scotland, only to find that the two women with Langton were Nell Keene and her maid. As I mentioned, they had been taken there under false pretenses, and Miss Keene asked me to escort her ashore."

"All very confusing," the policeman said. "I hope you're not suggesting that Langton came all the way from London to San Francisco to kidnap Miss Keene because she preferred to ride in your boat rather than his?"

Ken smiled at the seeming absurdity of his story. "No, there's more to it than that. Miss Keene also testified against Langton in court. So you could say we both put him in jail. After the sentencing, he vowed to settle the score. He's obsessed with Miss Keene, and perhaps he thinks he might get to me through her as well."

"You've kept up your friendship with Miss Keene over the years?" Laird asked curiously.

Ken nodded. "In a roundabout way. Maggie Tolley, her wardrobe lady, was my late wife's maid for many years, and they kept up a correspondence. After I saw Miss Keene safely from Scotland to London, she said that if she ever did an American tour, she would make sure she scheduled performances in Salt Lake City. She did come to Salt

Lake, and that's when Karen and I renewed our acquaintance with her. Her schedule was published in the newspapers, so Langton would have known she was stopping in Salt Lake City and San Francisco. Perhaps he felt that if he kidnapped Miss Keene, I would come to her rescue, and he could take his vengeance on both of us."

"And you *have* come to her rescue."

"I guess I have. As I mentioned, Langton's involvement in Miss Keene's disappearance is only a theory, but I know he's capable of anything. I believe his assault on her at the embassy in San Francisco was a botched attempt to kidnap her. However, Police Chief Doherty is of the opinion that she got away and is on her way to Australia."

"And what do you think?"

"I really don't know. But we need to find Langton, whether he has Miss Keene or not. There'll be no peace for her or me until Langton's locked up again."

"Just out of curiosity," Mackenzie began, "how did Scotland Yard identify Langton's cat's-paw, Gandy, so quickly?"

"It wasn't hard," Ken said. "Gandy has a scar from his eyebrow to his chin and is well known in London's underworld."

The policeman was silent for a moment.

"You've come a long way from Salt Lake City on pretty slim evidence," Mackenzie said. After a moment's pause, he thoughtfully added, "It's strange that Langton would risk recapture in order to get revenge. He must really have it in for Miss Keene and perhaps you as well."

Ken nodded. "It does seem strange. But Chief Inspector Soames of Scotland Yard warned me that Langton is the sort of man who won't rest until he has retribution."

Laird stroked his chin. "Yes. History is full of such people—Napoleon, for one. When he escaped from Elba, he could have retired to live in peaceful obscurity. But something in him wouldn't allow him to do so. He couldn't resist one more kick at the can."

"Let's hope Langton's boldness in showing up in San Francisco will lead to *his* Waterloo," Ken said. "Speaking of my coming here on slim evidence, it was actually my father who talked me into it. As you may know, he's a senior editor at the *Deseret Evening News,* where I work. He wanted me to get away for a while and gave me the assignment to investigate Miss Keene's disappearance and to write a travel piece on this area. My wife died not quite three months ago, and I guess I haven't been much use at the newspaper office."

"I'm sorry to hear about your wife. She must have been young. Any children?"

Ken nodded. "Three, including a new baby. Fortunately they're in good hands while I'm off gallivanting."

A knock sounded at the door, and the desk sergeant poked his head in. "Sorry to disturb you, sir," he said, "but Mr. De Cosmos insists on seeing you. He says it is of the utmost gravity."

The police chief looked at Ken and rolled his eyes. "I assure you, I'll be just a moment."

"Of course," Ken said. "I can wait outside."

"That won't be necessary. In fact, I'd like you to meet him. He's quite a character, always putting a flea in my ear about something. All right, Yates," Chief Inspector Mackenzie said, nodding at the desk sergeant, who held the door for a tall, thin man dressed in a top hat and old-fashioned frock coat, and carrying a big-handled walking stick. The chief and Ken stood to greet the newcomer.

"Mr. De Cosmos," Chief Mackenzie said, "permit me to introduce Mr. Sanderson of Salt Lake City. He's a newspaperman like yourself."

"Salt Lake City?" De Cosmos said, shaking hands with Ken. "An interesting community, to be sure. I wintered there back in '52 and '53 on my way to the goldfields of California. Are you a Mormon?"

"Yes, sir," Ken said, waiting for a negative reaction, but De Cosmos's deep-set eyes showed no reproach.

"Despite how your people are depicted in the press, I found them to be hospitable," De Cosmos said, taking a seat. Ken and Chief Mackenzie also sat. "The Mormons had settled the Great Basin only a few years before I arrived and had a dearth of this world's goods, but they freely shared what they had."

The man's words pleased Ken.

"I'm glad you had a good experience in the Valley," Ken said.

De Cosmos acknowledged Ken's words with a nod and continued. "Although not yet thirty years old, I was able to give Governor Young some sound advice." Chief Mackenzie and Ken exchanged amused glances. "I warned him of the folly of removing the seat of government from Salt Lake City south to the Pauvan Valley. At first, he disregarded my advice. However, he soon found the wisdom of my words and, as you know, moved the legislature from Fillmore back to Salt Lake City. As for the practice of polygamy, which was officially announced just before I arrived there, I advised Mr. Young in no uncertain words to abandon the practice. It has taken a long time, but I understand my advice has finally been accepted."

Ken wanted to tell this somewhat egotistical old man that the change in policy regarding plural marriage, announced the year before, had nothing to do with his advice, but politeness restrained him.

The man continued. "And what brings you to our fair city, Mr. Sanderson?"

Ken hesitated, wondering how much he should say. "I'm here regarding the disappearance of the actress Miss Nell Keene and her maid," he finally said.

"Have you heard about the disappearance, Mr. De Cosmos?" Laird asked.

De Cosmos glowered almost contemptuously at the chief inspector. "Let me remind you, sir," he said, his voice going up an octave, "I am a newspaperman through and through. Daily, I read every paper available in this corner of the empire." Having made this statement, he dismissed Chief Mackenzie's question and turned back to Ken. "Are you personally acquainted with Miss Keene, Mr. Sanderson?"

"Yes," Ken said. "We met in Scotland five years ago and have recently renewed our acquaintance."

De Cosmos nodded. "While I am, of course, sorry that Miss Keene and her maid have vanished, I must say I am much aggrieved that an English actress would come all the way to the west coast of North America and perform in Los Angeles and San Francisco while ignoring the capital of British Columbia. Have we not theaters and companies here as well? I immediately dispatched a letter of protest to the editor of the *San Francisco Chronicle*. When you see her—and I have no doubt she'll show up sooner or later, as actresses are prone to publicity-seeking behavior—please extend my personal invitation for her to perform here. In fact, I will depart now and compose a missive to that end. I shall have it hand delivered to this office forthwith."

He rose to leave, and then, remembering why he had come in the first place, turned to Laird and added, "Chief Inspector Mackenzie, I really must insist that you do something about the drunken sailors, mostly Americans, cluttering up the footpaths of the inner harbor. A body cannot walk two feet unmolested. This travesty must be seen to instantly!"

"Duly noted, Mr. De Cosmos," Laird said. "And now, with your permission—"

"And another thing," De Cosmos continued, "Why is the *Prince Albert* continuously tied up at the government dock? I discussed this with Premier Robson the other day, and he agrees with me that the police boat should be policing, not sitting idle. It should be patrolling the inner passage and showing the flag. Floods of foreigners are sweeping over us, and we must impress upon them that this is firmly a part of Canada and the British Empire. Had it not been for the prompt action of my old nemesis, Governor Douglas, during the Fraser Valley gold rush of '58, there's no doubt the stars and stripes would be flying over British Columbia today! " After rapping his cane on the hardwood floor for emphasis, he concluded with, "Good day, sirs."

Wrapping his cloak around him, he exited the room with a flourish.

Laird smiled at Ken. "Well, what do you think of our illustrious Mr. Bill Smith?" he asked.

Ken's eyebrows lifted. "Bill Smith?"

The policeman laughed. "That's what his parents named him: William Alexander Smith, to be exact. He was born in Nova Scotia, and, as he mentioned, he spent some time in Utah and California. While in California, he had his name legally changed to Amor De Cosmos. I once asked him why he changed it, and he said he knew he was destined for greatness, and Bill Smith was too common a name. He chose his new name because to him it symbolized what he loved most—'Love of order as shown in the movement of heavenly bodies.'"

Ken thought of the Prophet Joseph Smith, whom he regarded as the greatest man of the nineteenth century. "To my mind, greatness is not found in one's name," Ken said, reflectively, "but in the way one lives his life."

"Well said," Laird responded sincerely. "Obviously, Mr. De Cosmos is entering his dotage now, but in his day he was a powerful influence in British Columbia. He founded two newspapers and led the movement to join the colony of British Columbia with Canada. He was even the premier of the province for a short time and also served as a member of the Canadian parliament in Ottawa. Unfortunately, he seems to be unaware that he's no longer in government."

"It's sad that senility is overtaking him," Ken said.

Laird nodded. "I'm afraid we may have to commit him to an asylum eventually. He's prone to using that heavy walking stick as a weapon, especially on the heads of drunken sailors. In the meantime, we put up with him. I've no doubt that before the day is out an invitation for Miss Keene to perform here will be hand-delivered, as he promised. Now, back to your reason for being here. It shouldn't be too hard to find out if anyone has purchased an island recently. Let's take a walk to the records department."

It had showered while Ken was in the police station. Now, as he walked beside the policeman, he breathed in the fresh, blossom-scented air with pleasure.

"Victoria surely is a city of flowers," Ken said.

Laird nodded. "It's the climate. Mild and damp."

* * *

After some research, the men found that over the last six months there had been several land purchases on the islands in the Strait of Georgia but only one of a whole island—Peregrine Island, purchased by one Selwyn Langley.

"Can you describe Mr. Langley, the man who recently purchased Peregrine Island?" Ken asked the clerk.

The clerk shook his head. "No, sir. It was arranged through an agent, Randolph MacCauley."

"MacCauley, eh?" Laird said. "Let's go, Ken my boy. I know him."

"Sorry, Chief Inspector," the real estate agent said in answer to the policeman's inquiry. "It was handled by Mr. Langley's agent, Cecil

Hardy. I never laid eyes on Langley. He must have some money, though. No quibbling—paid full price."

"It could be Langton," Ken said. "He's very rich. And the names Selwyn Langley and Stephen Langton do sound remarkably similar."

Laird smiled. "I worry we're grabbing at straws, lad." He rubbed his chin in thought. "Surely you must have an address for the purchaser, Mr. MacCauley."

Mr. MacCauley searched his files. "Ah, here it is. 2978 Hobson Street, Piccadilly Circle, London, England. It's strange that he didn't give a local address, because, as I recall, the signed paperwork came back to me in a few days."

"Mm," Laird said. "Perhaps he's on Peregrine Island. Thanks, MacCauley. If you hear from Langley or Hardy, please let me know."

Ken and Laird returned to the latter's office.

"Tell you what, lad," Laird said. "The wife's been pestering me to take her to Salt Spring Island to visit her sister. She and her husband are trying to get a farm going there. Since the premier and Mr. De Cosmos want to see the police boat on patrol, I'll commandeer it, and tomorrow morning we'll go by way of Peregrine Island." He smiled. "It'll be a treat to get out of my office and onto the boat. How does that sound?"

"First rate," Ken said. "And like my father said, at the very least I'll be able to see some of the world's most beautiful scenery."

The policeman smiled. "Your father should take his own advice."

Chapter 11

Ken's blood surged with excitement as the *Prince Albert* left Victoria's inner harbor, slicing through the whitecaps with ease. "It's not a fast boat or a new one," Laird had said when they first went aboard, "but it's well built and serviceable."

"Please tell me all about the area," Ken said to Laird, who was at the wheel. "As I mentioned, I'm working on a story for my paper."

Laird nodded. "Ogden Point," he said, directing Ken's attention at the shore to their right as the boat rounded a point of land and nosed into the Strait of Juan de Fuca.

As the steamboat cut through the surf on its way to the Gulf Islands, Laird gave a running commentary and Ken furiously scribbled in his notebook. Mrs. Marjorie Mackenzie, a few inches taller than her stocky husband, was of pleasant face and manner. Dressed in a warm tweed coat, she sat quietly knitting across from Ken. Two crew members completed the boat's complement.

"There are about two hundred islands here in all." Laird continued. "Peregrine is one of the smaller ones. It's just this side of Salt Spring—"

"Look!" Mrs. Mackenzie exclaimed.

Ken's gaze followed her pointing finger, and his heart leapt at the sight of the glistening, black-and-white bodies of three orcas arching in the sun. The whales paralleled the boat for several minutes before the pod moved off and disappeared.

Ken's heart raced. "I've never seen such a sight," he said.

Mrs. Mackenzie smiled. "I've seen them many times, but I never tire of it. Each time is like the first. Are you hungry yet, Mr. Sanderson?"

"I had a good breakfast only two hours ago," Ken replied, "and already I'm famished."

"It's the sea air," Mrs. Mackenzie said with a smile. "It quickens the appetite."

The policeman's wife produced a hamper and handed Ken and her husband sandwiches wrapped in butcher paper. She withdrew a bottle of milk.

"I know you Mormons don't use tea," she said, smiling.

Ken gave her an appreciative nod and thanked her. After a brief, silent prayer of blessing, he tucked into the thick brown bread slathered with butter and a thick slice of cheese. While they ate, it began to rain, sending them under the cover extending from the wheelhouse. It was only a brief shower, and soon the sun was peeking from between woolly clouds.

"What will you do if Selwyn Langley truly is Stephen Langton?" Ken asked Laird as they ate.

"Arrest him in the queen's name," Laird said without hesitation. "Generally speaking, on this edge of the empire I don't inquire about a man's past, and I've even been known to turn a blind eye to bench warrants for minor infractions. If I arrested every expatriate with a questionable background, the Victoria Jail would be full to overflowing. But, if you identify Langton as an escapee from Newgate, I'll gladly clap him in irons and put him on the next ship to England."

Ken nodded. "If I do see him again, I'll have no trouble identifying him. How much farther to Peregrine Island?"

"Not far. I won't be able to stop long as I have a lot of work in my office. I plan on leaving Mrs. Mackenzie at her sister's and returning to Victoria immediately. As I mentioned, Peregrine's not a large island, so we should be able to look it over quite quickly."

Suddenly, a staccato sound echoed across the water.

They listened as the noise grew louder.

"Sounds like hammering," Ken said. "Maybe Langley's building himself a house."

A few moments later, the police boat rounded the point of a large island.

"That's it," Laird said, pointing to a small, rocky island with a stand of Douglas fir at the center and some spindly, twisted oaks toward the edges. A scruffy tugboat sat at anchor in a scenic, half-moon bay. "Looks like there's no dock, so we'll anchor beside that tug and go ashore in the dinghy," Laird said. "Do you think that's Langton's boat?"

Ken shook his head emphatically. "Absolutely not. Langton wouldn't be seen dead in that. The launch he had in Scotland was all spit and polish. Also, his coach and four were meticulous. If that boat belongs to the owner of the island, I believe we've drawn a blank."

Laird nodded. Turning to his wife he said, "We shouldn't be long, love."

Marjorie Mackenzie nodded. "Be careful, Laird. Who knows what you might find. While you're gone, I'll catch up with my knitting."

"I'll be careful," Laird said. He turned to the crew members. "Put the dinghy in the water, boys, but stay here with Mrs. Mackenzie. I'll row." To Ken he said, "We'll go over the starboard side." Laird smiled at Ken's hesitation. "The right side."

Minutes later, Ken and Laird stepped ashore and pulled the small boat up onto the gravel beach beside a large rowboat as ill-used as the tug. The hammering increased as they climbed over some driftwood logs, up a slight bank, and through an ankle-high patch of salal, wet from the recent rain. In the corner of a cleared area, a small frame-building had been raised on a foundation of cemented rock. Curiously, the one small window in the building was barred.

"Looks like a jail," Laird said.

Ken nodded and sighed. "It couldn't be Langton's place. I can't believe his pride would allow him to build such a small structure."

Three men were perched precariously atop the building nailing cedar shakes to the roof. They stopped hammering when they saw Ken and Laird approaching them.

"Morning, gents," Laird said genially. "Sorry to disturb you. I'm Chief Inspector Mackenzie from Victoria, and this is Mr. Sanderson. And who might you be?"

Before answering, the oldest of the three glanced at the others, his brow furrowed. He returned his gaze to Ken and Laird. "John Bellamy," he said in a gruff English accent. He nodded at his companions. "These are m' boys."

"Pleased to meet you," Laird said. "We're looking for Mr. Selwyn Langley."

"He ain't 'ere," Bellamy said quickly.

"Do you know where he is?" Laird asked.

"Never met the man," Bellamy said. "All my dealings 'ave been with Mr. Cecil 'Ardy."

"Then where is Mr. Hardy?" Laird asked.

"Gone to Victoria in Mr. Langley's fancy boat, I reckon," Mr. Bellamy said.

"A fancy boat?" Ken asked, his interest piqued.

The younger of the two sons spoke up. "Slickest boat you ever saw, mister," he said. "Teak deck, oak cabin, polished brass everywhere. Yes, sir. Slickest boat you ever saw—"

"Enough," Bellamy said, cutting off his son. "Get back to work, boys. We's already behind schedule." So saying, he turned his back and pounded a nail with more force than necessary, splitting the shake. Cursing under his breath, he turned to glower down at Ken and Laird.

Undeterred, Ken barreled ahead. "Can you describe Mr. Hardy to us?" he asked. "What he looks like?"

"Say, what's this all about?" Bellamy asked.

"Police business," Laird said sternly. "Answer the question and be quick about it."

Mr. Bellamy looked at Laird suspiciously. "He's an Englishman like me, Mr. 'Ardy is," he said. "With all the rights an' freedoms of an Englishman."

Laird smiled at the implication.

"We're not here to abridge your rights, Mr. Bellamy, just to get a few facts."

"How tall and how old is Mr. Hardy?" Ken asked impatiently.

Mr. Bellamy pursed his lips, focusing his gaze on Ken, and said, "Not tall—short man 'e is. Maybe fifty years an' bald. An' if you don't mind, we'd like to get back to work afore it pours again."

Ken's heart sank, and he heaved a sigh. *Another wild goose chase,* he thought, *Just like Scotland all those years ago.* Turning to Laird, he shook his head and shrugged his shoulders. "It's not him, I'm afraid."

"One last question and we'll leave you be," Laird said evenly. "Do you know when Mr. Langley got back from San Francisco?"

Mr. Bellamy stared down blankly.

"Didn't know he'd been there," he finally grunted, grabbing another shake. "Can we get back workin' now?"

"Of course," Laird said. "Thanks for your help."

Father and sons bent to their work, and Ken and Laird headed for the dinghy.

"Well, we're back to square one," Laird said, disappointment evident in his voice. "Hardy is definitely not Langton, and we've no proof Langley is."

"True," Ken said gloomily. "But the mention of the fancy boat is a possible clue that Langley could be Langton."

"Maybe," Laird said more cheerily. "We'll keep investigating. And if nothing comes of it, you'll still have gotten a boat ride in the most beautiful place in the world."

Ken smiled. "I guess," he said. "But I sure hoped this would be Langton's lair, so we could rescue Miss Keene, and I could get back home to my children."

By the time they had rowed to the police boat and climbed aboard, Ken's spirits felt somewhat lifted. He breathed deeply of the fresh, tangy air.

"We ate only a little while ago, and I'm already famished!" he said.

Laird laughed. "Don't despair. We'll soon be at Salt Spring, where Betty'll feed us a wee bit of lunch. She's almost as good a cook as Marj."

Marjorie Mackenzie smiled at her husband's diplomacy.

As they continued on to Salt Spring Island, Ken felt the disappointment of the failed venture sink in. He hung onto the railing and stared down at the restless waves. He wondered if this whole trip to the Pacific Northwest was an exercise in futility.

Noticing Ken's somber countenance, Laird attempted to cheer him up.

"A story's told about a famous mariner," Laird began with a twinkle in his eye, "who for over forty years had worked his way up from cabin boy to captain. His first mate had been with him for fifteen of those years and greatly admired him. There was one thing that puzzled the first mate, though. Every morning the captain would open a desk drawer, take out a slip of paper, and read it with great concentration. When the captain finally retired and was replaced by the first mate, the latter, eager to solve the riddle of the slip of paper, opened the desk drawer, withdrew the paper and read, 'Port is left. Starboard is right.'"

Ken laughed, and Marjorie Mackenzie, who had apparently heard the story many times before, smiled and shook her head.

When Laird had run out of history lessons and humorous stories, Ken concentrated on the scenery as the boat threaded its way among the many forested isles.

"What are those trees with the peeling bark?" he asked Mrs. Mackenzie. "Their cinnamon color certainly stands out among the evergreens."

"Arbutus," she said. "Actually, they *are* evergreens—one of the few broadleaf evergreens in Canada. They're rare in other parts of the world, but as you can see, they're plentiful here."

As the *Prince Albert* chugged past an island, Ken's attention was riveted on a huge bald eagle perched atop a leafless snag jutting out at a forty-five-degree angle from a gray cliff. Suddenly the bird plummeted toward the blue-green water. With practiced grace, it quickly rose again, a writhing, silver fish clasped in its talons.

Ken turned to Laird, who had also been watching the eagle, and smiled. Laird nodded, a proud, proprietary smile on his broad, friendly face.

"Are these waters warm enough to swim in?" Ken asked after a few minutes.

Laird shook his head. "Not really," he said. "They're pretty cold all year round. I've heard of people falling overboard and going right to the bottom in minutes. It's the initial shock that gets them. If they survive the shock, they can last about ten or fifteen minutes. Of course, there are always exceptions. One man I know of lasted three hours clinging to boat wreckage."

"Although there are a few beaches," Marjorie added, "where the water is shallow and the sand goes out a long way. On a hot day, the sun's able to warm the water enough to be pleasant for bathing. But if one goes out to the deep water, it's always cold."

"One more question," Ken said, directing it to Laird. "Is it true what Mr. De Cosmos said about the Americans almost taking over this area in 1858?"

Laird smiled and tilted his head slightly. "Yes and no. Forty years earlier, what is now British Columbia was called New Caledonia and was part of Old Oregon—the land between California and Alaska. The southern part of Old Oregon was called Columbia. Both Britain and the United States claimed all of Oregon, but they finally agreed to joint occupancy of the region. As you may recall from your history lessons, in 1844, American presidential candidate James Polk decided that the whole region should be part of the United States. He campaigned on the political slogan 'Fifty-Four Forty or Fight!' In other words, if the U.S. didn't get all of Oregon, it would go to war with Britain. When Polk became president, however, the U.S. and Mexico went to war, and Polk was in no position to fight Britain as well, so in 1846, they reached a compromise."

1846, Ken thought, *the year the Saints were driven from Nauvoo.*

"The U.S.," Laird continued, "got Columbia, which became Washington and Oregon, and Britain got New Caledonia, which became British Columbia, including all of Vancouver Island or Vancouver's Island, as they called it then."

"I just remembered," Ken said. "President Brigham Young once suggested that Vancouver Island might make a good home for the members of our church."

"Really?" Laird said. "I didn't know that."

"I hope Laird isn't boring you, Mr. Sanderson," Marjorie said. "His father was recruited in Scotland by the Hudson's Bay Company when he was only a youth. He spent his whole working life in the service of the company. There isn't much Laird couldn't tell you about company history, which is just about impossible to separate from early British Columbia history."

Ken shook his head. "I'm finding it very interesting," he said. "In fact, I'm familiar with some of the information from school." He turned to Laird. "What's significant about 1858, the year Mr. De Cosmos mentioned?"

"In 1858," Laird said, "British Columbia experienced an invasion of gold seekers, mostly Americans up from California. At that time, the colony on Vancouver Island was firmly in the hands of the old Hudson's Bay Company man, Governor James Douglas, but the mainland was basically unorganized territory. With the help of a few Royal Navy gunboats and a small force of Royal Engineers, Douglas 'showed the flag,' as Mr. De Cosmos termed it, and took control of the mainland, firmly establishing British law. The mainland was then organized as the colony of British Columbia. Later, the Vancouver Island Colony and the British Columbia Colonies were joined, and Victoria, which had been the capital of the island colony, became the capital."

"So this beautiful island could have been part of the United States," Ken said. "And a home for the Latter-day Saints."

"And the whole area west of the Rockies and north of California could have been British," Marjorie Mackenzie countered with a smile. "Before the treaty of 1846, the Hudson's Bay Company pretty well ruled that vast territory from its headquarters at Fort Vancouver, which is now Vancouver, Washington.

Ken looked thoughtful for a moment. "You know, I read something about that. I believe the Hudson Bay fur traders even went as far south as Utah."

"They did," Laird said. "In fact, the Ogden Point we passed on our way out of the Victoria harbor was named for the same man as Ogden, Utah, was—Peter Skene Ogden, a chief factor of the Hudson's Bay Company."

Ken jotted down this information. "My readers will enjoy that little tidbit," he said. "I appreciate the voyage and the history lesson."

As the *Prince Albert* plowed through the blue-green waters toward Salt Spring Island, Ken leaned on the rail and gazed across the beauty that surrounded him, but his mind was not idle. He thought about the unpredictability of life and how one event influenced another. Had it not been for the Mexican War, all of Old Oregon might have been part of the United States; and, closer to home, if it hadn't been for that same war, Ken might now be a citizen of the Mexican empire rather than the United States. This thought led him to wonder just how much Heavenly Father influenced events in the lives of nations and individuals. He thought about the principle of foreordination. What was foreordained in one's life and what was happenstance?

As Ken ruminated on this, Laird approached him and said, "Let me have your notebook and pencil, and I'll give you something to chew on." Laird turned to the last page of the notebook and wrote in bold, block letters: ABLE WAS I E'RE I SAW ELBA. "See what you can make of that."

Ken studied the cryptic sentence for several minutes. *Obviously it has something to do with Napoleon,* he thought. *Is it some kind of code?*

Ken had still not come up with an answer when Salt Spring Island came into view. He shrugged and put his notebook and pencil in their usual place, the inside pocket of his coat jacket.

Except for being larger and much rockier, Salt Spring was very much like Peregrine. After navigating a short inlet, the *Prince Albert* anchored in a beautiful horseshoe bay surrounded by rocky cliffs to the west and gentle, treed slopes to the east. A handsome, rock-faced church adorned the hill behind the bay, and Ken wondered where all the congregants were, as there were no signs of habitation. He asked Laird about this.

Laird smiled. "It's a big island, and the people are spread far and wide, especially in the fertile areas. Settlers began arriving here as far back as 1859. Are you ready for a short hike?" Ken nodded. "Marjorie's sister and husband live about a mile up the Burgoyne Valley, straight ahead."

Ken, Laird, and Marjorie went ashore in the dinghy, which they pulled up onto a pebbled beach.

* * *

Marjorie's sister, Betty, and brother-in-law, Malcolm, glad for company on the quiet island, welcomed their guests profusely. Despite Laird's insistence that he and Ken couldn't stay long, they all sat down to a delicious meal of Chinook salmon caught that very morning.

"It's too bad you've come all this way to find out Langley probably isn't Langton after all," Malcolm said after hearing Ken's story. "What will you do now?"

Ken shrugged. "I guess I'll do a little more detective work in Victoria and then head back to San Francisco and see if I can pick up Langton's trail. Even if he didn't kidnap Miss Keene, he'll continue to be a menace to her and to me if he isn't caught. On the other hand, I don't want to spend too much time away from my children."

"We could go through the records again," Laird said, "and check out other purchases on the islands.

Ken nodded. "I guess we could," he said with little enthusiasm.

Chapter 12

"A wire for Mr. Sanderson in care of you, sir, from San Francisco," Sergeant Yates said to Laird when he and Ken walked into the Victoria Police Station after returning from Salt Spring Island. "It's on your desk. Oh, and there's also a letter for Miss Nell Keene. Mr. De Cosmos asked if you would deliver it to her, Mr. Sanderson."

"Told you it would be here," Laird said with a smile. "Mr. De Cosmos's mind may be slipping, but he still follows through with what he says."

Laird handed the telegram to Ken.

"It's from Chief Doherty," Ken said. "He's decided to check out a couple of possible witnesses in the Nell Keene case this weekend. They live in the Sierra Nevada mountains. When he mentioned them before, I asked if I could go with him if he decided to visit them."

"You may as well," Laird said. "I'll keep my eyes open up here and let you know if we get a line on Langton."

Ken placed De Cosmos's letter for Nell in the inside pocket of his coat.

"Thanks, sir. Do you know when the next boat leaves for San Francisco?"

"Tomorrow morning early," Laird said.

"I guess I'll be on it."

* * *

As the San Francisco boat steamed away from Victoria the next morning, Ken stood at the stern and looked back at the busy harbor with its forest of masts and smokestacks filling the sheltered bay. He wished that circumstances were such that he could have stayed longer. But his goal was to find Nell or at least assure himself that she was safe. Perhaps accompanying Chief Doherty to the mountain home of Mr. Hawkins and son would yield the answer. As the boat steamed into the Strait of Juan de Fuca, Ken drank in the panorama of ocean, verdant shoreline, and the misty mountains.

Ken arrived in San Francisco late in the evening, and early the next morning he was at the police station. He waited a half hour before Chief Doherty showed up.

"Mr. Sanderson," the policeman said, "you're an early bird. How was your trip to British Columbia?"

"Fruitless," Ken said. "But I very much enjoyed the scenery and Chief Inspector Mackenzie's hospitality."

Chief Doherty nodded. "It's a beautiful place to visit," he said. "Now to business. According to the *Sacramento Chronicle,* a preacher, Reverend Bailey of Placerville, near Sacramento, got an interesting letter from a man named Hawkins up in the Sierra Nevadas. It was mailed from the Sequoia Trading Post. The man asked the preacher if he would consider performing a marriage in the Hawkinses' home. He offered to pay the extravagant sum of one hundred dollars if the whole thing were treated in strict confidence. He didn't give the names of the couple to be married, but we think the intended bride could have been Miss Keene."

Ken looked skeptical. "Why would you think that?"

"You'll recall that the suspects I mentioned were called Hawkins and that they wore old-fashioned clothing and could do with haircuts. Well, we figure since the Hawkins who wrote the preacher lives in the mountains, he might be one and the same person. When Sergeant Blunt read the story, he saw a possible connection. What if Hawkins planned all along that he or his son marry Miss Keene and is taking advantage of her predicament? In other words, their scheme might have been to befriend Miss Keene, entice her to go to their home, and force her into marriage. It wouldn't be the first time that lonely men, in a fit of cabin fever, concocted such a harebrained scheme. I'll admit it's a bit of a long shot, since Mr. Hawkins is apparently a respectable man, but stranger things have happened, and it's all we have to go on."

"I suppose you contacted the preacher," Ken said. "Did he agree to marry the couple?"

The policeman shook his head. "We communicated by wire. He turned Hawkins down in a letter. Among other reasons, the Episcopal church requires the names of those to be married so that the preacher can post banns for three Sundays before the wedding. Also, Reverend Bailey was suspicious of the whole affair."

"How did the press get ahold of the story?"

Chief Doherty smiled. "Apparently, Mrs. Bailey read the letter and told a friend—in the strictest confidence. The next thing they knew, it was in the local newspaper. Later, it was picked up as filler in the *Chronicle.*"

"Must have been a slow news day," Ken said wryly.

The policeman nodded his assent. "The preacher answered Mr. Hawkins's letter, inviting the prospective bride and groom to come see him in Placerville. As far as I know, he hasn't heard back from them. Since Mr. Hawkins's letter was mailed from the Sequoia Trading Post, I figured we'd start there and then go on to the Hawkinses'.

"Thanks for inviting me along."

"Glad of the company. But you'll have to find your own way back if I decide to stay in the mountains for a while. If we can get this case wrapped up, I'd like to take some time off for a little fishing."

"That would be fine."

"Okay, then. We'll leave at first light tomorrow. I'll bring enough gear for the both of us. We may have to rough it a bit. Where are you staying?"

"The Grovesnor." Ken paused at the door. "This afternoon I'd like to do a little snooping. Can you suggest anyone for me to talk with?"

"I think we've interviewed everyone quite thoroughly. But you could talk to Old Wylie, the caretaker at the Orpheum. He wasn't much help when we talked to him, but maybe you can get something useful out of him. You could also talk to the folks at the Palace."

Ken went directly from the police station to the Palace Hotel.

"What can you tell me about Mr. Hawkins and his son, who were registered here when Miss Keene disappeared?" he asked the desk clerk on duty, a skinny youth with a pockmarked face and protruding teeth.

"Who wants to know?" the clerk asked cheekily.

"Ken Sanderson, of the *Deseret Evening News.*"

"Another reporter. You gents never give up, do you? Well, I'll tell you what I told the others. It's against the Palace's policy to give out information on its guests—except, of course, to the police, and I've told them all I know. So my advice is for you to go see Chief Doherty."

Ken next took a cable car to the Orpheum Theater.

"Mr. Wylie?" Ken said, coming up behind the caretaker.

The man quickly stuck a bottle in the bottom drawer of a battered desk and turned around, wiping his mouth with the back of his blue-veined hand.

The old man peered at Ken through rheumy eyes. "Who are you?" he asked.

Ken introduced himself, and for the next fifteen minutes, they talked about Miss Keene. The caretaker had nothing to add to what Ken already knew.

Ken was about to leave when he thought of one more question. "By the way, do you know what happened to Sir Lionel Freeport, Miss Keene's manager?"

Concern caused the old man's mouth to fall open, revealing his one remaining tooth.

"No. What happened to him?"

Ken smiled. "That's what I'm asking you. Do you know where he is?"

"Oh, I see what you mean." The old man laughed at his own mistake. "He's Down Under."

"Dead?"

The old manned grinned. "No. Australia. He was only here a few days, and then he up and heads off to get things ready for Miss Keene. The rumor is they's getting hitched."

Ken nodded. "Anything else you can tell me?"

Mr. Wylie slowly shook his head, then his vacant eyes lit up. "No . . . 'cept one o' the newspaper men came before all the others."

"Before Miss Keene disappeared?"

The old man strained to remember. "I think so."

"Was he local?" Ken asked.

"Don't think so. Talked kinda funny. From Boston, I figure."

"What did he look like?"

"'Bout your height. He wore a beard. A false one, I figure."

Langton, Ken thought.

"A false one?" Ken asked. "How could you tell?"

The old man smiled. "When y've been 'round the theater as long as I have, y'know such things."

"Did you tell the police about this man?"

The man frowned. "Not really."

"What do you mean, 'not really'?"

The man scratched his hairless scalp for a few seconds. "Well, I was goin' to tell them, but I'd had a few drinks, and . . . and they treated me as if I didn't know what I was talking about, so I shut up."

Ken thanked the caretaker and went to his hotel room. For a long time, he lay on top of the covers and contemplated all he'd learned about Nell's disappearance. *If she hasn't gone to Australia, is she in danger from Hawkins? Hopefully our trip to the mountains will yield the answer. What have I accomplished so far? Nothing.*

Ken sighed and rubbed his temples as the unanswered questions kept sleep at bay. *Should I have left the matter to the police? I should be home with the children . . . I miss them so much. Why did Karen die? I miss her more than I can stand.*

Almost in despair, he lay pondering the twist of fate that had led him to this room, and the gnawing in his stomach returned with a vengeance. Throughout the long night, he tossed and turned. The gray light filtering through the streaked hotel window the next morning was a welcome relief. He was dressed and waiting in the hotel lobby when Chief Doherty arrived in a buggy driven by a policeman.

"Hop aboard, Mr. Sanderson," Doherty said. "Sergeant Blunt'll drive us to the wharf, where we'll catch a steamboat for Sacramento."

Near noon, they arrived at Sacramento and managed to get tickets on an eastbound train on the Sacramento and Placerville Railroad. The station agent told them to get off at Latrobe, a small town west of Placerville and the closest town to the Sequoia Trading Post. Seated in a comfortable coach, the two men discussed the scenery as the train carried them into the green, rolling foothills. Ken expressed surprise.

This was not the rough, wild country his father had told him about from his gold-mining days on the American River.

"It's changed a lot since those days," Chief Doherty said.

Ken could see it had as they passed herds of cattle grazing on green, oak-bordered hills interspersed with orchards and vineyards.

Arriving at Latrobe in the late afternoon, they hired horses and continued on to the trading post. It was getting dark by the time they arrived. Proprietor Emile Watkins, a dwarf-like old man with kindly black eyes and a decided stoop, welcomed them. Mr. Watkins ushered Ken and Doherty into the store, a large room filled with barrels, boxes, dry goods, and a myriad of trade items hanging from the ceiling. One wall of the room was dominated by dozens of framed photographs, mostly of outdoor scenes.

Chief Doherty was vague in describing the purpose of their mission to the mountains, hoping that Mr. Watkins would bring up the subject of the Hawkinses.

"Since the fur trade slowed to a trickle," Mr. Watkins said as the three of them sat around the lit stove, "we don't get many customers these days—mainly a few curiosity seekers from Placerville and sometimes San Francisco. They come to see what an old-time trading post looks like, and they sometimes buy a few things. If it wasn't for the Hawkinses, I'd be out of business. They're a father and son who live about a day's ride from here. I'm kind of their link with the outside world. They order things through me, books mainly. They must have over a thousand books in their library."

"Tell us more about the Hawkinses," Chief Doherty said.

"Odd fellows, the Hawkinses, but honest as the day is long," the trader said.

Chief Doherty considered Mr. Watkins's words before asking, "Not the type to, say, kidnap women, I suppose?"

The trader looked surprised and vigorously shook his head. "Oh, I wouldn't think so," he finally said. Then he appeared to have a second thought. "But they are an odd pair. One thing I do know is that Abraham Hawkins treats women well. He was always the gentleman to his late wife. Yes, sir, always a gentleman. Abraham is not yer typical mountain man. No, sir, not by a long shot. Strange as it may seem—him living away up here and all—he's a very learned old gentleman with an aristocratic bearing. His wife, a well-educated woman, died a while back, and the loss made him even stranger than before. Grief and isolation can do that to a body."

Ken glanced around the room and wondered if Mr. Watkins spoke from experience.

"What's the son like?" Ken asked.

"Ben's a good boy," Mr. Watkins said. "Very quiet and polite, but being raised in the woods, he's never learned to mix much. Schooled at home by his mother, you know. I asked him once why he doesn't go down to the Saturday-night dances at Placerville and meet some other young folk. I even offered to let him stay here free on his way. He told me he had once before, and then he hurried off."

"When's the last time you saw them?" the policeman asked.

The trader thought for a moment. "A few weeks ago, I guess. Abraham asked me if I knew any preachers. I gave him the name of a Rev'rend Bailey in Placerville." Chief Doherty glanced at Ken and nodded as the trader continued. "Abraham sat down right away and wrote a letter to Mr. Bailey." He smiled. "I asked Abraham if he was suddenly in need of religion. He shook his head. Haven't seen either of them since that. Rev'rend Bailey wrote back. I still have the letter. Abraham and Ben come down every few months to get supplies and to play chess with me. Abraham loves chess."

"Is there another way to their cabin?" Chief Doherty asked. "I mean, would a person have to pass by here to get to their place?"

"There're two ways to get to the Hawkinses' place," Mr. Watkins said. "Overland by a wagon road from Latrobe, and a bridle path from here. The wagon road's on the east side of the river where the Hawkinses' place is. The bridle path's on this side of the river. They use the path if they don't have much freight. It crosses the river at a ford about a mile north of the their place, so they need to double back when they use it. They've built a rope bridge across the gorge near their place. It saves them the two miles. Abraham's always involved in some new project." Chief Doherty nodded and, for a moment, he was deep in thought. Mr. Watkins took the opportunity to ask, "What's all this about a woman being kidnapped? Why would Abraham and Ben kidnap a woman?"

"Two women," Doherty said. "As wives, we figure."

The trader's eyes went wide. "You must be joshing. Old man Hawkins involved in kidnapping? Never. Besides, where would they get the women?"

"That's what we're here to find out," Doherty said. "Have you heard of Nell Keene, the English actress?"

Mr. Watkins thought for a moment and nodded. "I have. A visitor left a copy of the *San Francisco Examiner* a while back, and it had an article about her coming to the city. I usually don't read papers myself. Most of it's depressing news. Wars here and earthquakes there." He chuckled and added, "But Miss Keene's image caught my eye. I'd sure like to get her in front of my camera."

"Well, Miss Keene did come," Doherty said, "and then disappeared. We're trying to find out what happened to her."

Mr. Watkins shook his head in disbelief. "And you think the Hawkinses might have something to do with it? Come to think of it, they borrowed the paper telling 'bout the actress coming to Frisco." The trader thought for a moment before adding, "I guess they could have something to do with it. I told you they was strange. But you said two women."

"Miss Keene's maid, Marian Treadwell, has also disappeared," Ken said.

"Anything else you can tell us about the Hawkinses?" Chief Doherty asked.

Mr. Watkins shook his head. "Nope. All I can say is they's good people, man and boy."

"You say it takes about a day to get to the Hawkinses' cabin?" Ken asked.

The trader nodded. "A day and a bit. You'll have to camp overnight along the way. Got enough gear? It gets plenty cold in these mountains, even at this time o' year."

"We've got gear," Chief Doherty said.

"Do you think we could go part of the way tonight?" Ken asked, impatient to be on his way.

"Not a chance," Mr. Watkins said. "There're some pretty deep gorges. If you value your life, you'll stay here and go in the light. I have guest rooms I rent out."

Ken suppressed his impatience. "I suppose you're right."

"By the way," Mr. Watkins said. "Even though the Hawkinses live in the mountains, they don't live in a cabin. It's more like a mansion. You'll see."

"One last question, Mr. Watkins," Chief Doherty said. "Any good fishing spots hereabouts? I brought along my fishing rod just in case I get a chance to use it."

The trader smiled, got up, and walked over to the wall covered with photographs. "You'll pass several good fishing lakes on your way to the Hawkinses' place." He pointed to a lake scene. "This is Mary Lake, one of the best."

"Did you take those photographs, Mr. Watkins?" Ken asked. "I've been admiring them ever since entering the store."

"I did," Mr. Watkins said, proudly. "Photography's become my hobby, you might say."

That night Ken and Chief Doherty slept in one of Mr. Watkins's guest cabins. Ken wondered if he would find Nell at the Hawkinses' place, and the thought brought him pleasure. From all he'd learned about the Hawkinses, he doubted that Nell and Marian were in danger.

At first light, Ken awoke and realized it was Sunday. He felt bad about traveling on the Sabbath, but he rationalized that this was an ox-in-the-mire situation. After a surprisingly tasty breakfast of Mr. Watkins's special crepes with butter and honey, he and Chief Doherty were on the trail. Both men had bedrolls tied behind their saddles and haversacks on their backs.

"Watkins wasn't exaggerating," Chief Doherty said as they briefly halted the horses and stared down into a rocky gorge through which white water tumbled. "It would have been madness to try this last night. Even in the light we'll have to be careful."

Ken nodded his agreement. "I can't wait to meet the Hawkinses. They seem to be the key to this whole mystery. I wonder what we'll find at the mansion in the mountains."

Chief Doherty shook his head.

Hour after hour they threaded their way through evergreens and rocks along a somewhat overgrown trail. Around noon, they reached the shores of a beautiful lake.

"Must be Mary Lake," Chief Doherty said. "Let's lunch here, and I'll try my luck with my fishing rod."

Ken wanted to protest the delay, but he was sore from riding and welcomed the respite. They dismounted, and the policeman took the haversack off his back, handing it to Ken. He then untied his bedroll from the back of the saddle and withdrew a small bundle of bamboo rods. As Ken looked on, the fisherman fitted the various rods together into a fishing pole. He then added a reel from his haversack.

"There we are," he said. "You get a fire going and the frying pan out of my pack. I'll go catch us some trout." He smacked his lips. "I can taste 'em already."

The policeman's luck was good, and before long, two speckled trout were sizzling in the frying pan and two more waiting to go in.

"This is delicious," Ken said as he separated another tender piece of trout flesh from the bones and popped it into his mouth. "I never was much of a fish eater, but I think I'm converted. The salmon I had up in British Columbia was just as delicious."

After lunch, they were on their way again. That night, they camped beside another pretty lake. Despite his proximity to the fire and being wrapped in two blankets, Ken hardly slept. When facing the fire, his front got too hot and his back too cold. When he turned his back to the fire it was the opposite, and the cold seeped up from the ground into his bones. Well after midnight, the long, lonesome howl of a wolf sent chills of a different kind through him, causing him to sit bolt upright. Leaning over, he threw a handful of sticks on the red coals. When the sticks burst into flames, he felt a little safer. Glancing over at the snoring policeman, he shook his head with wonder. Neither the cold nor the wolf howl had disturbed Chief Doherty's slumber. After what felt like an endless night, Ken was glad when the sky began to lighten and he could get up from the chilly ground.

"I didn't get much sleep last night," Ken said at breakfast. "I almost froze to death."

Chief Doherty smiled. "Mr. Watkins wasn't exaggerating when he said it gets cold at night. I was so tired I didn't notice the cold, but when I woke up, I was half frozen. Typical early summer weather in these mountains, cold at night and warm in the day. On the way back, we'll have to prepare our beds better."

Before noon, they heard the Rubicon River before they saw it. In the bright sunshine, they followed the river several miles.

"There's the rope bridge Watkins told us about," the policeman said, loud enough to be heard above the river's roar.

They dismounted beside a small, neat hay shed and an empty lodgepole-pine corral.

"From what Watkins said about Mr. Hawkins," Chief Doherty said, "I don't suppose he'd mind if we fed and watered the horses."

The horses taken care of, the policeman withdrew a pistol, checked the mechanism, and returned it to his pocket. Ken looked on quizzically.

Chief Doherty shrugged. "'Be prepared' is my motto," he said. "Let's go."

Halfway across the swaying rope bridge, Ken stopped and gazed with fascination at the white water below, swooshing its way between two jagged cliffs and plummeting to a pool at the bottom of the gorge. After a minute or so, he pulled his eyes from the spectacle and gingerly followed in the policeman's footsteps across the bridge.

"Never could stand heights," the policeman said when Ken joined him.

The first sign of life was a plume of smoke curling lazily above the trees. Topping a hillock, they looked down into a lovely valley and stared in wonder at the domesticated scene before them. Dominated by a handsome, oversize, saltbox-style house modified with a huge, covered deck around three sides of the building, the valley could have been in Massachusetts or Vermont. The house fronted on a widening of the river, in essence a small lake. A neat log cabin stood just south of the main house, and a green lawn swept down to the water. Sheep grazed on the hillside behind the main house, and a stream with a waterwheel on it ran down the hill and into the river. Behind the cabin, fruit trees, their blossoming branches adding to the beauty of the scene, stood in neat rows.

In front of the cabin was an old stove with something boiling on it. To the left of the stove, a young man and woman were working at a table. The woman, dressed in a sober gray riding habit, had her raven hair tied at the nape of her neck with a yellow ribbon. She was ladling a red mixture into a glass bottle. Even though she had her back to him, Ken immediately recognized Nell.

"Miss Keene!" he exclaimed.

Chapter 13

"It smells delicious," Nell said as she ladled a strawberry mixture from the bubbling pot into a glass bottle.

Ben was teaching her to put up strawberry preserves. They were working happily at an old stove set up in front of the cabin that had been the Hawkinses' first home in the Rubicon Valley. Ben watched Nell's happy excitement, and it filled him with confusion. He knew in his heart that they could never be married, yet he thrilled to be in her presence. Glancing up, he saw two men coming over a hillock toward them. He stared guiltily at the newcomers, as if he'd been caught participating in a less-than-honorable endeavor. Nell, whose back was to the men, saw the change of expression on Ben's face and turned to see what had caused it. Her face filled with sunshine and recognition.

"Ken!" she exclaimed excitedly. Turning to Ben, who was eyeing the men suspiciously, she said, "That's my friend Mr. Sanderson from Salt Lake City."

Ken smiled at Nell's happy expression as he and Chief Doherty approached. "Nell . . . Miss Keene," Ken said, suddenly aware that his heart was thumping faster. "Thank goodness you're safe. This is Police Chief Doherty from San Francisco."

"Police chief?" Nell asked. Then, nodding toward Ben, she added, "And this is Benjamin Hawkins. His father is in the main house with Marian."

Nell beamed, thrilled to see Ken again. She felt a little guilty at how thrilled. Through force of will and acting ability, she composed herself. She glanced at Ben, inviting him to welcome Ken and Chief Doherty.

Ben looked from Nell to Ken to the policeman. "What do you want, gentlemen?" he asked.

"What do you think we want?" Chief Doherty said sternly. "We're here to take Miss Keene and her maid back to San Francisco. Do you have any objections?"

Ben bit his lower lip and shook his head. "Of course not," he said defensively. "They came by invitation and are free to go when they like."

"Do I have to go back to civilization?" Nell asked playfully. "Ben here is teaching me to make strawberry jam, and I'm having a wonderful time!"

Chief Doherty's brow furrowed. "Strawberries at this time of year?" he asked.

"Oh, yes," Nell said. "They have a huge greenhouse heated by a hot spring. It's marvelous."

Despite his joy at seeing Nell again and despite her enthusiastic greeting, Ken was a little put off by her jovial attitude. After all, he had gone to great lengths to find her, and she was acting as if she were on a picnic. However, he didn't dwell on it, as Marian, who was walking out onto the porch of the main building, caught his attention.

"Miss Treadwell!" Ken exclaimed. "We've come to . . . to rescue you and Miss Keene."

The words were no sooner out of his mouth than he realized the audacity of his statement. He smiled sheepishly at Nell, who tilted her head and raised her eyebrows as if to say, "We all make mistakes."

"Rescue us?" Marian asked. "Why ever would we need rescuing, Mr. Sanderson? We're here at Mr. Hawkins's invitation, and he and Benjamin have treated us royally." She waved them to her. "Please come through."

Ken marveled at the change in Marian Treadwell. No longer was she the mousy maidservant in Nell's shadow. The proprietary tone of her voice and her confident carriage both evidenced a new status.

Ken and Chief Doherty walked past Ben, who stepped aside and eyed them suspiciously. They paused to let Nell precede them into the house. Inside, they were led into a huge parlor, one wall of which was lined with books. The master of the house sat on an overstuffed chair in the middle of the room. His handsome, aristocratic face, albeit rather pale for a man of the mountains, showed welcome as he nodded at the two strangers.

The policeman, a wry smile on his lips, said, "Mr. Hawkins, I presume?"

"The same," Mr. Hawkins said with a smile.

"This is Police Chief Doherty and Mr. Sanderson, Mr. Hawkins," Nell said.

"Welcome, gentlemen," Mr. Hawkins said. "To what do we owe this pleasure?"

Ken and Chief Doherty sat down on chairs provided by Marian. Nell and Marian remained standing.

"Miss Keene and Miss Treadwell left San Francisco in rather a hurry," Chief Doherty said. "And some people, especially the British ambassador, felt they might have met with foul play. We're delighted to see that the ladies are well."

Nell inhaled and sighed. "I'm sorry to have caused so much trouble, Chief Doherty," she said. "Perhaps I should have told someone where we were going, but I didn't want a certain man—a very dangerous man—to know."

"Langton," Ken said.

"Exactly," Nell said. "He was masquerading under the name of Sir Reginald Cripps from South Africa and was wearing a false beard, but I knew who he was almost immediately. He tried to force me to leave the British embassy with him, but I escaped his grasp. Fortunately, Mr. Hawkins and Ben were leaving for their home just as I returned to my hotel, and Miss Treadwell and I came with them."

"You should have gone directly to the police station, Miss Keene," Chief Doherty chided. "We would have given you protection and perhaps have been able to arrest this fellow, Langton. We learned much about him while investigating your disappearance, but he is nowhere to be found now. We feel it is safe for you to return to San Francisco, and, of course, you'll have police protection."

"Thank you, sir," Nell said. "Although I'm having a wonderful time here, it seems I have some fences to mend in San Francisco, especially with the British ambassador. And I'll have some explaining do when I finally get to Australia." She dragged out the last words, and it seemed to Ken that there was reluctance in her voice. She shrugged her slender shoulders and added, "I would have gone back to the city earlier, but Mr. Hawkins has been sick." She turned and smiled at Ben, who was standing by the door. "I'll never forget my stay here. It's been a wonderful lark. Ben has taught me about the fauna and flora of these woods, and, as you saw, he was teaching me the fine art of putting up preserves."

"Well, we'd best get you back to San Francisco as soon as you ladies are ready," Chief Doherty said. Turning to the old man, he asked, "I don't suppose you'd mind us using your wagon to transport the ladies as far as the railroad?"

"*Lady*," Marian corrected with a smile. "Miss Keene is going, but I'm staying."

"Staying?" Ken said, glancing first at Marian and then at Nell.

Chief Doherty also looked to Nell for an answer.

"Yes, gentlemen," Nell said. "Much to my sorrow in losing her, Miss Treadwell has decided to stay."

"As Mr. Hawkins's wife," Marian proudly clarified. "I've been a spinster long enough, and this home needs a woman in it again. When Mr. Hawkins is fully recovered from his illness, we're going down to Placerville to wed."

"Congratulations, Miss Treadwell," Chief Doherty said, glancing around the pleasant room. "I'm sure you'll both be very happy here."

"Thank you, sir," Mr. Hawkins said. "Ironically, we went to the city to get Benjamin a wife, and I got one instead."

"My only regret," Marian said, "is leaving Miss Keene's service. We've been together a long time. I don't know how she'll get along without me."

Nell smiled. "It won't be easy, Marian. You've been a wonderful friend and companion. But I'll survive. You know I always land on my feet." She turned to the men. "I'm ready to leave when you are, gentlemen."

Chief Doherty glanced at Ken, who shrugged as if to say, "I guess Miss Treadwell's old enough to make up her mind." Doherty then turned his gaze to Ben, who had been standing quietly by the door. "How do you feel about this, son?"

Ben glanced at the smiles on his father's and Marian's faces and nodded. "I'm glad, sir," he said. He then crimsoned slightly and, glancing at Nell, added, "I reckon I'll try the Saturday-night dances at Placerville again."

His remark brought smiles all around.

"Go with them to Latrobe, son," Mr. Hawkins said. "See they get there safely. Miss Treadwell's made up a list of things she needs. You can fetch 'em for her." He turned to Nell. "Are you an equestrienne, Miss Keene?"

"Yes, sir," Nell said. "I love riding."

"Good," Mr. Hawkins said. "Rather than going on the wagon route, I think you'd enjoy the bridle trail. It's more scenic. Of course, you would have to camp in the open. Perhaps a lady like you wouldn't find that appropriate."

Nell smiled. "I think the last time I spent any time in the wilds was when Mr. Sanderson and I were temporarily stranded on an island in Loch Lomond. And I found that a great lark."

It was agreed that Nell would have her night in the wild. Mr. Hawkins asked Ben to take two horses upriver, across the ford, and back down to where Ken and Chief Doherty's hired horses were corralled.

"Don't be long, Benjamin," Marian said. "We'll all have lunch before you leave for town."

"Miss Keene, why don't you show Chief Doherty and Mr. Sanderson around the place while we're waiting?" Mr. Hawkins suggested.

"I'd be delighted," Nell said. "Come, gentlemen."

"Not me," Chief Doherty said. "I need to ask Mr. Hawkins a few more questions for my report. You go ahead, Mr. Sanderson."

Chapter 14

"Let's go to the orchard first," Nell said as they exited the house. "It's so pretty with the blossoms. I'm dying to ask you some questions."

Away from the others, Nell felt a little shy in Ken's presence. She guiltily tried to suppress the butterflies that had taken to flittering in her stomach, knowing Ken had recently suffered a devastating loss and that she herself was committed to marrying Sir Lionel. Nevertheless, she could not deny that she was delighted to see Ken again.

Nell looked at Ken's kind face and was reassured that he was likewise glad to see her. When she smiled and he quickly looked toward the mountains, she wondered if he might not have similar feelings. But brushing the thought away, she resolved inwardly that she would rein in her feelings. She indeed felt a kinship with this man, and she was touched that he had come so far to "rescue" her. But she knew that the timing could not have been more wrong. They walked to the orchard in silence and sat together under an apple tree. Nell breathed in the blossom-scented air and slowly exhaled.

"How wonderful," she said at last. "I'm glad we've a few private moments to converse in this lovely place. My first question—I can understand Chief Doherty coming here, but why are you here?"

"Why indeed?" he said wryly. "When I learned from the wire service of your disappearance and that Langton had resurfaced, I thought I could be of some help to the police and perhaps repay, in some measure, all that you and Lord Darnley did for Karen and me in England."

Nell dismissed Ken's talk of obligation with a wave of her hand and a shake of her black tresses.

"You owe me nothing," she said sincerely. "But thank you so much for coming to my rescue anyway. I feel safe here, but knowing that Stephen Langton is still lurking out there frightens me. At the embassy dinner when I realized who was under that false beard, my blood ran cold. Hence our quick exit from San Francisco. While I appreciate your taking the trouble to find me, I feel terrible to have dragged you away from your children. Please tell me about Utah. How are the children, Maggie, Jack, and everyone?" Nell paused. "And how are you?" she added quietly.

Ken smiled sadly, and Nell suppressed the urge to take him in her arms like a child, seeing the depth of his loss in his eyes.

"The children are well," Ken began slowly. "They miss their mother very much . . . They don't understand. Sometimes I don't either."

"I'm so very sorry," Nell said quietly. For a moment, she was lost for words. Then she said, "The love you shared is a rare thing in this world. I'm ashamed to have been the cause of bringing you out here when you're needed so much at home."

"It wasn't your fault. And I don't blame you for fleeing Langton the way you did. Actually, I needed to get away. I wasn't much use at the newspaper office, so my father arranged for me to come out here on assignment. I've also been up to British Columbia."

She gave him a quizzical look. "British Columbia? Why?"

Over the next few minutes, he told her of his trip to Canada.

"Please forgive me for dragging you into this experience," Nell said, her hazel eyes concerned.

"Nothing to forgive," Ken replied. "The children are in good hands. Maggie and Jack are looking after Ainsley and Gage. Doris, Jonathan's wife, is caring for baby Karen. I won't say I don't miss them—I do, more than words can tell—but I know they're being well cared for."

They fell into silence, each waiting for the other to speak. They turned toward each other, and in an instant their eyes met and parted just as quickly. Nell knew she was not the only party with mixed emotions—pleasure at being together but guilty for feeling that pleasure. They turned from each other and studied the blossom-laden fruit trees.

"Perhaps I should show you around now," Nell finally said, picking up a fallen blossom and stroking its delicate petals.

"Yes," Ken said, leaping to his feet.

Politely, he helped her up. As Ken took Nell's gloved hand in his, their eyes met again, and Nell felt an unspoken understanding pass between them. Whatever the future held, now was not their time. They would honor, for now, the commitments they had made, both past and present. And they would keep their emotions in check.

"What would you like to see first?" she asked, feeling more composed.

"You mentioned a hot spring?" he asked. Nell nodded, and they walked toward the blue-green hills a short distance away.

By the time they arrived at the spring bubbling out of the hillside, the tension of the orchard felt far away. Nell explained to Ken that the hot water had been the clincher in the Hawkinses' decision to settle there. It flowed into a stream, which continued down to the Rubicon River. By hand, the Hawkinses had first dug a pool and lined it with flagstones. Later, they had built a gazebo-shaped building over it to protect them while bathing. Later still, they'd tapped the water to heat the greenhouse and the main house.

"Amazing," Ken said, impressed by the Hawkinses' ingenuity. "I guess it's true what they say about Yankee know-how."

Nell nodded her assent. "You came across the rope bridge, didn't you? So you saw the waterfall."

"Yes."

"Well, Mr. Hawkins's next project is to build a contraption there to make electricity. He's been reading everything he can get on Mr. Edison's work and hopes to have electric power here in the near future. Can you imagine?"

Ken smiled. "Yes, I can imagine, now that I've seen what he's done here. What other marvels does the Hawkins estate hold?" he asked.

At that moment, Chief Doherty approached them. "Lunch is ready," he said. Glancing around, he shook his head in wonderment. "You've got to hand it to old Mr. Hawkins. This place is a paradise in the wilderness."

During lunch, the topic turned to why Mr. and Mrs. Hawkins had settled so far from civilization.

"I never would have recognized the beauty of living a life such as this if it had not been for Mrs. Hawkins," Mr. Hawkins said. "Before we met, all I could think of was making money and expanding my business enterprises. She showed me a better way of life, teaching me that there was more to life than business. With my wife's encouragement, I decided to give up the bleak world of commerce and live my life in a different fashion. After much study and thought, I sold my factories, and we began the search for a place where we could live closer to nature. It took us two years, but we finally found this beautiful valley."

"You certainly are to be commended for what you've done here," Ken said, waving his hand to include the surroundings. "How could you build all this without outside help?"

Marian answered for her husband-to-be. "Mr. and Mrs. Hawkins built all this by themselves. There isn't much that Mr. Hawkins can't do." She smiled proudly.

"Even the boards for the house?" Chief Doherty asked. "Surely you must have hauled in finished lumber."

"No," Mr. Hawkins said. "We felled the trees, seasoned them, cut them into boards with a water-driven sawmill, planed them by hand, and built this house. It's true that we did buy a few manufactured items, hinges and such, mostly through Mr. Watkins at the trading post, but almost all this is of our own making. We slowly built this house while we were living in the log cabin."

"Amazing!" Chief Doherty exclaimed. "Any regrets about living out here?"

Mr. Hawkins glanced at his son, who had returned across the rope bridge early that afternoon after delivering to the corral the horses he and Nell would ride to Latrobe.

"Only one," Mr. Hawkins said. "We should have arranged for some playmates for Benjamin as he grew up. I guess the poet Mr. Donne was right. 'No man is an island.' It would have behooved my late wife and me to be a little more involved with mankind. If we had, it might not have been necessary to go to such extremes to find Benjamin a mate." He looked across the table at Marian. "But all's well that ends well. God truly does work in mysterious ways."

Nell smiled and saw Ken glance in her direction. As the group ate in silence for several minutes, enjoying the homegrown food, Nell thought about Mr. Hawkins's statement. She could not help but wonder, as she glanced again across the table again at Ken, if the events of the past month had been more than mere happenstance.

Chief Doherty broke the silence. "Would you mind if I stayed here a few days and did a little fishing?" he asked Mr. Hawkins. "Now that this case is wrapped up, I'm going to take a few days off."

"You're more than welcome, sir," Mr. Hawkins said.

"Would you mind escorting Miss Keene to San Francisco alone, Mr. Sanderson?" Chief Doherty asked. "If it's all right with you, Miss Keene," he added.

Nell glanced at Ken and saw the hesitation in his eyes.

"Let me defer to Mr. Sanderson," she replied.

Ken paused. As much as he was intrigued by the thought of spending more time alone with Nell, he knew that it would be impossible. She was promised to Sir Lionel Freeport, and he was still grieving his beloved Karen. The opportunity was tempting, but the timing was wrong. In Ken's mind, the situation demanded a chaperone.

Coming to his aid, Nell quickly said, "Chief Doherty, are you sure you don't want to return to San Francisco with us so that you may be properly credited for solving the supposed kidnapping case?"

The policeman shook his head. "No. I'll let Sergeant Blunt get the glory. It was he who made the connection between the letter Mr. Hawkins sent to Reverend Bailey and your disappearance."

Nell tried again.

"The trip really would be all the more enjoyable," she said, turning to Mr. Hawkins, "if *two* handsome men escorted me to San Francisco. Would it be permissible for Benjamin to accompany us there? I would like to buy him some modern clothes and have his hair cut in a more . . . more fashionable style."

Mr. Hawkins glanced at his son, who nodded enthusiastically. The father pursed his lips and turned back to Nell.

"Accompany you, yes, Miss Keene," he said. "But as much as I appreciate your kind offer, Benjamin can buy his own clothes and pay for his own haircut."

"Very well," Nell said. "When he returns home, you won't recognize him—neither will the girls at the Placerville Saturday-night dance!"

Everyone smiled, including Ben.

"It's settled then," Chief Doherty said. "As soon as you get to town, Mr. Sanderson, let the sergeant know the facts and, of course, that there'll be no charges laid. He'll take it from there." Turning to Nell, he added, "Be prepared for a deluge of reporters, Miss Keene. They'll be—" The policeman suddenly interrupted himself. "You're a reporter, Mr. Sanderson. Maybe you'd like to file a story with your paper and scoop the others. It's big news."

Ken's face lit up at the prospect.

"I'll do that," he said enthusiastically. "It's the least I can do for my employer, considering all the time I've had off."

"One more thing," Chief Doherty said. "Please let the livery stable man know that I'll return his horse in a few days."

Ken nodded, satisfied with the plans for their departure. Nell smiled and turned to her maid. "Marian, will you help me get ready to leave?"

When the two women were alone in Nell's bedroom, Nell said, "Any doubts, Marian? Mr. Hawkins is quite a bit older than you."

Marian smiled. "You're one to talk, Nell. Lord Darnley was older than you by more than Mr. Hawkins is older than me."

"That's true," Nell agreed with a smile. "Apparently you've changed your mind about such things. If I recall correctly, you were quite concerned when Lord Darnley told you he was marrying me."

Marian smiled and sat on the bed. "Concerned is an understatement. I was aghast, especially when he asked me to stay on as your maid. As you know, I had served the first Lady Darnley for over twenty-five years and nursed her till her death. I thought Lord Darnley had lost all reason when he told me he was going to marry a young snippet of a girl and an actress at that. I absolutely refused to be your maid."

"Tell me again. What changed your mind?"

Marian sighed and looked back in her mind.

"Flattery, I suppose. When Lord Darnley asked me to stay, he told me that my great experience and wisdom were needed to help you to adjust to your new station. He went on to say that I would grow to love you as he did. He actually pleaded with me to stay."

"That must have been a sight, a lord of the realm pleading with a ladies' maid."

Marian smiled. "Indeed. But it worked, and I have not regretted my decision."

"I'm sorry I won't be able to attend your wedding, Marian. But I must get back to San Francisco and on to Australia. Sir Lionel will be beside himself by now."

"Speaking of Sir Lionel . . ." Marian hesitated.

"Yes, Marian?" Nell prodded gently when Marian did not speak for a few moments.

"I know it's not my place to say anything," Marian began slowly. She paused again. "But I have not been able to shake the thought from my mind all day."

"Please, Marian, what is it?" Nell asked.

"I think Mr. Sanderson would be a better choice for you than Sir Lionel," she said in a rush. "I don't know him well, but he impresses me as a good man, even though he is a Mormon."

Nell's cheeks colored, and she sighed as she pondered Marian's words.

"Mr. Sanderson is a good man and would make any woman a good husband," Nell finally said. "But I promised Lord Darnley I'd marry Sir Lionel, and I could never live with myself if I went back on my word. Besides, Mr. Sanderson has just lost the love of his life and is in no condition to marry again for the foreseeable future. And he would never marry someone of another religion, and I don't know if I could change. We are dear friends. I, too, question why our paths continue to cross, but it's all so impossible. All I can do is continue to be his friend. Who knows what the future holds for us." Nell was lost in thought for a moment. She took a deep breath and smiled at Marian. "Well, I best get ready to go."

Marian sighed. "I suppose. Will you wear that outfit for the ride to Latrobe?"

"Yes. I'll send it back with Ben. It's fortunate that the late Mrs. Hawkins was not much bigger than me or you."

Marian smoothed the skirt of her borrowed frock. "It still feels strange wearing Mrs. Hawkins's clothes. Will you send my things back with Ben as well?"

"Certainly, along with some outfits for your trousseau." Marian started to protest, but Nell put up her hand. "No argument, Marian. It's the least I can do, since I won't be at your wedding."

"Thank you, then, dear."

Neither of them spoke for a moment. Marian carefully folded Nell's lavender dress and placed it in a haversack Ben had provided. Nell stared out of the window at the verdant valley.

"It certainly is a lovely spot," she said. "I think you'll be happy here."

Marian sat on the bed again and thought about Nell's words. "I know I will be. Funny, but I'd given up the quest for married bliss a long time ago. Like most girls, when I was young, I longed for a Lochinvar to come on his white steed and sweep me into his arms." She paused and smiled ironically. "It's been a long time coming, and my Lochinvar has white hair rather than a white horse." She paused again. "To be mistress of this beautiful estate is a long way up for a woman who's been in service since she was fifteen." She turned to look at Nell. "My only regret is leaving your service. Lord Darnley was right. I have grown to love you . . . love you like the daughter I never had."

Nell left the window, and the two women embraced.

Marian and Nell made their final farewell at the rope bridge. Marian remained on the east side of the river, while Ken, Nell, and Ben crossed over the swaying bridge to the west side.

"Hurry back, Benjamin," Marian called loud enough to be heard over the churning water. "You have a wedding to attend."

Chapter 15

Nell, Ken, and Ben wound their way along the narrow trail toward the trading post. Ben led the group, and Nell and Ken brought up the rear. Every so often, especially if she saw a bird or an animal, Nell would turn in her saddle and smile back at Ken. Her smile never failed to set his heart beating a little faster. About suppertime, they reached the lake Ken and Chief Doherty had camped at on their way to the Hawkinses'.

"What a beautiful sight!" Nell exclaimed. "May we camp here for the night? I must admit it's been a long time since I've been in a saddle, and I'm . . . well, it's been a long time."

Ken smiled. "I know what you mean. What do you think, Ben?"

Ben looked up at the sun. "We still have lots of daylight, but I guess it wouldn't hurt. There's a little wild hay meadow near here where we can pasture the horses."

"By the way, Miss Keene," Ben said as they were setting up camp. "You ride very well, especially for a city person."

"Thank you, Ben," she said with a smile. "But I'm not wholly a city person. As the wife of a peer with a country estate, it was *de rigueur* to participate in fox hunting, although I always thought it rather silly for a whole bunch of well-dressed people to be following a batch of baying hounds that were chasing a defenseless little animal." She smiled and thought for a second before adding, "I recall Mr. Oscar Wilde remarking at a dinner party I attended that the sight of an English country gentleman galloping after a fox was 'the unspeakable in full pursuit of the uneatable.'" The two men laughed. "When I asked Mr. Wilde if this was a line from one of his plays, he remarked, 'Not yet, but it will be.'"

While Ken kindled a fire and Nell unpacked the food Marian had sent with them, Ben disappeared. He returned ten minutes later with an armful of wild hay and placed it near the fire.

Nell smiled. "Are the horses sharing their supper with us?" she asked.

Ben grinned. "Nope. I'll be back in a few minutes with some more."

The three of them sat on the hay as they ate their supper.

* * *

Nell sighed contentedly. The stars winked down upon them, and the fire cast shadows on the faces of her friends as they talked. Even though she had come here to escape from Langton, she was grateful for the experiences she'd had in this beautiful place and to have met the Hawkinses. She was also grateful to have been reunited, if only briefly, with Ken Sanderson. She smiled as he shared a story with Ben from his adventures in England.

During a lull in the conversation, Ben stirred the fire and asked Ken, "I've been wanting to ask you something ever since I heard you're from Salt Lake City." Ben prodded the fire. "Is it true that the Mormons have given up polygamy?"

Nell glanced at Ken for his reaction.

Ken nodded. "Yes, we have. President Woodruff, our prophet, ended the practice."

"Interesting," Ben said. "Except for that aberration, I find much to be admired in your church. Although my mother wasn't a religious person per se, she insisted that I learn about all religions. If Miss Keene doesn't mind, I'd like to hear more about what you believe—to compare, if you will, with the things Mother and I studied."

Nell didn't mind.

"Well," Ken began, his face bright. "Before I talk about specific beliefs, I'd like to set the stage, which will hopefully put my beliefs in context. The Church of Jesus Christ of Latter-day Saints is the restoration of the primitive Church established by the Savior in the meridian of time, or when He lived on earth and preached His gospel. He established a Church with Apostles, prophets, and so forth. After Christ's ascension, the Apostles administered the Church. However, after they were killed—almost all of them suffered martyrs' deaths—the Church began to fragment, and this fragmentation continued to the present day."

"I've wondered why there are so many Christian churches," Nell said.

Ken acknowledged her remark with a nod and went on. "In 1830, through Joseph Smith, Christ restored His Church to the earth, and it became known as The Church of Jesus Christ of Latter-day Saints. So the Church is not another fragment of the original Church, you see. Rather, it is a restoration of the original Church. With that said, now I'll explain some of the specifics."

For the next two hours, Ken outlined his beliefs and fielded questions, mostly from Ben. Nell made a few comments, but for the most part she remained quiet throughout the discussion. It was plain to Ken, however, that she was listening intently.

The moon had risen, silvering the landscape, when Ben finally ran out of questions.

"Thank you, Mr. Sanderson," Ben said. "You've explained your beliefs well and corrected some misunderstandings I had. I appreciate your candor. I now have quite a different picture of your church from the one Mother and I gained from books."

"My pleasure," Ken said. "If you don't mind, I'd also like to add a personal note. I truly believe the things I've told you. I know that Joseph Smith really did see and converse with God the Father and Jesus Christ, and I know that the Book of Mormon truly is the record of God's dealings with the peoples of the American continent. President Wilford Woodruff is God's prophet on the earth today. I bear this solemn witness to you in the name of Jesus Christ, amen."

Neither Nell nor Ben knew how to respond to Ken's heartfelt declaration.

Several moments ticked by in silence, until Nell rose from her seat by the fire and pointed to the stunning reflection of the moon on the water. She smiled. "Before retiring, I think I'll go down to the shore for a better look," she said.

"I'll go with you," Ben said quickly. "You never know what you might run into at this time of night."

"Thank you, Ben," Nell said and glanced toward Ken. "Perhaps you'd like to join us, too, Ken?"

Even in the dim light, Ken could see Ben's disappointment. It was obvious that in spite everything, the young man still had feelings for Nell.

"Thanks anyway," Ken said, "but I think I'll tend the fire. It needs some more wood. You two go ahead, and maybe I'll join you later."

Ken had no sooner got the fire blazing than Ben was back.

"Is Miss Keene still down at the lake?" Ken asked.

"Yes," Ben said glumly. "I think she'd like you to join her."

"Did she say so?"

"No. But I think she would."

Ken looked toward the lake.

Ben grabbed up an armful of wild hay. "I'll fix up our beds."

Ken found Nell sitting on a log near the lapping water. His mind went back to the day he first met her.

"You look very much the way you did that day on the island on Loch Lomond," he said.

She turned and smiled at him. "Strange, but I was just thinking of Loch Lomond, too. It seems a lifetime ago, although it was only about five years or so."

"A lot has happened in those five years."

She nodded her agreement and moved so he could join her on the log.

"Our few hours on the island seem like moments out of time," she said. "It's strange. I almost felt reluctant to leave the island, even after all that had happened. Life is so full of choices between feelings and duty."

Ken nodded. "Yes. I think of it as the David/Joseph dichotomy."

Nell's eyebrows lifted quizzically.

Ken explained. "Life often presents us with a choice between doing what we would like to do and what we ought to do. When King David saw Bath-sheba bathing, he should have averted his eyes and gone about his business. Rather than doing so, he gave in to the strong feelings she aroused in him and eventually became an adulterer and murderer. Joseph, on the other hand, allowed his sense of duty to God to rule over his passions when he spurned Potiphar's wife."

Nell smiled mischievously. "Of course, Mrs. Potiphar may not have been as attractive as Bath-sheba."

Ken grinned and nodded. "Maybe you're right. But the point is, Joseph ran from temptation while David embraced it. Of course, most of our choices are not as monumental as those of David and Joseph, but they are still important, because the sum of those choices equals who we are. As a man 'thinketh in his heart, so is he.'"

Nell contemplated Ken's words. Her admiration for him grew. He seemed so sure of who he was and what he believed. He seemed so sure of the answers to questions Nell had asked herself all her life.

"I've never been quite sure of who I am," Nell admitted. "As you know, I grew up in the slums of London, often wondering where my next meal would come from, and ended up married to Lord Darnley, with all that this world has to offer. Even though I learned to speak and act properly, I've never felt at home in London society. I guess in many ways, I'm still trying to find a home."

Ken looked at her. The moonlight fell across her face, and her eyes were reflective as she looked out across the lake. He found Nell's candor refreshing. In his limited experience, most people who lived their lives in the limelight were rather egotistical.

"To some extent," Ken said, "we all suffer from homesickness. This life, of course, is not our real home."

Nell turned so that she could look into his face. "Not our real home? What do you mean?"

"Our real home is with God, our Father in Heaven. As I mentioned at the campfire, before we came to this earth we lived with God. Coming here is only a brief training stint. I believe when we return home to God, we'll fully understand why we felt so out of place here."

"Perhaps you're right." She sighed. "Maybe when Sir Lionel and I marry and return to London, I'll feel a little more settled."

Her words sent a pang through Ken, but Nell had said it with such hesitancy that he was prompted to ask, "It's really none of my business, but why are you getting married in Australia?"

Nell smiled. "Sir Lionel's older brother, Francis, is archbishop of New South Wales and head of the Freeport family—actually, from what I understand, Lady Freeport, Lionel's mother, runs things. Anyway, Francis insists on meeting me before Lionel and I get married. While no one has actually said so, I'm sure it's to see whether they approve of my entering the family. They know, of course, that I'm from the lower classes and an actress."

"I would think that having been married to Lord Darnley would qualify you," he said with a trace of sarcasm.

She shook her head. "Not really. The Freeports have always felt superior to the Darnleys. The two families are connected by marriage. My late husband's first wife, Sir Lionel's aunt, was a Freeport."

"Well, I don't know the Freeports, but I know you, and my one concern is whether Sir Lionel is good enough for you."

"Thank you, sir," Nell said with a smile.

Ken paused and gathered the courage to ask the question foremost on his mind. "Are you sure you want to marry him?"

She heaved a sigh and was silent for a moment. "Actually, I don't have much choice in the matter. On his deathbed, my husband expressed his desire for me to be well settled and avoid fortune hunters. He extracted my promise to marry Lionel."

"Why did Lord Darnley choose Sir Lionel? Is he well off?"

"His family is. Francis, advised by his mother, controls the family's vast fortune. Sir Lionel receives an annual allowance. When he marries, he'll have a certain sum settled on him, and he'll also inherit one of several family estates, Freeport Park in Herefordshire. Of course, his brother must approve of the marriage first."

Ken shook his head in disgust. "It all sounds so very archaic, cold, and businesslike. What about love?"

Nell smiled sadly. "It's the way the upperclass lives. And it's not all bad. As for love, my mother married for love and lived to regret it. Until I married Lord Darnley and was able to rescue her from poverty, she lived a hardscrabble life full of misery. I owe a great deal to my late husband, and I am resolved that I will not break my promise to marry his nephew, but sometimes . . ."

"But sometimes?"

Nell sighed and touched Ken's shoulder with her gloved hand. Then she shook her head, as if chiding herself for having said too much.

"I'm sorry to have said so much about my personal matters," she said, sidestepping the question. "Thank you so much for coming all this way to rescue Marian and me. You say Maggie is looking after the children?"

Ken was reluctant to leave the subject behind but gave in to Nell's obvious desire to do so.

"Yes. She and Jack are living at my house," he said. "Maggie is in her glory with the children, and Jack is enjoying fixing things. You may recall that I'm not very skilled when it comes to manual labor."

Nell laughed, remembering his attempt to row a hired boat in Scotland. "I recall you had a bit of a problem sculling on Loch Lomond." For a moment, neither of them spoke. Then Nell said, "I believe I told you that my mother was religious and that I attended a Methodist Sunday school. When you mentioned King David, it took me back to those days. I recollect how much I admired young David who slew Goliath. Later, when I learned that David became an adulterer and a murderer, I was completely disillusioned. How could the pure, honorable, heroic David become a murderer? What do you think led to his downfall?"

Ken shrugged his shoulders. "I don't really know. Perhaps he wasn't able to handle power. William Pitt wrote that 'unlimited power is apt to corrupt the minds of those who possess it.'"

Nell smiled. "How do you come up with these quotations? I can never remember things like that. Sometimes a quotation does come to my mind, but I've never any memory of where it came from."

Ken shrugged modestly. "I'm a newspaperman, and it's my business to come up with quotations. If I wrote only my own words and thoughts, nobody would read my articles. Anyway, a rich and powerful man like King David might also have fallen victim to the idea that he could have what he wanted when he wanted it."

Like Stephen Langton, Nell thought with a shudder.

"Are you cold?" Ken asked.

"Just a little."

"Here, take my coat."

He removed his coat and placed it around her shoulders. Guilty pleasure filled her as the warmth of Ken's coat embraced her. She was grateful for the semidarkness, as she knew she must be blushing.

Ken continued their discussion. "I believe that if David had been less prideful and more patient, he would not have fallen. Even before he became king of Israel, his pride and impatience showed. Are you familiar with the story of David and Abigail?"

Nell was enjoying the moonlight, the lapping lake water, and Ken's presence so much she didn't want the evening to end. "No. But I'd like to hear it," she said.

"Well," Ken began. "In a nutshell, Abigail's husband, Nabal, offends David by withholding supplies from David's small army. David's pride is wounded, and he decides to kill every male in Nabal's household. When Abigail hears about David's murderous plans, she has her servants load donkeys with provisions, intercepts David, and pleads with him to take the supplies and spare her household. David accepts her intercession and repents of his plan. Not only that, but he is so impressed with Abigail that, after Nabal dies, he takes her to wife. There's much more to the story, but what I've told you is enough to illustrate David's fatal flaw. Rather than waiting for the Lord to avenge him against Nabal, David set out to do so himself. Fortunately, Abigail intervened and saved David from himself."

Nell nodded thoughtfully. "If I may play devil's advocate for a moment," she said. "You mentioned love before. What if David's attraction to Bath-sheba hadn't been merely physical? What if he truly had fallen in love with her and she with him? If I remember correctly, out of all of David's sons, God chose Solomon—David's son by Bath-sheba—to rule in David's stead. Would David and Bath-sheba have been denying happiness and destiny to remain apart?"

Ken was impressed by Nell's reasoning. He paused, and when he answered it was with a question.

"Ultimately," he said, "where does true happiness lie?"

Nell nodded thoughtfully. "In doing what's right?"

Ken smiled. "That's what I believe also. The Prophet Joseph Smith once wrote that 'happiness is the object and design of our existence' and that the path to it is 'virtue, uprightness, faithfulness, holiness, and keeping all the commandments of God.' I know that if we do our best, God will bless us with happiness. The trouble is, some of us seek to obtain God's blessings before He is ready to give them to us. If, for dynastic reasons, God meant for David and Bath-sheba to get together to fulfill Israel's destiny, He would have provided a way. Patience is the key. It truly is a virtue."

"But isn't patience sometimes an excuse for doing nothing?" Nell asked with a wry smile. "How do we know when to be patient and when to take action?"

Ken nodded thoughtfully. Nell's question confirmed to him again that Nell was not simply a beautiful woman, but an intelligent one as well.

"I've struggled with that question myself," he said. "I guess it's up to us to act—while remembering to seek and heed divine inspiration."

"Divine inspiration?" Nell mused. "How does one come by that?"

Ken smiled. "By prayer, by the Holy Ghost, and by the Light of Christ."

"I know a little about prayer and the Holy Ghost," Nell said. "But what is the Light of Christ?"

Ken's breast burned within him. The feeling led his memory back to the upper room of the London mission home, where he, Karen, and Jonathan Kimball had spent many happy hours discussing the gospel. *Can anything be more satisfying than talking about the gospel and feeling the Holy Ghost permeate our very beings?* Ken thought.

"As Latter-day Saints," Ken answered, "we believe that everyone born into this world has what we call the Light of Christ in him or her. Among other things, it teaches a person what is right and wrong."

"Like a conscience?"

"Yes."

She smiled. "Let me play the devil's advocate once more. Do you recall the line from Shakespeare about conscience making cowards of us?"

"I thought you couldn't remember quotations?"

She smiled. "Somehow that one stuck."

"Yes. I believe it comes from Hamlet's soliloquy."

"Do you think that conscience make us cowards?" Nell asked.

Ken shrugged, momentarily lost in thought.

"Perhaps from a worldly standpoint," he said. "Sometimes when a person does the right thing, people equate it with cowardice. For example, Joseph fled from Potiphar's wife rather than standing up to her. Some could say he acted in a cowardly fashion, but I believe he did exactly the right thing."

Nell nodded thoughtfully and then grinned mischievously. "Did your conscience tell you it was improper to accompany me alone to San Francisco?"

Ken could feel his cheeks color. "I . . . I guess so. I probably appeared rather prudish and maybe even cowardly, but we're to avoid even the appearance of evil, and since you're sort of betrothed—"

"You needn't be ashamed," she interjected sincerely. "I admire your . . . your desire to do the right thing." She gave an involuntary shudder. "As much as I'm enjoying our philosophical tête-à-tête, I guess we should go back to camp. Even with your coat, I'm beginning to get a little chilly."

Ken nodded. "It is getting rather cold." He rubbed his arms briskly. "I hope Ben has a good fire going. Speaking of Ben, he looked a little glum after leaving you here."

Nell sighed. "I'm afraid he misunderstood my asking him to accompany me to San Francisco, and I felt it necessary to make it clear that we could only be friends. I tried hard to be gentle, but I guess I hurt his feelings."

"He's young," Ken said. "And young hearts tend to heal quickly."

They returned to the camp to find a neat little shelter made of branches overlaid with pine boughs. The floor was strewn with the wild hay Ben had gathered. On the opposite side of the roaring fire, Ben had strewn the rest of the hay.

"For me?" Nell said, nodding at the shelter.

Ben nodded shyly. "Those extra pine boughs are for you to put over your blankets."

"Over the blankets?" Nell asked.

"Yes," Ben said. "They'll help keep you warm. There are some for us too, Mr. Sanderson. I'm off to check on the horses."

"Thanks, Ben," Nell and Ken said in unison.

"Speaking of hurting one's feelings," Ken said as he and Nell sat together in the warmth of the fire, "there's something in the inside pocket of my coat for you."

"For me?" she said, slipping her hand inside the coat she still wore. She withdrew Ken's notebook.

"The other pocket," he said.

She handed him the notebook and from the other pocket withdrew a folded and sealed sheet of paper, and broke a wax seal, squinting her eyes as she tried to read the contents by firelight. "I'm afraid I can't read this spidery scrawl. Do you know what it says?"

Ken smiled and nodded. "It's an invitation from Mr. Amor De Cosmos, the former premier of British Columbia, for you to perform in Victoria. You hurt *his* feelings when he heard you were performing in Los Angeles and San Francisco and ignoring the capital of British Columbia."

She nodded thoughtfully. "I seem to be hurting feelings all around. But in this case, the blame falls on Sir Lionel. Except for my request to perform in Salt Lake City, he chose the other venues. As soon as I can, I'll write to this Mister—"

"De Cosmos."

"And tell him that I'll pass his suggestion on to my business manager for future reference. How should I address the letter?"

"I think 'Mr. Amor De Cosmos, Victoria, British Columbia, Canada' should be sufficient. He's a local character; everyone knows him. By the way, if you ever *do* get the chance, you really should visit Vancouver Island. It's one of the most beautiful places I've ever been. I was only able to see the southern part and the islands in the Strait of Georgia—that's the body of water between the island and the mainland—but what I saw was magnificent."

"So I've heard. Last year at a society to-do in London, I met a Mrs. Joan Dunsmuir from Victoria. Her husband had died a year earlier, and she and her three daughters were doing the grand tour of Europe. Apparently, they are extremely well off and live in a brand new castle overlooking Victoria. Mrs. Dunsmuir invited me to visit. Perhaps I'll accept her invitation and Mr. De Cosmos's as well someday."

"You'd enjoy it," Ken said.

He glanced down at the notebook in his hand and smiled. Turning to the last page, he held it up to her and asked. "What do you make of that?"

Even by firelight Nell could read Laird's bold script. ABLE I WAS E'RE I SAW ELBA.

"It's a palindrome," she said without hesitation. "One can read it backward or forward."

Ken turned the book so that he could read it. "You're right," he said with chagrin. "How did you figure it out so quickly?"

She raised her eyebrows and shrugged as if the answer were obvious. "I'm brilliant, don't you know!" Then she smiled broadly and admitted, "Actually, I've seen it before—at a soiree for the London literati."

"The London literati? It must have been exciting to rub shoulders with such people," Ken said with awe in his voice.

Nell shrugged and sighed. "At first, yes. But after a while I became bored with such gatherings, each person trying to outdo the other with witty remarks. Cynicism abounds in such circles. It all rings so phony, so hollow. I find society parties anything but uplifting or soul satisfying. I wouldn't attend them at all if it weren't for Sir Lionel. He enjoys them."

The mention of Sir Lionel spread a pall over the conversation, and Nell looked quietly down at her hands. Not knowing what else to do, Ken poked at the fire, sending yellow flames and sparks upward. After a long pause, Ken turned to Nell.

"On the right outside pocket of my coat you'll find a book," he said. "I'd like you to have it."

"You certainly make use of your pockets," she said as she withdrew the book.

Ken nodded. "That's the Book of Mormon."

Nell took the book of scripture and examined it thoughtfully.

"Thank you," she said, leafing through the pages and placing De Cosmos's invitation inside. "You sparked my interest in the book when you mentioned it earlier. I can't promise you I'll read it right away, but I am interested."

At that moment Ben returned, and the three of them agreed that it was time to retire. Before drifting off to sleep, Nell recounted to herself the day's events, and a warm feeling spread through her. *Is this feeling from the things Ken said about his church?* she wondered. Her thoughts turned to the kindly expression in his brown eyes. *Or am I falling in love with him despite my resolve?*

On the opposite side of the fire, Ken, too, thought of the glorious day and thanked his Heavenly Father that he had had the opportunity of sharing the gospel with Nell and Ben. *Maybe Nell will join the Church,* he thought. *And maybe . . .* He quelled his next thought and settled into the bed of wild hay. Ken drifted off to the sounds of the fire crackling and did not awaken until dawn painted the eastern sky a rosy pink.

Chapter 16

From her horse, Nell gazed back wistfully at the lake and then at Ken. Deep in her heart, she knew that something wonderful had happened the night before. She also knew, however, that neither she nor Ken would act on the feelings that had crept so close to the surface as they'd watched the moon ripple across the lake. Nell flashed Ken a friendly smile before urging her horse forward.

They reached the trading post in the late afternoon. When he learned who Nell was, Mr. Watkins couldn't do enough for her. And when he discovered that Nell and her escorts would be too late to catch the train from Latrobe to San Francisco that day, he was delighted. He had no trouble talking them into staying at the trading post rather than going on to the Latrobe Inn.

Mr. Watkins fed the trio well, and the three travelers clapped as Mr. Watkins regaled them with his talented fiddling that evening. After several songs, the trader got out his chessboard.

"I'll leave the chess to you men," Nell said. "Would it be possible for me to bathe, Mr. Watkins?"

"Of course, Miss Keene," he said jumping up. While he scurried around to get things prepared for her, Nell watched Ken and Ben play chess.

"All ready, Miss Keene," Mr. Watkins said later. "I've set the tub up in front of the fire in your cabin and filled it with warm water."

Ken's heart leapt when Nell rejoined the group later in her lavender frock. Her scrubbed face, completely free of makeup, shone. A raven braid of still-damp hair hung over her left shoulder.

The three men leapt to their feet and gazed at her with unabashed admiration.

"Please be seated, gentlemen," Nell said. "I only came in to hang up this outfit." She held up Mrs. Hawkins's riding habit. "Do you mind if I use the drying rack, Mr. Watkins?"

"Of course not, Miss Keene," the trader said. "Let me lower it for you."

After hanging up the outfit, Nell said, "Good night, gentlemen. Thank you so much, Mr. Watkins, for your hospitality. After riding two days and sleeping outdoors, it was heaven to have a bath and to wash my hair."

"You're very welcome, Miss Keene," the trader said.

"I think I'll retire, too," Ken said. "I'm no match for Ben at chess, and I need to write up the saga of Nell Keene's return to civilization so that I can file it when we get to San Francisco."

The next morning Mr. Watkins served a hearty breakfast of bacon and eggs, and Nell and her escorts prepared to leave.

"How much do we owe you, Mr. Watkins?" Ken asked.

"Here's your bill, Mr. Sanderson," the trader said. "I've put Ben's charge on his father's account."

Ken paid the trader, and he and Ben went out to saddle the horses, leaving Nell with Mr. Watkins.

"And my bill, Mr. Watkins?" Nell asked.

The trader grinned. "Your stay is gratis, Miss Keene. Gratis, that is, with a catch."

"A catch?"

He nodded. "All I ask is that I be permitted to take your image and hang it on my wall."

Nell smiled. "I'd be happy to oblige, Mr. Watkins." She looked down at the gray riding habit she was wearing. "Had I known, however, I would have worn the frock I had on last night instead of this old thing. It's rather wrinkled from my rinsing it out and hanging it to dry." She smiled. "Oh, well. I guess it can't be helped."

"You look lovely," the trader said.

"Where would you like me?"

"Outside," the trader said, "next to the Sequoia Trading Post sign. I want evidence that the famous Nell Keene visited my humble post."

At Latrobe, Ken returned his hired horse and advised the livery stable operator that Chief Doherty would need the other horse a few more days. Ben arranged for his two horses to be boarded until he returned from San Francisco. At the train station, they bought tickets for the next departure to San Francisco.

"You're in for a treat," Ken said to Nell as they sat in the train car watching the landscape pass them by. They had just reached Benicia on the east side of the Carquinez Strait.

"What kind of treat?" Nell asked.

Ben looked on curiously, and then his faced cracked in a smile when he caught on.

"You'll see when we get to the water," Ken said.

"Ben?" Nell asked.

"You'll see," he said.

Ken smiled to see the expressions on Nell's face as the train left the land and pulled onto the huge ferryboat *Solano*.

"It's gigantic!" Nell exclaimed. "It's big enough to take the whole train!"

"I understand it's the biggest ferryboat in the world," Ken said. "I came this way from Salt Lake City and, like you, was amazed at its sheer size."

The three travelers stared out the window as the train—engine, cars, and all—pulled completely onto the ferryboat. When the train came to a stop, Ben quickly moved toward the door, eager to explore the gargantuan boat. Ken helped Nell out of the carriage and onto the deck. They walked over to the side of the boat.

"What a refreshing breeze," Nell said.

"Quite a sight, ain't it?" said a decidedly Irish voice to their right.

Ken and Nell turned to see a little man sitting on a capstan and smoking a slim pipe. Nell smiled. The scene reminded her of a picture she'd seen as a child of a leprechaun sitting on a toadstool. The man took the pipe from his mouth and, with a quick motion of his hand, indicated that the sight he was referring to was the *Solano*.

"It certainly is," Nell said.

"Are you quite familiar with the boat, sir?" Ken asked.

"Aye, lad," the man replied. "Know it from stem t' stern."

"Would you mind giving me some information about it?" Ken asked, pulling out his notepad and pencil.

The Irishman's eyes lit up, and he took a long pull on his pipe as if to gather steam for the stream of words that poured from his lips. "'Tis a marvel altogether," he said. "Four hunnerd and twenty-four feet long, a hunnerd an' sixteen feet wide, three t'ousand five hunnerd tons, two big sixty-inch bore engines—the biggest ferryboat in the whole world, don't you know!"

"It certainly is impressive," Ken said. "And the mountains equally so. What are they called?"

"Aye, that they are," the man said nodding to the north. "Yonder's Mount Tamalpais and the one t' the east's Diablo." With hardly a pause, the man turned the conversation back to his beloved boat. "It be runnin' these ten years w' nary a problem, the *Solano* has."

For the next several minutes the little man talked nonstop of boilers, hinged aprons, vertical beam engines, balanced rudders, smokestacks, longitudinal trusses, hydro-powered counterpoises, accumulators, pumps, and so forth. When he had run out of technical jargon, he launched into a dissertation on the ability of the great boat to withstand the eight-mile-an-hour tides the *Solano* had to contend with. Ken and Nell listened patiently but were glad when the man finally said, "Best hop aboard the train, folks. We've arrived at Port Costa. Only takes nine minutes crossing the straits, don't you know."

Ken thanked the man and put away his notepad. He and Nell were about to head for the train when the man said, "Did ye hear the one about the Irishman that come runnin' down to a ferryboat and found it four feet from the pier? He sorely needed to catch the boat, so he took a flyin' leap and landed on the deck. A deckhand says to him, "Ye didn't have to do that, sir, the ferry's comin' in!"

The Irishman went into convulsions of laughter at his own joke. He continued laughing as Ken and Nell politely excused themselves and slipped away to reboard the train, where they found Ben waiting for them. After a few minutes at the Port Costa station, the train chugged off toward San Francisco.

"What do you think of the *Solano,* Ben?" Ken asked.

"I think it's a great feat of engineering," Ben said. "Last time we were on it, my father spent the whole time on the bridge talking to the captain. Living in isolation has its advantages, but there are lots of things we can't learn from books. When I get home I'm going to encourage father to come to town more often."

"I'm sure Miss Treadwell would support you in that," Nell said.

For several minutes, the three were lost in their own thoughts. Nell, saddened by the fact that she and Ken would soon be parting ways, was suddenly struck by an idea to delay their departure.

"Have you ever seen me perform on the stage, Ken?" she asked.

"Only once," he said. "A long time ago in London. It was before I met you. I was with Karen and my cousin Jonathan."

"Ah, yes," Nell said. "I believe you did tell me about that. You were accosted by a pretty orange seller."

"Yes," Ken said. "Why do you ask?"

Nell shrugged. "No reason of importance. It's just that you didn't get a chance to see me perform in Salt Lake City, and I was thinking of doing another charity performance of *Sweet Lavender* before I leave for Australia—my way of making recompense for all the fuss I made in fleeing San Francisco. If I can arrange it, will you attend?"

"I'd like that very much," Ken said.

Ken wondered if Nell's decision to do the charity performance had anything to do with the fact that it would further delay her trip to Australia, but he didn't voice his thought.

"How about you, Ben?" Nell asked. "Can you stand one more performance? Perhaps I can introduce you to my understudy. She's a nice girl."

Ben looked skeptical. "Please don't take offense, Miss Keene," he said. "But I think I'm through chasing actresses. As much as I'd like to stay and watch you perform, I should be getting back home. I have a wedding to attend."

They shared a hackney cab from the train station to the Palace Hotel.

"Thanks for everything, gentlemen," Nell said as she emerged from the cab. "Are you sure you won't take a room here?"

"No thanks," Ken said. "It's a little too rich for me. I'll stay at the Grovesnor. You, Ben?"

"I'll stay there, too," he said. "I'll be spending enough of my father's money on new clothes."

Nell nodded. "I'll see you both here for breakfast tomorrow, then."

As Ken watched Nell enter the Palace Hotel, a warm feeling spread through him. He had not felt in such high spirits for many months.

The two men reboarded the hackney, and Ken directed the driver to take them to the police station, where Ken thanked Sergeant Blunt for his skilled work in cracking the case of the Nell Keene "kidnapping." He asked the sergeant to continue to be on the lookout for Langton, especially now that Nell was back in the city. He also arranged for a police escort to accompany Nell whenever she left the hotel. Finally, he asked Sergeant Blunt to let the British ambassador know that Nell had returned safely.

That evening, Ken and Ben checked into the Grovesnor Hotel. After putting the finishing touches on his article about Nell's disappearance, Ken left Ben at the hotel and went to the telegraph office to file his story. As he pondered the events of the preceding weeks, he felt satisfied with the happy resolution of Nell and Marian's disappearance. He looked forward to spending the next few days in Nell's company. However, as he thought about this, a sense of unease began nibbling away the corners of his contentment.

As he mulled over his thoughts, he understood the reason for the feeling. It would take several days, if not weeks, for Nell to get back onto the stage—and he had promised Ainsley that he would return to Utah as soon as Nell was safe. Ken knew that it was more than this. He could no longer deny that his feelings for Nell were changing, and it frightened him. It had been less than four months since Karen's death, and he was not quite ready to have another woman by his side. Besides, Nell was promised to Sir Lionel and had no intentions of breaking her vow to her late husband.

But she doesn't love him. Can I in good conscience say nothing and watch her leave for Australia to marry a man she doesn't love? He was concerned about the impropriety of interfering. Nell's question about the dilemma of whether one should be patient or whether one should take action came into his mind. *I told Nell that it's through divine inspiration we know when to take action. I'm very much in need of that inspiration now.* When he returned to the hotel, he knelt beside his bed and poured his heart out to his Heavenly Father.

After climbing back into bed, Ken continued to deliberate on whether he should spend more time in San Francisco with Nell. One minute he felt sure that his conscience was making a coward of him, the next minute he felt sure that he should head home immediately. Finally, he fell into a troubled sleep.

The next morning Ken found the lobby of the Palace Hotel in an uproar. A crowd of noisy reporters hurled questions at a beleaguered Nell. She held her head high and answered the questions with poise, but Ken could tell that she felt overwhelmed by the rapid-fire questions. Ken forced his way through the crowd to her side. Holding up both hands, he called for quiet. The reporters ignored him.

"Gentlemen, gentlemen," Ken said louder. "Miss Keene has nothing further to say." The crowd gradually settled down. "Thank you, gentlemen." He continued in his normal voice. "If you want more of the story, please consult one of the wire services. AP probably has it by now."

"What do you mean?" a small bespectacled man asked. "Miss Keene only returned last night."

"I mean," Ken said, raising his voice for emphasis. "You've all been scooped by the humble *Deseret Evening News* of Salt Lake City. Really, the only thing left for you to do is to file your stories as quickly as possible and try to scoop each other."

In less than a minute, the lobby was devoid of reporters.

Nell stared at Ken in amazement.

"Thank you, Ken," she said admiringly as she sighed with relief. "This time I *did* need to be rescued!"

Ken smiled. "And now the bad news. I'm sorry, but I won't be able to attend your charity performance. I really should be getting back to Utah. Among other things, I promised Ainsley I'd return as soon as you were safe. However, the train doesn't leave until this afternoon, so I'll have a few hours to spend with you and Ben. I'll need to be on the three o'clock ferry in order to catch my train in Oakland."

Nell sighed and felt a pang of sadness. "I'm sorry you can't stay longer," she said. "But I understand completely. Your children need you." Then looking toward the door, she asked, "Where's Ben?"

"He's talking with the doorman. He should be here shortly."

Nell's two escorts joined her for breakfast in the opulent Palace Hotel Restaurant.

"I asked the desk clerk about men's clothing, and he directed me to Frith's down the street," Nell told Ben as the three of them waited for their order. "They have a good selection of ready-to-wear clothing." Ben nodded appreciatively, and after breakfast they set out to find the clothing store.

At Frith's, Nell picked out shirts, ties, socks, shoes, and two suits for Ben.

"I hope your father has deep pockets," Nell said with some concern when she looked at Ben's bill.

"Don't worry, Miss Keene," Ben said with a smile. "If it will help get me a wife, he'll gladly pay."

After seeing to Ben's needs, Nell turned to Ken. "And now, gifts for your children," she said.

"Gifts?"

"Of course. You can't return home empty handed. I saw a lovely doll for Ainsley and a crocheted blanket for the baby. While I'm getting them, you can pick out something for Gage."

He smiled at her, touched by this gesture. "Come to think of it, I did notice a model steam train Gage would like."

That afternoon the three dined for the last time at the Palace Hotel. Despite his resolve to leave, Ken prolonged the meal as long as he could. He could see that Nell was in no hurry to end their time together either. Seeming to sense that the two would appreciate a moment to say good-bye, Ben stood to return to the Grovesnor.

"Good-bye, Mr. Sanderson," he said. "I'll leave you to say good-bye to Miss Keene." Then he turned and walked away.

"I suppose this *is* good-bye," Ken said after Ben had gone. "I must be going or I'll miss my train." After a moment he added, "Will you be coming back through Utah on your way home?"

Looking at his kind, sincere face, Nell wanted to say yes. But she knew it was a promise she could not keep. "No. I'm afraid not," she replied. "After our marriage, Sir Lionel and I plan to honeymoon in Australia for a fortnight or so and then visit New Zealand. From there, we'll go home to England by way of the Suez Canal."

She could see that these were not the words Ken wanted to hear, but he simply nodded. She accompanied him out of the hotel and into the hot afternoon.

"Good-bye then, Miss Keene."

"Good-bye, Mr. Sanderson," Nell replied quietly.

For a moment, neither spoke and neither turned away. Nell desperately reached for some way to change her charted course, and Ken struggled silently with whether he should follow his heart or his head.

Out of the corner of his eye, Ken saw a cab pull up.

"Ah, there's a cab," he said as evenly as he could. "I must go. Good-bye, Nell,"

"Farewell, Ken. Give the children my best."

Ken handed his baggage to the driver and climbed into the cab. As the vehicle pulled away, he waved, and she raised a delicate, gloved hand to return the gesture. A great emptiness swept over him as the cab threaded its way through heavy traffic on its way to the ferry that would take him across the bay to Oakland and the Central Pacific Station.

He longed to tell the driver to turn the cab around. But to what purpose? His destiny lay in Salt Lake City with his children and hers lay in Australia and England with Sir Lionel Freeport. The die had been cast.

Chapter 17

Ken arrived in plenty of time to catch his train. After a frustrating wait, the train slowly chugged its way east on its two-day journey to Utah Territory. Later, when the train pulled onto the *Solano,* Ken remained in the carriage, only opening the windows to take advantage of the cool breeze.

The train again began chugging away. As the pain in his stomach intensified, Ken closed his eyes. A wave of loneliness washed over him. *Why do I feel this way?* he wondered. *Returning home is the right thing to do. So why do I feel I've let something precious slip from my grasp?*

He remembered the moment five years before when he and Karen had had their first disagreement and he thought he'd lost her. The way he had felt then was so similar to the way he felt now. *But why should I feel this way now? I'm not in love with Nell . . . Or am I?* Ken mused. He could not deny that he enjoyed the time they had spent together. *But is it only because I'm lonely and miss Karen so much? No.* He shook his head.

But what does it matter? She's chosen to marry Sir Lionel. Should I have tried to stop her? He sighed. *It's too late now.*

He thought of the discussion he'd had with Nell about the contrast between David and Joseph. David had made the wrong choice and was probably happy for a time; Joseph had made the right choice and was thrown into jail. Ken knew that ultimately, though, David had suffered great anguish while Joseph had been blessed beyond his imagination. These thoughts gave Ken some solace. *Like I said to Nell, if it is God's will, God will provide a way. It would be a great sin to force the issue. Nell is betrothed, or nearly so, to Sir Lionel and has pledged to her late husband to marry him. Unless that fact changes, I have no right to think of her as anything other than a friend.*

After a short stop in Sacramento, the train was on its way again, traveling into the night. A little after midnight, the train screeched to a halt, waking Ken and the other passengers.

"Sorry, folks," the conductor said, entering the car from the rear. "Avalanche. Snow on the tracks. It'll take a few hours to remove. Sorry."

The sky was lightening in the east when the train started on its journey again. As much as Ken loved the mountain scenery, he was glad when the train issued forth from the mountains and rattled and swayed its way across Nevada's flatlands, stopping briefly at Reno and Elko. As he got closer to home, Ken's spirits felt brighter, especially as he thought about seeing his children again.

The children were asleep when Ken finally arrived at home. He peeked into their rooms, and his heart burned within him to see them again.

"Papa, Papa!" Ainsley cried, running into her father's arms the next morning.

Gage was close behind. The three of them hugged for a long time while Maggie stood by beaming.

"Let's eat breakfast quickly and go get baby Karen," Ken said. "It's so good for us all to be together again."

"Where's Jack?" Ken asked Maggie when they were back home. The baby was asleep in her new blanket, and the two older children were playing with their new toys. Ken and Maggie sat across from each other in the parlor of Ken's home.

"At the temple site," Maggie said. "He volunteers there for a few hours ev'ry day. It's good he's not here. There's something I want to bend your ear about." Maggie paused as if not knowing how to start. Ken smiled encouragingly and waited. "Well, it's like this, Brother Sanderson," she began. Ken smiled at her use of "Brother Sanderson" rather than her former "Mr. Ken." "Since you've been away, Jack an' me've learned the gospel from Brother Kimball and your father. We've both accepted it."

Ken smiled broadly. "That's wonderful news, Maggie!"

She continued. "I would like to be baptized, but Jack won't agree. I mean he won't agree to be baptized himself, but he's all for me going ahead. But I don't want to join the Church without him." Maggie paused and sighed. "I don't know what to do. It's a turble d'lemma."

Ken nodded sympathetically. "Perhaps he has doubts about the restored gospel?"

"Oh, no," Maggie said quickly. "He believes ev'ry word of it. He told me so."

"And yet he refuses to be baptized?"

"Aye. I asked him what's holding him back, but he won't talk about it. Do you mind how Miss Karen was the same way?"

"I do. She refused to be baptized because of something in her past. Perhaps the same thing is holding him back. It seems whenever a person decides to join the Church, Satan throws obstacles in the way." Ken put his hand on Maggie's shoulder. "Don't despair, Maggie. I'll talk to him when he gets home. Now, there's something I want to talk to you about. On the way home from San Francisco, I decided that I'd like you and Jack to continue living here if you like. There's lots of room. Of course, I'll pay you a salary for keeping house."

"We'll gladly stay here until you find another missus, Brother Sanderson, but there'll be no talk of a salary. Jack and me've more money than we need. As soon as folks here found out he painted portraits, he can hardly keep up with the work."

"All right, Maggie, have it your way. If you're staying until I get married again, though, you may be here a long time."

"Not if your mother has anything to say about it!" Maggie exclaimed.

After supper that evening, Ken had a chance to talk with Jack alone in the parlor. "Well, Jack," Ken said. "Maggie tells me that you and she have had gospel discussions with Jonathan and my father. What do you think?"

"I believe ev'ry word," Jack said with conviction. "Ev'ry word."

"But you refuse to be baptized?"

"Aye, lad. A' old sailor like me could never be good enough to be a member o' the Church. Maggie now's a diff'rent kettle o' fish. I've tried to get her to join, but she won't."

"But, Jack, I know you. You're as good a man as I've ever known. Why do you say you're not good enough to join the Church?"

Jack's sea-scarred face took on a thoughtful look as his mind went into the past. "Ye've only known me since that day on Gray Street when ye told me ye liked m'scribblin' and threw a pound note into m'cap. It's true I turned over a new leaf that day, but it would scorch yer ears to know the things I done afore then. Sailors lead a wicked life o' drinkin' and carousin' wi' fallen women—and brawlin' in pubs from Calais t' Calcutta. Losin' m'leg slowed me down a mite, but these hands is stained, lad. M'wicked life 'as put me beyond the pale. I could never be a member o' the Church."

Ken vigorously shook his head. "If you mean by 'beyond the pale' that you are beyond the reach of Christ's Atonement, you are mistaken. With all due respect my friend, I don't think you fully understand the far-reaching affects of the Atonement yet. Christ died for our sins, Jack. All of them. The scriptures are full of examples of those whose lives were on the wrong track but who were forgiven. Let me read you something." Ken took a large Bible from its stand, turned to the book of Isaiah, and read, "'Come now, and let us reason together, saith the Lord: though your sins be as scarlet, they shall be as white as snow; though they be red like crimson, they shall be as wool.'"

Ken then took a copy of the Book of Mormon from the shelf and turned to the book of Alma. Then he read the story of King Lamoni's conversion.

Jack remained silent for a long moment before saying, "Thanks, lad. But I still ain't convinced that an old reprobate like me 'as a place in the Church. Why can't Maggie go ahead and join without me? I've pushed 'er to do it till I'm blue in the face."

"Of course she could go ahead without you, but she wants you both to be one in the gospel. Is there nothing I can say that'll change your mind?" Ken implored. Jack shook his head, and Ken tried another tack. "Have you met President Woodruff since you came to the Valley?"

Jack smiled. "Met him? I've not only met 'im but I've been 'ired t' paint 'is portrait! I'm supposed to see 'im about it tomorrow."

"Good. When you see him, will you talk to him about your . . . your situation?"

Jack sighed. "All right, lad."

That night Ken lay awake for a long while wondering what more he could say to Jack to help him understand. Suddenly it hit him. It was not his job to convince Jack; it was the job of the Holy Ghost. This realization was a balm to Ken's mind, and before long, he was sleeping peacefully.

He didn't see Jack again until the following afternoon. The latter had just returned from seeing President Wilford Woodruff.

"Well, Jack," Ken said, "what has President Woodruff to say about your situation?"

Jack raised his bushy eyebrows and smiled sheepishly. "About the same as ye said, lad. Is Maggie about?"

"Yes. She's in the kitchen. I'll get her."

Jack nodded and sat down on a sofa in the parlor. His rugged face was pensive when Ken and Maggie joined him.

"Well," he said. "Ye'll both 'ave yer wish. I tried m'best to shock President Woodruff w' tales o' me wicked past, but it rolled off 'im like water off a sou'wester. When I was finished 'e just says, 'Brother Tolley, 'ave ye repented of yer sins and forsaken 'em?' I says I thought so, and 'e says, 'Then there's nothing to stop ye from joining the Church.'" Jack turned to his wife and gazed into her expectant face. "We're to be baptized tomorrow afternoon in City Creek, luv." Then turning to Ken he added, "I'd like fer ye to baptize us and Brother Kimball to confirm us, just like when Miss Karen joined the Church." He turned back to Maggie. "If that's alright with ye, luv?"

"Of course, Jack," a beaming Maggie said as she threw her arms around her husband.

Ken's heart swelled within him as he nodded his acceptance. He was about to slip out of the room and leave his friends to their happiness when Jack stopped him.

"Don't go yet," Jack said, "there's more news." He motioned for Ken to sit down across from him and Maggie. He paused for a moment before saying, "Your father and cousin taught me about a thing called foreordination, and I couldn't really fathom it. But President Woodruff said something that's made it clear as glass. 'E says when we met, ye and me, lad, on Gray Street, it was meant to be, that the Lord had a purpose fer me t' join the Church. And what was that purpose? For one, t' 'elp finish the inside o' the temple. I've been 'elpin' outside, as much as a one-legged man can, but can ye believe it? Me, Jack Tolley, workin' inside the Lord's house? But that's what President Woodruff said. I'm to use m'God-given talents t' paint murals. When I 'eard this, you could've knocked me down with a feather, as Maggie would say."

Ken smiled. "And to think that I lost sleep last night worrying about how to get you baptized when all along the Lord had it well in hand." He rose and put out his hand to Jack. "Congratulations, my friend."

For the rest of that day, warmth pervaded Ken's being. The knowledge that he would have the privilege of baptizing Jack and Maggie was like the anticipation he had felt as a child waiting for Christmas morning.

How I wish Karen could be here for the baptism, Ken thought as he checked in on his sleeping children, who looked so much like their mother, before going to sleep himself. *But maybe she will be* were his last thoughts before he fell asleep that night.

Chapter 18

"Ken, this is Sister Priscilla Reynolds," Elisabeth Sanderson said to her son at the post-baptism reception that was being held at her home. "Sister Reynolds is from Springville. Her husband passed on a while back."

Ken shook hands with the attractive young widow who appeared to be in her late twenties. They exchanged smiles, tacitly agreeing to tolerate Elisabeth's matchmaking.

"From Springville," Ken said. "That's a nice town."

"It is," she answered.

"Oh, I must go see how Maggie's doing with the ice cream," Elisabeth said, leaving Ken and Priscilla alone.

"I must apologize for my mother," Ken said. "She's determined to see me married again."

Priscilla smiled. "I can see that she means well. Likewise, my friends are constantly introducing me to eligible men. Has your wife been gone long?"

"Several months. She died from complications after childbirth. And your husband?"

"Two years. He was killed in a quarry accident while they were getting stone for the temple."

"I'm sorry," Ken said limply, and he could think of nothing more to say.

Priscilla, too, was lost for words. Elisabeth's return rescued them from an embarrassing silence.

Later that evening after all the guests had gone, Elisabeth asked Ken, "Well, what did you think of Sister Reynolds?"

"She's very nice, but if you have any hopes of getting us together, know that they are vain. It will be a long time, if ever, before I'm interested in a woman again." An image of Nell, her hazel eyes sparkling with laughter, suddenly popped into his head. His conscience pricked him, so he pushed the thought aside. "With the children, my work at the newspaper, and my calling with the elders, I have a full life."

"Of course, dear. I wouldn't think of meddling," Elisabeth said, a facetious smile on her lips. Ken raised his eyebrows, skepticism in his eyes. His mother went on. "However, Karen expected you to take another wife. She told me so. The Brethren also feel a man in your position should marry again."

Ken shrugged. "I know all this, Mother, but it's only been a few months. Maybe after a year or so I'll give some thought to such things, but right now I'm not interested."

"Of course, dear," Elizabeth replied. "But please be cautious that you don't let your timetable supercede the Lord's. I recall from Church history that on the suggestion of the Prophet Joseph, his brother Hyrum married Mary Fielding only one month after his first wife died in childbirth. Hyrum and Mary, as I'm sure you know, are the parents of Elder Joseph F. Smith of the First Presidency. I only mention this because I want you to be sensitive to the promptings of the Spirit in this matter. When the time is right, if you're living close to the Spirit, you'll know."

Ken smiled at his mother. "Thanks, Mother. I know you are only interested in my welfare and the children's."

* * *

Despite his decision to wait at least a year before calling on a woman, a month after the discussion with his mother, loneliness drove Ken to invite Priscilla Reynolds by mail to a dance in Springville. Her positive reply both pleased and scared him.

"Who are you?" a young boy asked Ken as the latter stood nervously on Priscilla Reynold's porch.

"Brother Sanderson," Ken said. "Is your mother ready?"

The young boy eyed Ken suspiciously. "Wait," he said, abruptly shutting the door.

As he stared at the closed door, Ken felt guilty from head to toe —guilty about even thinking of keeping company with a woman other than Karen. He contemplated bolting from the porch, leaping into his rented carriage, and heading back to the train station. The door suddenly opened.

"I'm sorry, Brother Sanderson," a blushing Priscilla Reynolds said. "Noal knows better than to leave you on the porch. Please come in." She settled him in the parlor. "I'll be ready directly."

From his seat on the edge of a sofa, Ken glanced up at a picture over the mantelpiece. It was of a distinguished man, perhaps ten years older than Priscilla. Ken assumed it was Priscilla's late husband. Under the stern stare of Brother Reynolds, Ken felt even more disconcerted. The minutes ticked slowly by.

What am I doing here? he thought. *I'm not ready for this.*

By the time Priscilla reappeared, Ken was almost ready to call the whole thing off.

"I'm so sorry for keeping you, Brother Sanderson," she said. "My son needed some persuading that going to the dance with you is appropriate behavior for his mother. I'll just run next door and let my mother-in-law know that I'm leaving. She will be minding Noal and the younger children, who are already asleep."

Priscilla soon returned.

"Your late husband?" Ken asked, nodding at the painting over the mantelpiece.

"Yes. He was . . . is a good man."

"I can see you loved him very much." Ken hesitated. "May I ask a personal question?" When Priscilla nodded, he asked, "How did you cope when you lost him?"

Priscilla sighed and sat down across from Ken. "It wasn't easy. But prayers, friends, family, and the scriptures got me through. There's one scripture in particular that really helped me. It's found both in the Book of Mormon and the Bible—Isaiah, chapter fifty-four."

"I'm not familiar with it, but I'll look it up when I have the chance." Ken smiled and stood. "I guess we should be going. The dance will have already started."

When they got to the dance, Ken helped Priscilla from the carriage and immediately withdrew his hand. She preceded him into the hall, and he left her briefly to take care of their coats. When he returned, she was surrounded by a bevy of women who immediately ceased their chattering when he came in sight. The coterie dissolved as he approached. He could feel as much as see their appraising stares as they retreated.

When he led Priscilla onto the dance floor, he felt that all eyes were on them. But his awkwardness slowly faded and, despite his initial misgivings, he found himself enjoying the music and Priscilla's company.

That evening Ken lay in bed at the Harrison Hotel thinking about the time he had spent with Priscilla. *Perhaps being married again wouldn't be so bad. The children need a mother, and, despite what I said to Mother, this half-life I'm living is intolerable.* He thought, as he had on many occasions, of the day he had first met Karen. It was plain to him that the fire in his bosom he had experienced at that time was missing in his first meeting with Priscilla. *Still,* he thought, *she is very nice. Maybe that fire only happens once in a lifetime. What would be so bad about marrying for companionship?* Suddenly Nell entered his mind. *Nell married Lord Darnley for security and, I suppose, companionship. They had a good marriage. It seems that in marrying Lionel Freeport she's chosen security over love once more.* Thoughts of Nell drove Priscilla from his mind, and the same feeling of loss he'd felt in parting with her invaded his peace. *I wonder how she's doing in Australia.*

Chapter 19

As Ken's hackney cab pulled away from the Palace Hotel, Nell felt a sharp pang of regret already forming in the pit of her stomach. *Why does fate continue to bring us together if we're not meant to be more than friends?* She sighed deeply, turned from waving good-bye, and slowly reentered the hotel.

"Good afternoon, Miss Keene," said a bellboy, tipping his pillbox hat.

Nell returned his greeting with a forced smile and continued to her room. She lay down on the bed and stared up at the ornate ceiling. Feeling very alone, she wondered why life had brought her here and left her alone. She was happy for Marian and Mr. Hawkins and wished them well. And she knew it was the right thing that Ken had gone home to his children. She thought of her feelings for Ken, and her head told her that she could never fit into his world, but her heart told her a different story. Her mind went back to the first love of her life, Davy Norris, whom she had walked away from to marry Lord Darnley. Had she done the right thing? Was it better to marry for security than love? *Why can't one have security* and *love?* she thought. *Certainly, the woman who marries Ken will have both.*

Then she thought of their discussion of religion. Religion was such an important part of Ken's life. The woman who married him would have to be a member of his church. *I guess Lionel was right. It would be impossible for me to become a Mormon and change my whole way of life. Besides, I've promised to marry Lionel, and I will not break my promise. In a few weeks, we'll be together again, and life will be back to normal.* Her mind dwelled on this thought for a moment. *But do I really want life to get back to normal?*

A flock of people was again waiting at Nell's hotel. On Nell's instructions, the concierge turned them all away, except for the theater manager and the British ambassador. The manager pleaded with her to accept another run of *Sweet Lavender,* as the publicity surrounding her disappearance would lead to more sold-out houses. She reluctantly refused, except for one charity performance, scheduled for a week from Saturday. Nell also had her passage to Australia rebooked for the Monday after the performance.

Nell also met with the British ambassador. The man was contrite, embarrassed that Langton had fooled him. He assured Nell that she had done the right thing in fleeing the dinner.

The next days were a blur of activity. Nell supervised Ben's haircut, shopped for Marian's trousseau, and saw Ben off. *How fine he looks in his new clothes,* she thought as she waved good-bye to him. *The girls will be flocking around him at the Placerville Saturday-night dances.*

After a frantic scramble, the cast was regrouped, and the charity matinee went forward as scheduled. It was a sellout. A cast party followed the performance. Late that night, Nell fell into bed completely exhausted. She slept through most of Sunday, forcing herself from bed in the late afternoon in order to finish packing. With the help of a maid supplied by the concierge, she was packed and ready for her voyage by Sunday evening. The next morning a policeman escorted her to the San Francisco dock, where she boarded the *S.S. Mariposa.*

For the first two days of the voyage, Nell hardly left her stateroom. On the morning of the third day, she went up on deck to get some fresh air. The sky was overcast, the wind brisk, and the waves boisterous. She leaned on the taffrail and drew in a deep breath.

"Excuse me," said a hesitant voice to her right. Nell turned to see a pleasant-faced young woman dressed in a plain, inexpensive dress and bonnet. The latter smiled and pushed a shock of blonde hair from her eyes. "Please forgive my boldness, but aren't you Miss Nell Keene, the actress?"

"I am."

"Oh, Miss Keene," the woman gushed, "I just loved you in *Sweet Lavender*. My mother and I thoroughly enjoyed your performance last Saturday. We were so glad to finally see you. We tried to get tickets to see you before your . . . your disappearance but couldn't. We were so worried for you and so glad when you returned safely, and we were overjoyed to get tickets for your final performance."

Nell gave the stranger an appreciative smile. "Thank you. Leaving the city so unceremoniously caused a few problems, but all was put right before I left. As for my role in *Sweet Lavender*, I did my best, but I think it's time for me to give up ingenue parts."

"Oh, no, you were just wonderful as Lavender."

A self-deprecating smile played on Nell's lips. "It's amazing what makeup can do. And you are?"

"Mrs. Randall Trescott—Sara."

Nell studied Sara Trescott. "You hardly look old enough to be married."

Sara smiled. "I'm one and twenty. My husband and I were barely married when he took off to Australia to take possession of his grandfather's sheep ranch." Sara sighed before adding, "I'm going there to join him."

For a moment neither of them spoke as they leaned on the railing and gazed out at the white-capped waves. Nell wanted to ask Sara why she was reluctant to join her husband, but the queasiness in her stomach prevented her from carrying on the conversation. She wondered if she were getting seasick but dismissed the thought as she'd had no trouble with this malady on her way across the Atlantic.

Without turning to look at Nell, Sara continued her story.

"I long to be with Randall again," she said. "But I fear what life will be like on a sheep station. When we first got word he'd inherited his grandfather's thousand acres, we were overjoyed. No longer would we have to get by on Ran's meager wage as a bank clerk and my even smaller wage as a housemaid. Ran quickly quit his position at the bank and shipped out to Australia, promising to send for me as soon as he was settled." She sighed. "I don't think the farm is all he hoped for. He hasn't actually said so in his letters, but it has been almost a year, and he still hasn't sent for me. My mother gave me the money for the passage. She can ill afford it as she's on a widow's pension and was saving the money to have her little house painted. Randall will be cross. He doesn't like accepting charity. I'm sure he—" Sara suddenly realized that she had been rambling on without a response from Nell. She turned to face her. "Why, Miss Keene!" she exclaimed. "You're white as a sheet. Please, let me help you below."

Nell nodded weakly and allowed her new acquaintance to assist her to her stateroom. Once Sara had made Nell as comfortable as she could, she went off to get the ship's doctor.

"Nothing too serious, Miss Keene," the doctor, a rotund, cheerful man, said after examining Nell. "I believe you're suffering from fatigue and a touch of *mal de mer.* All you need is rest." He withdrew a bottle from his black bag and handed it to Sara. "Give Miss Keene a spoonful of this every four hours. Keep her in bed for the next three days, give her lots of fluids, and she should be right as rain." Turning back to Nell, he added, "Let your maid do for you, and I'll drop in and see you again tomorrow."

"Thank you, doctor," Nell said. "But Mrs. Trescott is not my maid. Perhaps you could suggest someone to attend me."

"Please let me look after you," Sara said quickly. "I have nothing to do. It will be my great pleasure."

"There," the doctor said with a decisive nod. "Problem solved. See you tomorrow."

"Thank you so much, Sara," Nell whispered when the doctor had gone. "Would it be more convenient for you if you removed to the second bedroom?"

Sara opened the door to the other room and glanced in. "Oh, Miss Keene!" she exclaimed, "It's beautiful. It makes my shared cabin in steerage look like a hovel. I'd love to stay here with you."

Later, after she had moved her few belongings into the stateroom and seen to Nell's needs, Sara sat comfortably knitting in an over-stuffed chair while Nell slept. Several hours later, Nell awoke.

"Miss Keene," Sara said. "You're looking so much better. I don't think you were seasick, just exhausted."

Nell nodded her agreement and asked, "Is that a baby blanket you're knitting? Are you . . . of course not. Your husband has been gone for a year."

Sara sighed. "More's the pity. I'd love to have a wee one, but—"

"But?"

Sara took a deep breath. "Well, to be honest, I'm really not sure how things stand between Ran and me. Besides my feeling that the ranch is not all Ran expected, there's another thing." She hesitated. "On his way to Australia on the boat, he met some Mormon missionaries. I guess they must have been very convincing, because when he got to Sydney, they baptized him. I can't imagine what got into him to join himself to such awful people. He's always been so levelheaded. So you see, although I love Ran with all my heart, I'm a little fearful about our future. I don't know what to expect when I get to Australia. How will he have changed and what kind of place is this sheep farm?"

Nell began to sit up, and Sara was instantly at her side to prop the soft silk pillows behind her. Sara then drew a chair close to the bed and sat down.

Nell smiled reassuringly and patted Sara's hand. "I wouldn't worry about Randall joining the Mormon church. I'm glad to tell you that you've been misinformed about the Mormons. I'm sure that any changes you find in your husband will be for the better. One of my . . . my good friends is a Mormon, and a finer man you couldn't find. He was with the policeman who went looking for me. I've known him, Mr. Kenny Sanderson, for several years. We met in Scotland."

Sara listened attentively as Nell told her about her adventure with Ken in Scotland. When she was finished, she smiled sheepishly at Sara. "I'm sorry to have gone on so."

Sara smiled mischievously. "I think this Mr. Sanderson is more than a just a good friend, if you don't mind me saying so."

Nell closed her eyes and was silent. "Perhaps you're right, Sara. But there's nothing I can do about it. I'll soon be wed to Sir Lionel Freeport, and Mr. Sanderson will be only a memory, although a pleasant one I must admit."

Sara seemed about to respond but held her peace. After a moment she said, "Well, Miss Keene, I must see to our supper. Is there anything I can do for you first?"

"Only one thing," Nell said with a smile. "Stop calling me Miss Keene."

Sara smiled. "Okay, Nell. I'll be right back."

Later, when the two women had finished supper, Sara asked Nell to tell her all she knew about the Mormon church. Nell obliged by relating what she had learned from Ken, from her visit to Salt Lake City, and from the campfire discussion at which Ken had responded to Ben Hawkins's inquiries about the church.

"Perhaps it's not such a strange religion as I've been led to believe," Sara said. She smiled, revealing charming dimples. "At least I can rest assured I won't have to contend with Ran taking another wife now that the Church has given up polygamy."

Two days later, Nell was relaxing on a deck chair when the doctor stopped by.

"Here's a book on Australia you might find interesting, Miss Keene," he said.

Nell thanked him, and he left. She was well into the book when Sara joined her.

"What are you reading?" Sara asked.

Nell held up the book. "*All About Australia.* The doctor loaned it to me. I'm just reading about dingoes. Apparently they've become a real problem, especially to sheep farmers like your husband."

"Dingoes?"

"Yes. They're a kind of wild dog. Apparently they're not only a menace to sheep but other domestic animals as well. They've even been known to attack children. They're such a problem, the Australian government has built a fence all the way from Jinbour to Toowoon-ba—over three hundred miles—to keep them out of the sheep-raising Southwest."

"Toowoonba," Sara said with a smile. "What a funny name. Has the fence kept the dingoes out?"

"According to the book, the fence has only been up for about six years, but it seems to be helping. Reduction in the dingo population, though, has caused another problem—the Southwest is now overrun with rabbits and kangaroos."

"Come to think of it, I believe Ran wrote something about rabbits overrunning his place." She sighed. "I wonder what I'll find when I get there."

Nell smiled. "Don't worry, Sara," she said and patted the girl's hand. "I'll be there to help you just as you've helped me. And you're not alone in worrying about what awaits us. Lionel's description of his mother was anything but encouraging."

Seven days after leaving San Francisco, the ship docked briefly at Honolulu to drop off passengers and mail. Another seven days brought it to Apia, Samoa. The ship anchored off West Point, and passengers and mail were transferred by way of a small sloop. Six days later, the ship docked at the Union Steamship Company's wharf at Auckland, New Zealand.

The arrival of a ship from America brought hundreds of people to the wharf, and soon there was a crowd aboard. An Englishwoman recognized Nell almost immediately, and for the next hour, Nell answered questions about her American tour. She and Sara finally managed to free themselves from the friendly crowd and had no sooner returned to their stateroom than a cabin boy delivered a note from the mayor of Auckland inviting the two to an impromptu supper in Nell's honor.

"What an exciting life you lead," Sara said wistfully as she helped Nell with her coat when they had returned from the dinner.

Nell sighed. "I will admit my life on the stage has been exciting, but I'm ready to settle down now. I'd also like to have children before it's too late."

"Have you discussed children with your intended?"

The question took Nell off guard. She thought for a moment. "Now that I think of it, we haven't discussed children. I guess I just assumed he would want an heir."

Chapter 20

Four days after the brief stop in Auckland, the ship docked in Sydney, Australia. Nell had enjoyed the voyage and had recovered her strength; she was nevertheless glad to have the journey behind her. Soon she and Sara were on their way to the Freeport mansion.

Upon their arrival at the mansion, they were greeted by a dignified butler with a polished English accent. "Ah, Miss Keene," he said, "you are finally here. We have been expecting you for some time. My name is Cheevers. Please be seated in the parlor, and I will notify her ladyship that you have arrived."

The butler glanced at Sara and hesitated.

"Thank you, Mr. Cheevers," Nell said quickly. "This is my companion, Mrs. Trescott. We will both wait in the parlor."

"As you wish, Miss Keene," the butler said respectfully.

Sara's eyes were as big as saucers as she glanced around the ornate room. "Wow! What a place," she said. "Will you be staying here?"

"*We'll* be staying here," Nell said. "At least until I can arrange for you to join Randall."

"Miss Keene," said a tall, aristocratic old woman, completely ignoring Sara. "You have arrived at last. You were delayed?"

Nell and Sara rose to greet the woman. *She's just as Lionel described her,* Nell thought. *I must not let her dominate me the way she does her children.*

"I was, Lady Freeport," Nell said evenly. "Please accept my apologies. After we are settled, I will happily explain my tardiness." Motioning toward Sara, she continued. "This is my friend, Mrs.

Randall Trescott. May she lodge with me until we can arrange transportation to her husband's sheep station?"

Peering through a lorgnette, Lady Freeport examined Sara from head to toe.

"I suppose we could find accommodations in the servants' quarters," Mrs. Freeport said coldly.

"Actually, I would prefer she stayed with me," Nell replied.

"Oh, no, Miss Keene," Sara said. "I'll be happy in the servants' quarters."

Nell's voice became firm. "I wouldn't hear of it, Mrs. Trescott," she said, turning to face Lady Freeport. "I'm sure there is a place for you in my rooms."

Lady Freeport glanced at Sara and then at Nell. She heaved a sigh. "If you insist, Miss Keene," she finally conceded. "But I must say such things are not done, even here in the colonies. Lionel will hear about it."

"Speaking of Lionel," Nell said. "Where is he?"

"Sir Lionel and his lordship are not here and won't be for some time," Lady Freeport said in a voice that revealed that she had no qualms about Nell being separated from her son's company.

"May I ask where they are?" Nell asked.

Lady Freeport again sighed before revealing that because Nell had not arrived as planned, her two sons had left on a tour of the Church of England parishes throughout the province of New South Wales.

"I'm sorry I was the cause of friction between you and your future mother-in-law," Sara said as the two newcomers were unpacking Nell's things in the larger of two bedrooms of a cavernous suite.

"Think nothing of it," Nell said. "Lionel told me that his mother ruled the roost in the Freeport family, and I've determined to show her that she won't rule me. Your presence gave me a good excuse to do so. First impressions are very important. If one allows oneself to be cowed at the outset, it's very difficult to regain control. When I married Lord Darnley, I was completely out of my element and was constantly looked down upon by his aristocratic friends. It took me a long time and some embarrassing moments before I was accepted as the legitimate wife of a peer of the realm."

The two women continued unpacking in silence for several minutes. Then Nell said, "When we're finished here, I'll find out how to get you to your husband. May I see his address?"

Sara retrieved a slip of paper from her handbag and glanced at it.

"Strange-sounding place, isn't it?" she said, handing it to Nell.

Nell read the address aloud. "'Jumpbuck Sheep Station, Wagga Wagga, New South Wales.' It *is* a strange name—and rather redundant."

"Redundant?"

Nell smiled. "If I'm not mistaken, a 'jumpbuck' is a sheep, so it's really 'Sheep Sheep Station, Wagga Wagga'!"

Sara giggled, and in a lowered voice she chanted with glee, "Sheep Sheep Station, Wagga Wagga! Sheep Sheep Station, Wagga Wagga!"

Nell burst out laughing. They were both in fits of laughter when a knock sounded at the door. Nell wiped the tears from her eyes with a handkerchief and opened the door to the butler.

"Have we been making too much noise, Mr. Cheevers?" Nell asked.

The butler shook his head and smiled. "Not at all, Miss Keene. It's good to hear laughter in this ah . . . somber house. I've come to conduct you to luncheon. Her ladyship will not be joining you as she is otherwise engaged."

"I'm sorry to hear it," Nell said. "Mrs. Trescott and I were just discussing how to get to her husband's sheep station."

The butler turned to Sara. "Where is your husband's place, Mrs. Trescott?" he asked.

"Sheep Sheep Station, Wagga Wagga," Sara said quickly and again erupted with laughter.

"Jumpbuck Sheep Station near Wagga Wagga," Nell corrected with a broad smile.

The butler retained his professional detachment, but the twinkle in his eye told Nell that he was an ally in this big, cold house.

"Ah, Wagga Wagga," the butler said, "The place of many crows—that's what the name means. It's on the Murrumbidgee River, about halfway between Sydney and Melbourne. A day's journey on the steam train from here. I believe Jumpbuck Station is some miles this side of Wagga Wagga. A desolate area from what I know. Will you ladies be traveling alone?"

"I imagine so," Nell said.

Concern crossed the butler's face. "Australia is rather rough country," he said, "Settled by criminals, as you probably know. It's not advisable for two ladies to travel alone, although you should be all right on the train. Will someone be collecting you at Jumpbuck?"

Nell let Sara answer. "I'm sure my husband will meet us if we can get a telegraph message to him. Would that be possible?"

"Yes," Mr. Cheevers said. "You can wire him from the railway station." He paused before adding, "I'm still a little worried about you traveling alone, though." Suddenly, his eyes lit up. "I'll be right back." He quickly exited the room.

Nell and Sara exchanged quizzical glances and then returned to their unpacking. The butler was soon back, carrying a small, pearl-handled revolver.

"I'd like you to take this when you go to Jumpbuck," he said. "It was my late wife's. She was wont to carry it in her handbag when she went abroad. All you do is slide this safety catch over, and it's ready to fire."

"Thank you for your concern, Mr. Cheevers," Nell said. "But I don't like guns. Besides, I've traveled halfway around the globe without the need of a firearm. Unless Mrs. Trescott would like . . ."

Sara shook her head, and Nell didn't finish her sentence.

The butler sighed. "All right, ladies, have it your way. But I think you're making a mistake. Outside the city, this is a dangerous country."

Nell and Sara dined alone in the smaller of two dining rooms. That evening, they dined alone again. They were just finishing their supper when a maid informed Nell that Lady Freeport requested her presence.

"You wanted to see me, Lady Freeport?" Nell asked.

They were in the parlor of the older woman's suite. Lady Freeport was sitting at an ornate writing desk. She did not ask Nell to sit.

"I did," the old woman said. "It is not my custom to dine with servants. Until this Trescott person leaves the premises, I will not be dining with you. Furthermore, having her in your suite is most disagreeable to me. However, you have insisted on her lodging with you, and I have acceded to your wish. That will be all."

"Thank you for making your position clear, your ladyship," Nell said respectfully. "You need not distress yourself further on that score, as Mrs. Trescott and I will be leaving for the Jumpbuck Sheep Station near Wagga Wagga tomorrow." As she said these words, an involuntary smile played on Nell's lips. "If Sir Lionel returns before I do, please inform him of my whereabouts. Thank you."

The next morning, Mr. Cheevers accompanied Nell and Sara to the railway station. The three of them crowded into a small telegraph room.

"Would it be possible to get a telegram to Jumpbuck Sheep Station near Wagga Wagga today?" Sara asked the telegraph operator.

The man nodded. "Wagga, yes," he said. "Jumpbuck, no." Nell smiled, wondering if the brevity of the telegraphs he sent hadn't influenced his speech over the years. The man continued. "Course, a rider could take a message from Wagga t' Jumpbuck. It'd cost."

"It's important that Mr. Randall Trescott is informed of his wife's arrival," Nell interjected. "Please send the message, and I will pay the cost of the rider." Nell paid the fee, and the party walked toward the waiting train.

"Good-bye, ladies," Mr. Cheevers said later, as he waved to Nell and Sara from the railway station platform. "Keep warm, and don't let the dingoes get you."

"Thank you for your many kindnesses, Mr. Cheevers," Nell called through the open window. Holding up the large brown basket Mr. Cheevers had given them, she added, "And especially for the picnic basket."

"It's rather chilly this morning," Sara said to Nell once they were on their way. "It seems strange to have winter here and summer back in America."

After traveling for several hours, Nell eyed the picnic basket on the seat across from them. "I don't know about you," she said, "but I'm hungry. The aroma from that basket has been enticing me ever since we left. Shall we see what's in there?"

Sara smiled. "I thought you'd never ask. I'm starved."

Sara placed the basket between them on the seat, opened it, and began unwrapping cloth napkins.

"Mmm," Sara said. "Fried chicken, soda bread, strawberry preserves, milk, and . . . and a pearl-handled revolver!"

Nell's eyes went wide, and she slowly shook her head. "Mr. Cheevers appears to have had his way. Oh well, it won't hurt to keep it in the basket."

Six hours later, Nell and Sara were awakened from dozing by the train conductor. "Jumpbuck Station's only a few more miles," he said. "I suppose you have someone meeting you?"

"We do," Sara said. "My husband."

"Good," the conductor said. "Jumpbuck's not much—only a three-sided shed by the side of the tracks. No real station."

As they drew closer, Sara's face was glued to the window. Suddenly, she heaved a sigh. "He's not there!"

The train slowed to a stop, and the ladies and the conductor followed a porter who carried their baggage off the train.

"Mr. Cheevers was right," Nell said, glancing around. "It is rather desolate."

"You'd be well advised to go on into Wagga Wagga and meet your party there," the conductor said, checking his watch, anxious for the train to be on its way.

Nell glanced at Sara. "Perhaps he's right," Nell said. "We could send a rider from town informing Randall that you've arrived."

"I'd hate for Ran to show up and us not be there." She sighed. "I just can't wait to see him."

"We must be going, ladies," the conductor said, again glancing at his watch. "What will it be?"

Sara's disappointment moved Nell to ask the conductor, "When does the next train pass this way?"

"Not till the morning, I'm afraid," he said.

Nell considered this information and made a decision. "Go on, sir. We'll wait for Mr. Trescott."

The porter piled the baggage into the hut. The two women watched the train disappear down the tracks and surveyed the desolate landscape.

"We truly have traveled across the world," Nell said, looking around at the desolate land.

Chapter 21

"Shall we sit?" Nell asked, motioning toward a wooden bench in the hut.

"You go in, Nell," Sara said. "I'll watch out here."

Nell left her friend staring down the long, empty trail leading from Jumpbuck Station. She entered the hut and glanced around at the bare stud walls and up to the open, dusty rafters. An abandoned bird's nest clung to the vee where a horizontal beam met the wall. A multitude of spiderwebs spanned the rafters. *I hope the sheep station will be a little more accommodating than this shack,* she thought.

It was almost dark by the time Sara gave up her vigil.

"It's getting cold," she said, looking forlorn as she entered the shed. "We should have gone on to town, like the conductor said. I'm sorry."

"Don't worry," Nell said kindly. "Even if we have to spend the night here, it won't kill us. Growing up poor, I've spent the night in worse accommodations. Let's get my woolen cloak from the valise, and we can share it."

Soon they were sitting on the bench with their feet up on their baggage and Nell's warm cloak around them.

"This isn't so bad," Nell said. "Soon Ran will be here, and we'll look back on this and—"

Her words were cut off by a long, drawn out, howl. The women looked at one another, chills coursing down their backs.

"Dingoes," Nell whispered. "The book said they don't bark, but they do howl." She leaned over and pulled the revolver from the picnic basket. "How did Mr. Cheevers say this worked?"

Another howl sounded, this time closer. Nell slid the gun's safety catch off and waited.

"Look!" Sara whispered and clung to Nell's arm.

In the fading light, the women could see a doglike creature with glowing yellow eyes staring in at them, several feet from the doorless front of the shack.

"It is a dingo, all right," Nell whispered. "So much for the three-hundred-mile fence." She took a deep breath. "Away with you. Be gone!" she yelled. The wild dog didn't budge.

Sara joined Nell. "Be gone!" they yelled in unison.

The animal stood completely still. With trembling hands, Nell pointed the gun well above the beast and fired. The dingo loped off.

"Whew!" Nell exclaimed with relief. "Thank you, Mr. Cheevers."

But the respite was brief.

"It's back," Sara said, shuddering as she stared wide-eyed out through the doorframe. "And it's brought two others. I'm so sorry, Nell! I was sure Ran would be here."

"Don't fret," Nell said quickly. "The gun will keep them at bay."

Nell fired again, scattering the three wild dogs. But each time the ritual was repeated, the dingoes grew bolder. After several warning shots, Nell had had enough,

"That's it," she said firmly. "If they come back again, I'm *not* going to fire over their heads."

They did come back again. Nell aimed at the largest one and pulled the trigger. The metallic click caused her heart to sink.

"Sara," she said, "we're out of bullets. Are there extras in the picnic basket?"

Sara shook her head. "No. What will we do?" she asked, panic creeping into her voice.

"Quick. Up into the rafters."

The women threw a suitcase onto the bench, and while Nell shouted at the dingoes, Sara scrambled up into the rafters. Nell quickly followed. Almost immediately, the wild dogs rushed into the shed, ripped the picnic basket apart, and commenced devouring the contents. Suddenly, they stopped eating, stood frozen for a moment, then dashed out of the shed, the heftiest one with a chicken bone locked in its jaws.

Sara gave a nervous laugh. "Do you think all they were after was Mr. Cheevers's fried chicken?"

"Listen," Nell whispered. "Someone's coming."

"Maybe it's Ran."

"And maybe it isn't," Nell whispered. "Let's wait before we reveal ourselves."

"I have to sneeze," Sara said. "It's dusty up here."

"Put your finger under your nose."

Sara followed Nell's instruction, and the urge to sneeze passed. The squeak of a wagon wheel stopped in front of the shed, and seconds later they looked down on a lantern-lit black man. Nell and Sara held their breath and remained completely still as he inspected the luggage and the remains of the picnic basket. He then went outside.

Suddenly, Sara sneezed, and the man rushed back into the shed. He held up the lantern, and, wide-eyed, stared up at the women. They silently stared back. His face broke into an ear-to-ear grin.

"What you doin' up 'ere?" he asked.

"It's none of your business," Nell said, feeling more embarrassed than afraid. "Go away. We have a gun."

He ignored her threat. "Dingoes chase you up 'ere?" he asked, still smiling.

His friendly manner put Nell at ease. "Dingoes?" she said. "What dingoes? We always sit in the rafters of train sheds."

Sara burst out laughing. The man stared at them quizzically, seeming to debate whether Nell was being serious or not.

"Who are you, and what do you want?" Nell asked.

"Big fella, 'e send me fetch you," the man said.

"Big fella?" Nell said, turning to Sara. "Is Ran a big man?"

"No," Sara said. She then addressed the man. "What big fella?"

"Mista Randall. 'E send me fetch you."

"Why didn't he come himself?" Nell asked.

"Sick, missus. Very sick."

"I knew there was a reason he didn't come," Sara said, scrambling down from the rafters. "He must be awfully sick."

Nell quickly followed her, and the women looked on as the man, who the woman later learned was an aborigine called Burnu, piled their luggage into an open cart. Nell and Sara climbed into the cart and sat on the luggage. For the next half hour, the horse-drawn cart bumped along a rutted trail. It had no sooner stopped than Sara leapt from it and ran into the low-roofed cabin they had stopped in front of. She found her husband in a small bedroom at the back lying in a disheveled double bed.

"Ran," she cried, throwing herself down beside the bed.

His gaunt face, ashen in the lantern light, broke into a weak smile. "Sara," he whispered. "I can't believe you're here. When the telegram came, I managed to get out of bed, got dressed, and tried to hitch up the cart, but my strength failed me and I fell to the ground. Hours later Burnu found me. He got me back to bed and went to fetch you. I've been sick for a week." His eyes darted around the squalid room. "I'm sorry you had to find me like this and in such a place. I'm sorry—"

"Don't say another word," Sara interjected. "I'm here now. Soon you'll be well again." She inclined her head toward the main room. "I'm here with my friend, Miss Keene. She has been so good to me. Sleep, now, my love. In the morning, we'll talk some more."

Meanwhile, Nell had cleared a corner of the main room, and the aborigine, Burnu, had deposited her luggage there. She was busy hanging up a blanket to screen off the corner when Sara joined her.

"I found these blankets," Nell said. "But I couldn't find another bed."

"I'm so sorry to bring you here," Sara said as she helped Nell hang the blanket. "When we learned of Ran's inheritance, we pictured a big house with servants and all. This place is absolutely disgusting. No wonder Ran didn't send for me."

"Not to worry," Nell said. "Tomorrow we'll roll up our sleeves and have it shipshape in no time. In the meantime, let's find something to sleep on. I'm exhausted, as I'm sure you are."

A search produced six cured sheepskins. They laid the skins on the rough floor and overspread them with a blanket.

"This will do just fine," Nell said.

Sara sighed. "You're being such a good sport about all this, Nell."

Nell smiled. "This will be an adventure to tell my grandchildren. The expression on that man's face when he looked up and saw us dangling from the rafters was quite a sight to behold. Good night, Sara."

Sara left Nell and returned to her husband, whose heavy breathing indicated that he slept.

Over the next four days, the two women worked hard to make the cabin habitable, and Ran Trescott made a remarkable recovery. On the morning of the fifth day, he joined the ladies for breakfast.

"Are you sure you should be up so soon?" Sara asked.

"I'm feeling much better," Ran said, glancing around the room. "I hardly know the place. I'm embarrassed that it was such a mess when you got here." He smiled. "Did I understand Burnu right that you were chased up onto the roof of the train station by dingoes?"

Nell and Sara laughed.

"Up into the rafters," Nell said. "The beasts wouldn't go away. We were sure they wanted us for supper."

"Though they can be menaces, I doubt they would have actually attacked you," Ran said. "Did you have any food with you?"

"Yes," Sara said. "Fried chicken."

"Ah, that must have been what they were after. They have an acute sense of smell." He paused before adding with a smile, "You should have invited them into the shed to keep you warm. That's what the natives do. The colder it is, the more dogs they welcome. The aborigines' expression for a really cold night is a 'three-dog night.'"

Nell glanced at Sara. "Is your husband having us on?" she asked.

"Don't ask me," Sara said with a smile. "I'm a stranger here myself."

"By the way," Nell said. "Why does Burnu call you the 'big fella'? You're not a big person."

Ran shook his head. "It's got nothing to do with size. To the aborigines, the word *big* has many meanings. In this case it means boss. I certainly don't feel much like a boss, though. I haven't a clue how to run a sheep station." He grinned. "Although raising rabbits is another matter. I seem to have a knack for that. Have you taken a look around the place, Miss Keene?"

"I have," Nell said. "It's rather bleak country around here, but it has a beauty all its own. We passed through some really beautiful country on the way here on the train." She hesitated before adding,

"I'm sure with time you could build this place into a prosperous farm."

Ran considered this for a long moment. Then he turned to his wife.

"You haven't told Miss Keene?"

"No," Sara said. "I thought we'd tell her together."

"Tell me what?" Nell asked.

Ran shrugged. "About a month ago, I put the place up for sale with a broker in Sydney. I hoped to get enough to pay for my fare to San Francisco, and then our fare—Sara's and mine—to Utah."

"I see," Nell said. "How much are you asking for it?"

"One hundred pounds," Ran said. "That's about five hundred American dollars, but I'll take what I can get. I'm really not cut out to be a sheep farmer. Since joining the Mormon Church, my only desire is to gather with the Saints in Utah. There's a small branch of the Church in Sydney, but most of the members are leaving for Utah in about two weeks. I was hoping to go with them and surprise Sara in San Francisco. But the place hasn't sold, so it looks like we're stuck here a while longer. In the meantime, I hope to be well enough in a couple of days to accompany you back to Sydney. At least I'll be able to say good-bye to the other Saints as they leave."

"What are your chances of selling the farm?" Nell asked.

Ran sighed, and Sara slipped her hand in his. "According to the broker, not good, I'm afraid. But you never know. I've made it a matter of prayer, and as Lord Tennyson says, 'More things are wrought by prayer than this world dreams of.'"

"You sound like my friend Mr. Sanderson," Nell said. "He's a newspaperman and is always quoting something. Interestingly, he's a Mormon, too."

Ran leaned forward, interest evident in his pale face. "He's a Mormon? Where did you meet him?"

Ran and Sara listened intently as Nell recounted her first meeting with Ken in Scotland. Sara had heard some of the story en route to Australia. Nell also told them about her visit to Utah, and Ran pressed her for all the details about the place he called Zion.

Nell concluded, "I remember thinking that I could live in Salt Lake City. It has beautiful tree-lined streets and fresh, clean water flowing down from the mountains."

Ran looked at Sara with a wistful expression on his face. "Someday we'll be in Zion as well," he said.

Chapter 22

After breakfast Nell went for a ride on the old cart horse so that Sara and Ran could have some time alone. As she rode over the parched land, scattering rabbits in every direction, she wondered how she could help the young couple. She thought perhaps she could loan them the passage money to Utah, but she recalled Sara saying that Ran would not accept charity. On her way back to the farmhouse, an idea struck her. She smiled and urged the old horse into a canter. She was still smiling when Sara greeted her in the yard.

"You look like the cat that swallowed the canary," Sara said.

"I've just solved a tricky problem, which for the time being will remain a secret. How is Ran?"

"Much better. In fact, he thinks he'll be ready to accompany us to Sydney this weekend."

"That's wonderful, but you really needn't come with me. I'll be just fine traveling by myself."

Sara shook her head. "We want to go with you—anything to get away from this place. I wish Ran wasn't so stubborn. A Mormon family in Sydney offered to pay his way to Utah, but he refused. As I predicted, he was a little upset when I told him that I borrowed passage money from my mother, but then he kissed me and said I did the right thing." She paused, and her eyes surveyed the yard and ramshackle house. "A few days in Sydney will be welcome. Thank goodness we have Burnu to take care of things here. He's marvelous. I don't know how Ran would have gotten along without him."

Early Saturday morning, Burnu drove them in the wagon to Jumpbuck Station.

Ran looked inside the shed near the station. "You ladies climbed into the rafters in your frocks?" he asked.

Sara laughed. "We used our baggage as a ladder," she said. "When you have a bunch of hungry dingoes snapping at your heels, it's amazing what you can do."

The trip to Sydney seemed to go by quickly. Ran and Sara did more catching up on the months they had been apart, and Nell and Ran became better acquainted. When they arrived, they took a hackney cab to the home of Jedediah and Isabel Warren, Mormon friends of Ran.

"You are more than welcome to stay here, too," Mrs. Warren said to Nell as they all sat in the parlor of their large home. "And our services begin at nine tomorrow morning."

Nell smiled. "Thank you, that's very kind," she said. "But I'll be fine at the hotel. I will, however, accept your invitation to attend church services tomorrow. I listened to a sermon in the Tabernacle when I was in Salt Lake City and found it most enlightening. Later, a Mormon friend told me much about your doctrine."

One of the first things Nell did after checking into the Ambassador Hotel was to send a message to Mr. Cheevers letting him know she had arrived. Her message included an account of the dingo incident and her gratitude for the use of the revolver, which she promised to return to him.

Not long after Nell had sent off the note, a knock sounded at her door. She opened it to see the boy who had delivered her message to Mr. Cheevers.

"Mr. Cheevers sends his compliments, along with this letter," he said, handing Nell a sealed envelope.

Nell tipped the boy and sat down in an overstuffed chair. The envelope had only the words *Miss Nell Keen* written on it—no address and no postmark. Nell thought she recognized the handwriting and the misspelling. Hurriedly she opened it and read:

Frend Nell,

Greetings from me and Jack. We was so happy to lern you was found safe by Brother Sanderson. I call him

Bro. Sanderson cause me and Jack joined the Mormon Church. 'Twas a grand day. Bro. S. met a yung widow that day an' if his mum has her way they'll be wed by sumers end. By now your probly maried. We hope yur happy. Me and Jack is still wurking at Sanderson home. Jack spend his time at the tempel were hes doing murials on the walls. Ainsly, Gage and baby Karen is all well as we hope you and Sir Linel is.

Love,
Maggie & Jack

Nell stared blankly at the letter. *Ken might be married by now.* To her surprise, tears began rolling down her cheeks. *Why do I feel this way?* She chastened herself. *I will soon be married, too. It's only to be expected that Ken would marry. Any woman would be delighted to have him, children and all.*

A knock at the door interrupted her thoughts. She quickly wiped the tears from her eyes.

"Come in," she said, rising from the chair. Her heart remained with the letter as she looked at the man in the doorway, but she mustered enthusiasm and cried, "Lionel! You're back."

"I am," he said coolly as they embraced. Then he stepped back, searching her face. Nell wondered if he could tell she had been crying. He peppered her with questions. "Why in blazes has it taken you so long to get here? What are you doing staying in a hotel? Why are you not at my brother's home?"

Nell's openhanded gesture said as much as the words that followed, "After the extra three-week run—"

"Why did you take an extra three-week run?"

Nell shrugged. "I thought you'd be pleased that I was doing so well. At least I wrote and told you about it. Did you get my letter?"

"Yes, I received it. But even with an extra three-week run, you still should have been here weeks ago."

Nell sighed. "It's a long story. Can we talk about it later? It's getting late, and I'm exhausted."

"I suppose. But why are you staying in a hotel?" he asked.

"I thought it might be better for me to stay here. Your mother and I do not see eye to eye on some matters."

"She told me about your insisting that a servant live in your room and dine with you. Why would you do such a thing? I told you what mother was like."

Nell stiffened. "Just because you told me about her attitude, Lionel, doesn't mean that I accept it." She paused and her voice softened. "But now that you're here, I'll try to be more accommodating. If you like, we can meet with her in the morning and try to make amends."

Nell's words pleased Sir Lionel. "All right," he said, not unkindly. "But I don't want you to spend another night in this hotel."

"As you wish." Nell sighed.

"By the by," Sir Lionel said in the carriage on the way to his brother's house, "I missed you. Can we go back on an even keel—the way things were in London? There, I managed your career, we dined out with friends, we attended soirees—it was a great life."

For you, perhaps, Nell thought. *But for me there was always something missing.*

"I'll try," Nell said quietly, but in her heart she knew that it would be impossible.

Mrs. Freeport was still awake when they got to the mansion, and the meeting of reconciliation took place that night. It went well—at first. Now that Sara was no longer in the house, it seemed that the major cause of friction was gone.

"We'll talk no more of this unpleasantness," Lady Freeport said. "Tomorrow after church services, about one o'clock, several notables of the community will be here to tea, and I want you to meet them, Miss Keene."

"I would like that," Nell said. "I believe I'll be back by then."

"Back?" Lionel said. "You're not attending services with us?"

"No, I'm sorry, Lionel, but I've accepted an invitation to attend other services."

"What other services?" Lady Freeport asked suspiciously.

"The Mormon church," Nell said.

"The Mormon church!" Lady Freeport exclaimed, her pale face turning more pale.

Lionel caught his mother as she went into a swoon. He laid her on the nearest couch.

"Cheevers!" Lionel yelled. Then in a lower tone, he said to Nell, "Really, Nell. This is too much. If you don't want to marry me, just say so. You don't have to do such things to get out of your promise to Lord Darnley."

Nell stared in utter surprise. "I assure you, Lionel, such a thought has never entered my mind. I accepted the invitation to attend church with my friends because I like being with them. Furthermore, I had no idea that you had returned from gallivanting all over New South Wales."

After a few tense moments, the butler entered the room, assessed the situation, withdrew, and returned with a small bottle of smelling salts, which he wafted under the aristocratic nose of Lady Freeport. The old lady came to with a gasp and sat up. She didn't speak, but her eyes shot daggers at Nell.

"Mr. Cheevers," Nell said coolly, "would you be so kind as to arrange transportation to my hotel?"

The butler looked to Lady Freeport for guidance.

The old woman nodded. "By all means, Cheevers," she said. "Take this person from our presence!"

"Nell," Lionel protested at the door, "don't go. We can work this out."

"I have no doubt that you and I could work things out," Nell said sadly. "But your mother and I are another matter. It appears that you will have to choose between us. Good night."

Later that night, Nell sat on the bed in her hotel room, tired beyond measure and sick with worry. *Have I been uncharitable?* she asked herself. After some thought, she allowed that Lady Freeport's knowledge of the Mormons had undoubtedly been gained from the extremely biased press. *She probably doesn't know any better and thinks I'm after her son's money and position.*

Nell sighed. "Reality is mirroring art," she said, recalling a scene from *Sweet Lavender* where the aristocratic Mrs. Gilfillian reacts to the suggestion that Lavender is "innocent looking" by retorting, "Innocent looking! Do you think I will have my plans frustrated by a girl with ulterior motives and eyes like saucers?"

On the other hand, Mrs. Freeport's treatment of Sara was shameful. Could I be happy married to the son of such a woman? She thought of the early days of her marriage to Lord Darnley. Through patience and long-suffering she had been able to overcome all obstacles, especially the resentment her husband's grown children had shown her. Could she win Lady Freeport over? Did she want to win her over? *No,* she admitted. She had no desire to go through all that again. *Perhaps Lionel is right. Perhaps deep down I do want to scuttle our marriage plans.* An overpowering sense of relief filled her bosom at the thought. *I really don't want to marry Lionel. That's the truth of it. I really don't want to marry him.*

She picked up Maggie's letter from a writing desk and reread it. "I can't imagine how this letter found me, but it must have taken at least a month," she said out loud and sighed. "Ken is most probably married by now."

She thought of their parting in San Francisco, and a feeling of deep loss swept over her. She closed her eyes against the new tears that pricked at them. Through force of will, she switched her mind to the idea she'd had while riding at Jumpbuck. *If my plan works, Sara and Ran will soon be off to America, and I'll be alone. What should I do? Where should I go?*

No answers came, only tears.

Chapter 23

The next day, Sunday, she attended Mormon services at a rented hall. The accommodations were Spartan, but the feeling of love and acceptance was abundant. The main speaker, a missionary recently arrived from America, spoke about God's plan for His children on this earth, a topic Ken had explained at the campfire in California. The speaker quoted a scripture that Nell had often heard from her churchgoing mother: "Trust in the Lord with all thine heart; and lean not unto thine own understanding. In all thy ways acknowledge him, and he shall direct thy paths."

On hearing these words, she recalled her conversations with Ken and wondered if God had a path for her to tread. And if so, what was it? And how would she know whether she was on this path? As if responding to Nell's questioning thoughts, the missionary said that a negative answer to prayer sometimes came as a "stupor of thought," a phrase she had never heard before.

At the conclusion of the meeting, the missionary who had spoken approached her. "Miss Keene," he said. "I'm Elder Rolfson from Salt Lake City. I trust you received the letter from Brother and Sister Tolley that I delivered to the Freeport residence."

"I did," Nell said, and shook his hand appreciatively. "Thank you. I couldn't imagine how it had gotten here since it had neither an address nor a postmark."

Elder Rolfson smiled. "When Sister Tolley heard I was going to Sydney, she asked me to deliver it to you. She said you'd most likely be staying at the Freeports'. The butler there was most gracious. He said he'd make sure it was delivered to you."

After church, Nell, Sara, Ran, and Elder Rolfson ate lunch at the Warren home. Mr. Warren again offered to pay for Sara and Ran's passage to America, but, predictably, Ran refused. The sheep station would sell eventually, he said, and then they could go to America in good conscience. Nell felt warm inside knowing that she had a plan that would circumvent Ran's reluctance to accept charity.

Nell thoroughly enjoyed her day, but when she returned to her hotel room, loneliness again descended upon her. She even briefly entertained thoughts of not following through with her plan for Sara and Ran's passage money so that she would not be left all alone in a strange country, but the urge to help her friends was greater than her desire for company.

A good night's sleep refreshed her in mind and body. Dressed in one of her favorite frocks, a royal blue with white trim and a jaunty blue bonnet with a nautical flare, she entered the outer office of Mr. Oswald Greeley, estate agent.

"May I speak with Mr. Greeley?" Nell asked a young man with his nose in a book.

"Whom shall I say is calling?" he asked, barely looking up.

"Miss Nell Keene."

"Miss Nell Keene!" he exclaimed, jumping to his feet and knocking over the stool. "Miss Nell Keene the London actress?"

"The same," Nell said with a smile. "I'm surprised you've heard of me way down here."

"I . . . I've just come out from London," he stammered, his multitude of freckles taking on a rosy hue. "Jeremy Hoskins at your service."

"A pleasure to meet you, Mr. Hoskins," she said, taking and quickly releasing his bony hand. For a long moment, he seemed unable to do anything but stare.

"May I see Mr. Greeley?" she asked again.

"Of course, Miss Keene. I'm sorry for gawking, but you . . . you're even more beautiful than your picture . . . I seen it . . . saw it in the paper. I'll get Mr. Greeley." Turning abruptly, he tripped over a wastepaper basket and landed flat on his face. Nell started toward him with concern, but he was instantly on his feet, his face redder than his hair. He knocked on the door to the inner office, opened it, and excitedly announced Nell's presence.

Nell smiled at the clerk's antics, slipped past him, and entered the inner office. Oswald Greeley stood and motioned her to the chair in front of his desk. The estate agent was a round man—round face, round shoulders, and a round belly under his shiny black three-piece suit, the expanse broken only by a huge, gold watch-chain.

"Miss Keene," Mr. Greeley said, sitting down. "What an honor to have you in my humble office. How can I be of service?"

"I am interested in purchasing Jumpbuck Sheep Station near Wagga Wagga, sir."

The man's nose and brow crinkled. "Jumpbuck? Oh, Miss Keene, you wouldn't be interested in Jumpbuck," he said with disgust. "The land's poor and the buildings are run down. No, indeed. You wouldn't be interested in that bedraggled place. If you want something near Wagga Wagga, I have several estates for sale or let that would be much more appropriate for a lady of your station." A smile instantly replaced his frown. "If you would like something closer to Sydney, Avonlea is located just a few miles north of town on the beautiful Hawkesbury River. A magnificent estate of over two thousand acres, Tudor-style manor house, lovely lawns sweeping down to the river, fenced and cross-fenced. I could drive you there today at your convenience."

Nell waited politely until he was finished before saying, "Mr. Greeley, did not Mr. Randall Trescott engage you to sell his property, Jumpbuck Sheep Station?"

The ingratiating smile fell from his face, and he gazed at her warily. "He did, yes, Miss Keene."

"Then do you not think it would be in your client's interest if you attempted to sell said property?"

"Of course, Miss Keene, but—"

"No buts, Mr. Greeley. What is the asking price?"

"Two shillings per acre, one hundred pounds in all. The buildings aren't worth considering, though, and neither is the small flock of sheep."

"Would payment drawn on Barings Bank, London, be acceptable?"

The man's eyes lit up. "Most acceptable, Miss Keene. Most acceptable."

Nell handed him a draught for one hundred pounds. "Now, Mr. Greeley, I would like to list Jumpbuck Sheep Station for sale." She smiled inwardly to see the surprise on the estate agent's face.

"You just bought it, and you want to sell it?"

"That is correct. And this time, sir, I would be much obliged if you would do something in the way of trying to dispose of it."

"I shall, Miss Keene, I most definitely shall," Mr. Greeley replied contritely.

"Good. Please send the proceeds from the sale to the Piccadilly Circle Branch of Barings Bank, London, in care of Mr. Ernest Bowden, senior clerk. Now, please have the paperwork for the purchase and listing sent to the Ambassador Hotel for my signature. One last thing, Mr. Greeley, do not divulge to Mr. and Mrs. Trescott that I am the buyer. They are coming to see you today and—"

A knock at the door, which was quickly followed by a red-haired head poking into the room, interrupted Nell. "Sorry to disturb you, sir," Jeremy Hoskins said. "But a Mr. and Mrs. Trescott are here to see you. I told them you were busy and that they should make an appointment, but they insist on waiting."

Mr. Greeley looked at Nell for direction.

"They must not find me here," Nell whispered. "Is there another way out of the office?"

"I'm afraid not," the agent said.

"Where does that door lead?" She pointed to a paneled door at the side of Mr. Greeley's desk.

"Supply closet," the agent said.

Nell leapt up from her seat and opened the closet door. "Rather cluttered, but it will do," she said. "Please don't keep me in here too long." Smiling wryly, she entered the closet and closed the door.

"Invite Mr. and Mrs. Trescott in," Mr. Greeley said to the clerk, whose face, a portrait of astonishment, was still sticking into the room.

Nell smiled at Sara's squeal of pleasure when she heard that Jumpbuck Sheep Station had been sold. Moving slightly to get more comfortable in the crowded closet, she brushed her elbow against something hard, bringing it crashing to the floor with the sound of splintering glass.

Silence followed, and Nell could only imagine the looks on Sara's and Ran's faces.

"Mice," she heard Mr. Greeley say dryly and continue on as if nothing had happened.

The agent asked the young couple to come back later that day to sign the papers. He then quickly ushered them out of the office and returned to open the closet door. Nell stood inside, in a puddle of red ink. She glanced down at the broken ink pot and up to the estate agent.

"Sorry, Mr. Greeley," she said with chagrin. "It appears that I owe you for a pot of ink."

"Not to worry, Miss Keene," the estate agent said. "It's time Hoskins cleaned up the closet anyway."

"Thank you, sir," she said. "You are most kind. I'll be expecting those papers at your earliest convenience."

As she squished her way out of the office in her red-bottomed boots, the young clerk sighed. "Just think, sir," he said. "We had the great Nell Keene here in our office."

Mr. Greeley glanced down at the crimson footprints on the scrubbed wooden floor. "Yes, Hoskins," he said, wryly. "She's made an indelible impression."

The next morning, Nell met Sara and Ran for breakfast in the hotel restaurant.

"Nell, Nell!" Sara said, rushing toward her friend and sitting down at the table. "You'll never believe it. We've sold the sheep station and got the full price. It's a miracle!"

"I'm so happy for you," Nell said, hoping that her expression wouldn't give her away. "Does this mean that you'll be leaving for America with the other Saints?"

"It does," Ran said.

"Our only regret is we'll miss your wedding," Sara said.

"Maybe not," Nell said, shrugging and tilting her head slightly. "There may not be a wedding. We appear to have irreconcilable differences—Lady Freeport and I, that is."

A worried look crossed Sara's face. "Oh, Nell, I hope I'm not the cause of it."

Nell shook her head. "Not at all, Sara; it's much deeper than the little tussle we had over your staying with me."

Sara brightened. "On the plus side, you're free to marry someone else now."

"Someone else?" Nell said, blushing. "If you mean Mr. Sanderson, let me remind you that we are just friends. Besides, I just received a letter from my friend Maggie saying he's marrying a widow."

"Oh," Sara said. "What will you do?"

Nell patted Sara's hand. "Don't worry about me, my friend, I'll get by. I imagine I'll just go back home to England." At that moment, the waiter came for the order. When the waiter left, no one spoke for a moment. "When will you be heading back to Jumpbuck to pack up?" Nell asked.

"Tomorrow morning," Ran said. "Would you like to come with us?"

Nell shook her head. "No, thank you. I think I'll do some sightseeing. I've heard that the Hawkesbury River area is beautiful. I think I'll hire a hackney cab to take me there. Let me know when you get back from Jumpbuck, and we'll spend some time together before you leave for America."

Sara and Ran had no sooner left the restaurant than Sir Lionel appeared next to Nell's table. She politely invited him to sit down.

He heaved a sigh. "What a predicament. Mother has given me an ultimatum. If I don't give you up, she'll cut me off without a penny. She's even sweetened the deal by removing the requirement that I must marry before I can inherit the estate."

Nell looked surprised. "Can she do that? I thought your brother controlled the Freeport finances."

"He does," Sir Lionel replied slowly. "But, unlike me, he would never defy mother."

A fearful feeling swept through Nell. *Will he defy his mother? Will he choose me over the money? I'd be honor-bound to marry him. But I don't want to!*

"Unlike you?" she said. "You would give up your allowance and the Herefordshire estate for me?" She tried desperately to keep the apprehension out of her voice.

Sir Lionel heaved another sigh. "Ever since I was a child, I've dreamed of owning Freeport Park. I must say, you and Mother have created a moral dilemma for me." He paused and looked into her eyes. "There is something I must know, Nell. For a long time I've sensed that the only reason you agreed to marry me was because of your promise to my uncle. Is that so?"

Nell hesitated. "That . . . that's certainly part of it. But I do like you and appreciate you."

"But you don't love me."

Nell hung her head. "No, Lionel, I don't. I'm sorry."

Lionel nodded briskly, and Nell couldn't tell if he was disappointed or relieved.

"Right," he said. "At least you've solved my dilemma. Had you said yes, I would have had to choose between you and the estate. But since you don't love me, it simplifies things. I'm free to inherit, and you're free of your promise to my uncle." He stared across the table at her and shrugged. "I will miss you, Nell. You're one in a million."

"And if I'd said I loved you?"

He smiled, slowly rose from the table, and held out his hand. "We'll never know, will we? Good-bye, Nell. Like I said, I'll miss you, and I hope you'll miss me a little."

"I shall miss you, Lionel. I truly shall. You have been a good friend and excellent business manager. I'm glad we can part amicably."

When he had gone, Nell went to her room, lay on the bed, and wept from both relief at being free of Lionel and sadness for the very same reason. *Perhaps Ken was right,* she thought. *Perhaps if I trust God and am patient, He really will direct my path.* Despite her mixed emotions, she somehow knew deep in her soul that this course-correction was of God.

Chapter 24

For a long time, Nell lay on the bed thinking about what road her life would take now that she was free of the promise she'd made to Lord Darnley. She felt pained by the irony of the situation. *I'm free now, and Ken is probably not!* A knock at the door interrupted her thoughts. She dabbed at her eyes as she answered the door.

"Sorry to disturb you, ma'am," the bellboy said. "A gentleman wishes to see you in the lobby. His card."

Nell took the card and read: "Cyril Tompkins, Theatrical Agent."

"Thank you, young man," she said. "Please tell Mr. Tompkins I'll be down directly."

Ten minutes later, the agent greeted Nell in the lobby.

"Miss Keene," he said. "Welcome to Sydney. We're so honored to have you in our city."

"Thank you, Mr. Tompkins. How did you know I was here?"

The man smiled. "It would be impossible for a woman of your fame and beauty to remain incognito for long. Actually, your ship's steward told me. I tried to see you right away, but I was told you were in Wagga Wagga. Now that you're back, I have a business proposition for you. It would be a travesty if you came all this way and didn't perform for our theatergoing public. I know they'd thrill to see you, especially in *Sweet Lavender*. If you will allow me the great honor of representing you, I can set the wheels in motion. What do you say?"

The offer pleased Nell. Minutes before, she had been pondering her path, and here was a new opportunity. Was this the road she should travel?

"I'm flattered, sir," she said with a smile. "May I think about it overnight?"

"Of course, of course," he replied. "You have my card. Please inform me of your decision at your leisure."

Nell returned to her room, her heart beating quickly. She sat down in the overstuffed chair. *It's nice to be wanted,* she thought. *When one door shuts, another opens, it seems. It would be wonderful to be on the stage again. I'd probably have to commit for at least six months. Well, what else have I to do? With Sara and Ran going to America, I'll be all alone. Yes. I'll do it. But it would be a mistake to appear too eager. I'll let Mr. Tompkins know tomorrow.*

She got up from the chair and rang for the bellboy, who appeared in minutes.

"Please take this note to Mr. Greeley, the estate agent on Water Street."

The agent responded to her note within the hour, and soon Nell and Oswald Greeley were on their way in a pony and trap to inspect Avonlea on the Hawkesbury River.

"It's beautiful!" Nell exclaimed as she stood on the well-manicured lawns that swept down to the river. "You say it's for sale or for let?"

"Yes, either," Mr. Greeley said. "The former owner passed from this world earlier this year. She settled Avonlea on her two grown children in England, neither of whom wishes to remove to Australia. In the meantime, it's costing them a small fortune to keep it up. They would like to sell it, but they're prepared to rent it to get out from under the maintenance costs."

If I go back onstage, Nell thought, *I could take a flat in town and come here on my days off.*

For the next half hour, Nell and the agent inspected the house and grounds. As they did so, they discussed the rental and maintenance costs, including the salaries of the six servants who were presently employed there.

"As I may be staying in Sydney longer than I expected, Mr. Greeley, I will be in need of a home, and Avonlea has certainly taken my interest. May I let you know my decision tomorrow?"

"That would be perfectly fine."

Nell returned to the hotel elated. Her life was getting back on track. Soon she'd be performing again and living in the luxury to which she had become accustomed. After a late supper, she returned to her room, and for the rest of the evening studied her lines.

At precisely eleven o'clock, she retired. But sleep evaded her. Her thoughts turned to the events of the day, and she smiled when she thought of her escapade in the supply closet. *I'll surely miss Sara and Ran. It's strange how I keep running into Mormons—now even Maggie and Jack are Mormons. I wonder how it would affect me if I joined the Church? I certainly have nothing against the teachings I've heard. The people, too, are nice. And I wouldn't be joining because of Ken. He's probably already married. Maybe I should study further.* She mused on this. *Elder Rolfson is nice. I wonder if he's staying in Sydney for a while.*

Her mind turned to her decision to go back to the stage and to rent Avonlea. Try as she might, she couldn't recapture her former elation. *If God really does direct people's paths, I wonder if I should get some direction from Him.* It had been a long time since she had prayed, and for several minutes she pondered on whether she should do so. Finally, she slipped from her bed, got down on her knees, and asked God to confirm her decision to stay in Australia and rent Avonlea. To her great dismay, her former feeling of elation had completely dissipated and was, in fact, replaced by a feeling of uncertainty. *Is this the "stupor of thought" the missionary talked about?* She crawled into bed completely deflated. *That's what I get for asking. If I shouldn't go back to the stage and let Avonlea, what am I to do with myself?*

When it became apparent that sleep would not come, she rose and looked for something to read. She returned to bed with the copy of the Book of Mormon Ken had given her. Opening it, she found Amor De Cosmos's invitation to perform in Victoria, British Columbia. A picture of Victoria based on Ken's description entered her head, and a longing to go there gradually grew. A feeling of certitude completely dispelled the stupor of thought. "That's it!" she exclaimed aloud. "I can go with Sara and Ran as far as San Francisco and then take a ship to Victoria."

For a long time, she basked in the glow of the certainty and purpose brought by the Spirit and finally descended into a peaceful sleep.

The next morning, she wrote two notes of regret announcing her decision to leave Australia and had them delivered to Oswald Greeley and Cyril Tompkins.

They'll probably think I'm rather flighty, she thought as she pressed the seal into the wax on the second note. *No matter. It is better to do the right thing and suffer embarrassment than to do the wrong thing and suffer the consequences.*

The rest of the day was taken up with arranging for her passage to San Francisco and packing for the voyage. While she packed, she wondered about which route to take home to England after her run in Victoria. Should she go via Salt Lake City, or should she take the new Canadian route? Before leaving London, she had been urged by several friends not to miss the train ride through the Canadian Rockies and a stay at the newly opened, luxurious Banff Springs Hotel.

Perhaps I will take the Canadian route, she thought. *I don't think I could bear seeing Ken again if he's remarried.*

She was glad that she had come to Australia. Had she and Lionel married in London, she would be tied to a man she didn't love. Furthermore, she had gained two new friends in Sara and Ran, plus the other members of the Mormon Church who would also be taking the boat to America. Above all, she was content in the knowledge that her decision to go to Victoria was prompted by God. She could hardly wait to tell Sara and Ran that she was going with them.

* * *

Because of a storm, it took a few days longer than the usual three weeks to get from Australia to America. During the voyage, Nell spent her time almost exclusively in the company of the Saints. From this association and from reading the Book of Mormon, she had learned a great deal more about the Church. When she reached San Francisco, she was sorry to part with her new friends.

"I'll miss you terribly," Sara said as she and Ran stood with Nell in front of the Palace Hotel. They had shared a cab from the docks, and the cabbie stood waiting to take the young couple to Sara's mother's home. "We'll probably be in Utah around the time you are on your way home to England. You will stop in and see us, won't you?"

Nell hesitated and then answered with a question.

"You're not going directly to Utah?" she asked.

Ran shook his head. "No. Sara's mother paid for her fare to Australia with money she'd saved to paint her house, and I feel we should pay her back."

"I told Ran she won't take any money," Sara said with a smile. "So we've come up with a wonderful solution. Ran and I will paint the house for her!"

"And do any other repairs to the old house," Ran added. "After that, we'll be off to Zion. Good-bye, Miss Keene." He squeezed his wife's hand and said, "I'll leave you ladies to say your farewells."

"You will visit us in Utah, won't you, Nell?" Sara pleaded.

Nell wavered. She wanted to please Sara and to see Ken again, but if he were remarried . . .

She slowly shook her head. "I'm afraid not, Sara. I think I'll go back on the new Canadian Pacific Railway. I understand the scenery through the Rocky Mountains is spectacular. If you give me your mother's address, I'll write you from Victoria. In the meantime, please look up Maggie and Jack Tolley in Utah and give them my love."

Sara smiled mischievously. "No one else?"

Nell blushed. "You could say hello to Mr. Sanderson for me."

"I'll give him your love as well."

"Don't you dare! Just say hello for me."

Sara laughed and then grew serious. "I think you should know that I've decided to join the Mormon Church when we get settled in Utah. All the things I've learned during our voyage have convinced me of its truthfulness."

"I'm happy for you, Sara. I'll admit I've leanings that way myself. Perhaps when I'm back in England I'll look into it further. I know they have missionaries there. Both Mr. Sanderson's mother and late wife were baptized in the River Barle in Somerset. Who knows? Maybe I'll get baptized there, too."

As she waved good-bye to her friends, loneliness descended on Nell. She heaved a sigh and turned into the hotel.

"May I send a telegram to Victoria, British Columbia?" she asked the concierge.

Chapter 25

Ken stared at the sheet of paper in front of him. The sheet had two columns, one headed "Pros" and one headed "Cons." He was sitting in his newspaper office still pondering the list when his father approached him.

"Must be a compelling problem, Ken. I've seldom seen you so serious."

Ken smiled. "I'm trying to decide whether I should, to use Kipling's phrase, 'bite the bullet' and ask Sister Reynolds to marry me."

"Bite the bullet?" Gren said. "How romantic! Have you talked to your mother about this?"

"No. But she's talked to me. I guess it wouldn't hurt to discuss it with her again. What do *you* think about the matter?"

Gren shrugged. "As much as I'd like to help you, son, I'm a poor person to ask. If I ever lost your mother the way you lost Karen, I'd be hopeless. While I know it's often the right choice to marry again, I'd be hard pressed to know how to go about it. On the other hand, I can imagine how lonely you must be. Also, the children need a mother. Talk to your mother. She'll guide you aright."

"I would love to see you marry Priscilla," Elisabeth said that evening. "But having said that, I will not encourage you one way or the other. This must be your choice, with, of course, the aid of the Holy Ghost. I'm sure you've prayed about it."

"I have," Ken said in a discouraged tone. "but all I get is a neutral feeling, not for or against. Do you suppose I'm being left to make up my own mind?"

"Most likely. I feel that sometimes we try to evade our responsibility of making a choice and want the Holy Ghost to make up our minds for us. I don't think that's His role. I think He is to confirm our decisions, not decide for us."

"You're a great help, Mother," Ken said facetiously. "First you refuse to make up my mind for me, and now you tell me the Holy Ghost won't do it either."

Elisabeth smiled. "Surely marriage has come up in your discussions with Priscilla."

Ken nodded. "Yes, but only in a general way. I know how much she loves her late husband, and she knows how much I love Karen. I think because of that we've both avoided the topic. I have some newspaper business I need to attend to in Provo, so perhaps I'll take the train down and make a side trip to visit her. I can steer our conversation in that direction—see how she feels about marrying again."

Two days later found Ken and Priscilla having supper in the restaurant of "Beefsteak" Harrison's Hotel in Springville. They were almost finished with their meal when Ken summoned the courage to blurt out, "Priscilla, have you considered marrying again?"

A quizzical expression crossed her face, and then she smiled. "Of course. Have you?"

Ken nodded seriously. "Yes. I've given it a lot of thought lately."

A look of apprehension clouded her face. "And . . . and where have those thoughts led you?"

Ken inhaled deeply, then exhaled before replying. "Well, we've been keeping company for a while, and we get along well, and our children—"

She raised her hand to stop him. "Before you go on, Ken," she interjected, "Let me say that I've anticipated this moment since we first met. Now that it has arrived, I have something to say. May I speak first?"

With a sigh of relief, Ken said, "Please do."

"I very much appreciate our friendship. You are a fine man and would make any woman a good husband. But it would be tragic if we married and you discovered what I already know." She paused, then said, "You are in love, but unfortunately not with me."

Ken stared at her through surprised eyes.

After a moment, he said, "It's true that I'm in love with Karen. I always will be, but I think there's room in my heart for another woman. I've considered our friendship very much, and I think we could manage to—" Priscilla's raised eyebrows and wry smile halted him. He heaved a sigh. "Not a very romantic proposal is it?"

"No. Not very romantic at all. But when I said you were in love, I wasn't referring to Karen. If your late wife were my only competition, I would gladly accept you. But ever since I met you, I've suspected there is someone else."

"Someone else? Who?"

"I think you know, and if you don't know, your heart will soon tell you. I may regret this decision, but I think it's time for us to say good-bye, at least for the present." She rose. "May the Lord's choicest blessings be with you, Ken. If you do sort out your feelings and find yourself free to marry, please consider me."

Ken rose to his feet. With mixed feelings, he shook her outstretched hand. "I should at least walk you home."

She shook her head. "Good-bye, Ken," she said and quickly turned away.

Ken sat heavily on the chair, baffled by what had just happened. His hand went to his pocket and withdrew his carefully constructed list of pros and cons. *She didn't even give me a chance to use this,* he thought dejectedly.

On the way home on the train next day, Ken was still asking himself what had happened the night before. He pondered Priscilla's words: "You're in love, but unfortunately not with me." He knew she must have meant Nell. Thinking back, he realized he had talked of Nell quite a lot. *But that was only because she asked me about what I'd been doing since Karen passed away. And even if I were in love with Nell, she's married by now.* He thought about his conversation with Nell about David and Bath-sheba, and the irony made him smile. *Well, even if I am in love with Nell, I have no right to do anything about it. I'll not let the message of the David and Bath-sheba story be lost on me.*

* * *

"Well?" Elisabeth said eagerly the next evening as Gren came through the door from work. "Did Ken get back from Provo and Springville?"

Gren nodded. "He did."

"And?"

"Sister Reynolds turned him down."

Elisabeth's mouth fell open. "Turned my son's proposal of marriage down? How could she?"

Gren shrugged. "Apparently she thinks he's in love with someone else, besides Karen, that is."

"Who?"

"She wouldn't say, and Ken wouldn't talk about it."

Elisabeth sat down on the parlor sofa and sighed. "And I thought things were going along brilliantly." She shook her head. "Perhaps I'd best confine my efforts to medicine and leave matchmaking to others."

* * *

A month later, Ken was busy in his office at the *Deseret Evening News* working on an article on the dedication of the Jewish temple, B'Nai Israel, in Salt Lake City when an office boy approached him. "There's a man and woman to see you, Brother Sanderson," the boy said.

"Show them in," Ken said, rising from his chair.

"Brother Sanderson," the man said when he entered the room, "I'm Brother Randall Trescott, and this is my wife, Sara. We are friends of Miss Nell Keene."

The mention of Nell's name sent a spark of happiness through Ken. After shaking their hands, he invited the Trescotts to sit.

"And how is Miss Keene?" Ken asked as nonchalantly as his palpitating heart would let him.

"She was fine when we saw her last," Sara said.

"And her husband?" Ken asked.

Sara glanced at Ran and smiled. "She's not married," she said with great satisfaction.

Ken's eyebrows lifted. "Not married?" he said, unable to hide his delight. "What happened to Sir Lionel?"

"I won't go into all the details," Sara said, "but they parted as friends."

Ken's heart was now racing. "I suppose she went home to England," he said.

Ran shook his head. "No. Sara received a letter from her only last week. She's having a wonderful time in Victoria, British Columbia."

"Victoria!" Ken exclaimed, sliding to the edge of his chair. "What's she doing in Victoria?"

Sara smiled at Ken's reaction.

"Performing in *Sweet Lavender*," Sara replied. "In her letter, she says they're finishing up rehearsals, and the opening will be September eighteenth, this Friday. She says she's hobnobbing with the cream of Victoria society and living in a genuine castle. She mentioned some man that seems to know everybody and has much influence."

"Amor De Cosmos," Ken said.

"That's the one," Sara said. She hesitated, and the old refrain "In for penny, in for a pound" went through her head. "Pardon me for asking, Brother Sanderson, but I heard . . . have you remarried?"

"No," Ken said warily.

Sara's smile broadened, and then she said, "I'm sure Miss Keene would love to see you again. After she finishes in Victoria, she'll be returning to England on the Canadian railroad. If you want to see her, you'd better act fast. She *really* would love to see you."

Ken smiled at Sara's persistence. "What makes you so sure?" he asked.

"Oh, just a feeling."

Ken blushed. "Did she ask you to invite me?"

Sara shook her head.

Ken paused and thought for a moment before adding, "As much as I'd like to visit Victoria again, it would be very inconvenient to go there at present. My children, especially my oldest, have become extremely dependent on me. Except for when I'm here at work, they hardly let me out of their sight."

Sara's face fell.

"How thoughtless of me. I do understand." Her face brightened. "But she will be there for a while. Perhaps if things change, you could consider going to see her. I'm sure she'd welcome you."

Ken smiled again at Sara's obvious desire for him to visit Nell.

"I'll certainly consider it," he said. "Perhaps I'll write her."

"Good," Sara said, pulling a slip of paper out of her purse. "Here's the address where she's staying."

Ken took the address and reluctantly changed the subject.

"In the meantime, what are your plans?" he asked.

Ran shrugged. "We're not quite sure. We've come all the way from Australia to Zion, and now that we're here, we're not sure what to do. I guess the first thing is to get some accommodations. We were hoping you could give us some suggestions."

Ken smiled. "Well, any friends of Miss Keene are friends of mine. My house is rather full, but my parents have lots of room. I'm sure they'd be happy to put you up until you find something."

Ran and Sara exchanged thankful smiles.

"That would be most welcome," Ran said. "Our next task will be to find employment."

"What kind of work do you do?" Ken asked.

Ran looked at Sara and smiled. "My last job was as an unsuccessful sheep farmer, but I think I'm ready to go back to being a bank clerk. Sara has done mostly domestic service."

Ken nodded. "Leave it to me, and I'll see what I can do."

When Ran and Sara had gone, Ken pushed back his chair and put his feet on his desk.

So Nell's unmarried and in Victoria, he thought. *Maybe Karen and Priscilla are right.* Suddenly, a chilling thought hit him, and his feet clattered to the floor. *What if Stephen Langton is in British Columbia?*

Ken had no doubt whatsoever that Langton still lusted for revenge. The tranquility of the past few months had almost pushed thoughts of Langton from his mind, but the image of the criminal resurfaced with a jolt. Would Langton try again to kidnap her? What should he do? Where did his responsibility lie—in Salt Lake City or Victoria?

It was a long time before Ken got back to his story about the new Jewish temple and only after he wired Laird Mackenzie about his suspicions. Laird wired right back, assuring Ken that Miss Keene was well protected by the Victoria police and Mr. Amor De Cosmos.

Over the next week, Ken helped the Trescotts get settled into a small rented house, arranged for Sara's baptism, and helped Ran secure a position at Church-owned Zion's Savings Bank and Trust Company.

In the days following, the idea of visiting Nell in Victoria was never far from Ken's mind, but his responsibilities—especially to the children—outweighed his growing desire to see her again. One evening shortly after the Trescotts arrived in Salt Lake City, Ken was saying good night to his children when Ainsley broke into loud sobs.

Ken held her in his arms. "What's the matter, sweetheart?" he asked.

For several minutes, Ainsley didn't answer. She simply clung to her father and wept. Finally, the tears subsided and she managed to blurt out, "I miss my mama!"

Tears sprang to Ken's eyes as he tried to comfort his daughter.

"I do, too," he said softly. "I don't think we'll ever stop missing her. But we must be brave."

For a long time, he held his daughter in his arms. After a while, her tears turned to dry sobs, and finally she was silent. Ken thought she'd fallen asleep.

"Papa?"

"Yes, dear."

"Will we get a new mama, like Mama said?"

Ken tried to answer, but the words caught in his throat and warm tears ran down his own cheeks. Karen's words of praise for Nell came into his mind, and he suddenly knew that his desire to see Nell was not just a selfish whim but an inspired prompting.

"Yes, sweetheart," he said wiping his eyes. "Your mama always kept her promises."

* * *

"The poor little thing," Elisabeth said later when Ken told her about the incident with Ainsley. "I guess all we can do is give her as much love as possible."

Ken nodded and was silent.

After a while, he said, "I think there's something else I can do. The children need a mother, and I need a wife." He took a breath. "What do you think of Miss Nell Keene?"

Elisabeth stared at her son.

"Miss Keene? But isn't she married and in Australia or England?"

"No. She's single and in Victoria, British Columbia. Or so Brother and Sister Trescott tell me."

"I know that you and Miss Keene are good friends, but . . ."

"Isn't friendship a good basis for marriage?"

"Of course, but . . . I never thought . . . do you have feelings for Miss Keene? And do you think she has feelings for you?"

Ken nodded. "I like her very much, and I've been told she likes me as well."

"Who?"

"Karen, for one."

Surprise filled Elisabeth's face.

"Karen?"

Ken nodded. "Before she died, she strongly suggested that I marry again and hinted that Nell would make a good wife and mother. I completely dismissed the idea, of course. I was in no position to think of such things, and Nell was promised to Sir Lionel Freeport. But things have changed. According to Sister Trescott, the planned betrothal never actually happened."

Elizabeth looked thoughtful but did not reply, so Ken pressed on. "Sister Trescott says Nell is interested in joining the Church. She's read the Book of Mormon. I hate to leave the children again right now, especially Ainsley, but I feel that I should go to Victoria to see her. What do you think?"

Elisabeth took a deep breath before saying, "I've liked Miss Keene ever since I met her in England. And I'm delighted that she's interested in the Church. Yes. Yes, I think you should go see her. But first, talk it over with Ainsley. It wouldn't be right to leave her unless she agrees."

The next day at breakfast, Ken did talk with his daughter.

"Sweetheart," he said. "You once said that you liked Miss Keene and asked if she was coming back here. I've just found out that she's only a few days' train-and-boat ride from here. Would you like me to go see her and invite her to come visit us?"

Ainsley's face lit up. "Oh, yes, Papa." After a moment, she surprised Ken by asking, "Will she be our new mama?"

Ken shrugged and smiled at his daughter. "I don't know, dear. If I go see her, I'd be gone for several days. Can you be a brave girl and look after Gage and mind Auntie Maggie while I'm away?"

Ainsley considered her father's words before saying, "Yes. And Papa, I like Miss Keene. She's pretty and nice like Mama."

Ken breathed a sigh of relief.

"I promise I won't be gone long."

With his daughter's permission, Ken immediately set about making arrangements to go to Victoria. Without mentioning Nell, he apprised Laird Mackenzie of his intention by wire. Laird wired back immediately, saying that Marjorie insisted Ken stay with them. Laird added a cryptic postscript: *Miss Keene still here.*

Chapter 26

As the train pulled out of the Ogden station, Ken's excitement grew. A warm feeling spread from his heart, contrasting sharply with the utter loneliness he had experienced when he had parted with Nell in San Francisco earlier that year. On that occasion, he had hardly noticed the scenery, but now as the train rattled and swayed across the Great Basin and chugged through the Sierra Nevada mountains, he enjoyed each moment, seeing beauty in the flatlands and majesty in the mountains.

When the train reached the Carquinez Strait and pulled onto the *Solano,* he got down from the carriage and thoroughly enjoyed the fresh breeze on his face during the nine-minute crossing. He arrived in San Francisco in good time and immediately purchased a ticket to Victoria. The trip to Canada was equally enjoyable. When he arrived at Victoria, he wanted to seek out Nell immediately; however, having only Sara's endorsement to rely on, he wasn't completely sure how Nell felt about him. Since he would be staying with the Mackenzies, he decided to visit Laird first.

"Good morning, Sergeant Yates," Ken said. "Is Chief Inspector Mackenzie in?"

"No, sir," the desk sergeant said. "Would you care to wait? He should be back soon."

Ken waited, and soon he and Laird were chatting together in the lawman's office.

"Believe it or not," Laird said with a smile, "I wasn't really surprised to get your two telegrams."

"You weren't? Why is that?"

"As soon as Mrs. Mackenzie found out Miss Keene was coming to Victoria, she said, 'I daresay Mr. Sanderson won't be far behind.'"

Ken shook his head in amazement. "Women," he said. "I'm convinced they truly do have a sixth sense about these things. All except my mother, that is. She was trying her hand at matchmaking in Utah."

"Since you're here, I guess it didn't work."

"Right. It was close, though," Ken acceded. "Now that I'm here in Victoria, I'm not quite sure how to go about things. I can't very well walk up to Miss Keene and say, 'I'm here because I'm interested in you, and some say that you're interested in me as well.'"

Laird smiled. He thought for a moment before saying, "No. I suppose that wouldn't be appropriate. I'll tell you what. The wife and I still haven't been to one of Miss Keene's performances. It's been sold out ever since it opened—people have even been coming across the water from the mainland and from Washington State to see her. But I think I can wangle an extra ticket for tonight's performance. Afterward, you can go backstage and see her."

"You can get tickets to a sold-out performance?"

Laird smiled again. "Being the head of the Victoria police has its privileges, and I know they always keep a few tickets in reserve. Now, tell me all about how Miss Keene and her maid went missing—and especially about Stephen Langton's involvement."

Ken went on to give Laird all the details of Nell and Marian's flight to the mountains. He reiterated his concern that Langton still posed a threat to Nell and to himself.

That evening, Ken, full of anticipation, sat in the stalls of the Royal Victoria Theater with the Mackenzies. As he waited, he pondered on why the minutes leading up to the beginning of a stage performance always seemed to move at half-speed. At long last, the curtain went up. When Nell appeared on the stage, Ken couldn't take his eyes off her. *She must have given those lines a thousand times,* he thought. *But they seem as if they come from her mouth for the very first time. She surely is a superb actress.* His heart leapt as he realized that his admiration for her went far beyond appreciation for her acting prowess. He knew that he truly did love her. But did she love him?

After the last curtain call, Marjorie Mackenzie whispered, "That's your cue, Mr. Sanderson. Good luck!"

With some trepidation, Ken went backstage. As he stepped past the curtains, he and Nell saw each other at exactly the same moment. She was standing among a group of cast members. He froze, unsure of what to do next. *Do I run into her arms with all these people around? What if she doesn't have romantic feelings for me after all? Would I embarrass her? Myself?*

These thoughts coursed through his mind in a split second. When he was younger, he would have pushed such thoughts aside and impetuously rushed to her. But he had learned to control his emotions. He walked toward her as nonchalantly as his racing heart would let him. Taking his cue, she moved toward him as well, and when they were close enough, they merely shook hands.

"Mr. Sanderson," she said with a broad smile. "What a wonderful surprise."

"Miss Keene," he said. "I enjoyed your performance very much. You were marvelous."

She blushed and lowered her voice.

"Thank you, Ken. I'm . . . I'm amazed to see you here. Have you just come?"

"Yes."

"May I ask why?"

He smiled. "Yes."

She sighed and smiled. "Why?"

He felt dizzy to be so near her again. "To see you," he replied.

"No, I mean why have you come to Victoria? Surely you didn't come all this way to see me perform."

"No. I came to see you personally."

"Oh," she said, her hand going to her mouth and her cheeks coloring. "And now that you've seen me?"

He hesitated. "Now that I've seen you, I'm glad I came and would love to spend some time with you. Since it's late, may I see you to your lodgings?"

"Yes. Yes, I'd like that very much. But . . ."

"But?"

"But . . . I heard you had remarried."

Ken smiled. "Almost, but not quite. Priscilla Reynolds is a wonderful woman." He paused and then continued softly. "A wonderful woman who discerned that she couldn't marry me because she knew I was in love with somebody else."

"She did? May I ask who?"

Ken raised his eyebrows but didn't answer. Nell's cheeks crimsoned beneath her stage makeup, and her lips formed a brilliant smile.

"Please wait while I change into street clothes," she said quickly and was gone.

Half an hour later, she emerged from her dressing room in a pale blue frock and a navy blue, hooded cloak with a bright tartan lining. "All set," she said. As they walked toward the door, she asked, "Have you seen the harbor at night?"

"No. Only in the daytime."

"It's very pretty under a full moon like tonight. Also, I understand there's a beautiful sailing ship, *Serenity,* docked there. Shall we take a stroll and see it before you take me home?"

Ken nodded, and within minutes they were walking side by side along the foreshore of the inner harbor. It was a lovely fall evening.

"Do you like my cloak?" she asked, opening it to reveal the brightly colored lining. "I hardly need it this evening, but I love to wear it."

"Very much. It suits you. I remember you wore a tartan skirt when we first met."

She thought for a moment and smiled. "You're right—dark green, with a big silver pin."

"Did you purchase the cloak here in Victoria?"

"It was a gift from our mutual friend, Mr. De Cosmos. He gave it to me for coming to perform here. It's very warm and quite comfortable—Oh, look!"

They had reached the dock, and the object of Nell's delighted exclamation was the *Serenity,* a two-masted schooner, lit up like a Christmas tree and alive with activity.

"It surely is a beautiful ship," Nell said. "Sailing ships are so much prettier than steamships, especially when they're in full sail."

"I agree," Ken said. "We should enjoy them while we can. It seems that they will soon be a thing of the past." He nodded to a young man shouldering a barrel and heading for a loading ramp. "Are you setting sail tonight?" he asked.

"Aye, sir," the sailor said. "We're headin' for Honolulu with the tide."

"Ah, the Sandwich Islands," Nell said. "They're a paradise of lovely, sandy beaches, tropical fruit, and warm weather. I'd love to go there again and stay longer. We stopped for a few hours on my way to Australia."

"It sounds wonderful," Ken said. Then turning to the young sailor who was back for another barrel, he asked, "Does the *Serenity* take passengers as well as freight?"

"Aye," the sailor said, "a few."

Ken smiled mischievously at Nell. "Shall we—?"

"Mr. Sanderson, Miss Keene," a voice said from behind them.

"Sergeant Yates," Ken said, turning. "You're working late."

"Aye, that I am. I'd rather be home in bed, but the chief inspector assigned me to come down and see that the *Serenity* gets well away. Our regular constables don't like to patrol the waterfront at night." He sighed and looked longingly at the sailing ship. "I wish I was sailin' on it. Have you ever been to Oahu?" The question was directed to both Ken and Nell.

"Not I," Ken said.

"Briefly," Nell said. "Enough to make me want to go there again."

Ken smiled. "Miss Keene's almost convinced me to book passage on the *Serenity*."

The policeman nodded. "I know the feeling," he said. "Well, things look peaceful here. Would you like me t' see you two to your lodgings? It's not safe wandering around here at this time o' night."

Ken vacillated on whether to take the policeman's offer. His desire to be alone with Nell finally outweighed his concern for their safety.

"We'll be fine," he said. "But thanks anyway."

The policeman left, and Ken and Nell took one last look at the *Serenity* before heading for Nell's lodgings. They had only gone a short way when they came to a bench.

"I know it's very late," Ken said, "but I'm bursting to tell you something. May we sit for a moment?"

"All right," Nell said. "Actually, it doesn't matter how late I get in. I have a key to the castle." They smiled at one another. "But I do have a rehearsal in the morning."

Given the opportunity to speak, Ken felt suddenly nervous. He looked into Nell's dark eyes and longed to tell her what was in his soul, but he found himself speaking of others.

"Sara and Ran Trescott send their love, as do Maggie, Jack, and my parents," he said.

"How are Sara and Ran? Are they settling in well?"

"Very well. Ran's working at a bank, and Sara's found employment in the governor's mansion. Sara was baptized not long after they arrived in Utah."

Nell nodded. "Yes. She told me she wanted to. I've learned a lot about your church since we last saw each other, especially on the long journey from Australia to America. I've even read the Book of Mormon you gave me."

"And what do you think about what you've learned?"

She smiled. "I find much of it similar to what I was taught as a child in the Methodist Sunday School. However, the idea of heavenly messengers coming to earth in this century takes some getting used to. Other than that, the restoration of the gospel makes sense. I faithfully attended services aboard the ship from Australia, and by the time I reached San Francisco, I was almost persuaded to apply for baptism."

Nell paused and looked at Ken seriously. "However, I'm not sure if I could be a member of the Church and continue on the London stage. So much of London society revolves around parties where alcohol and tobacco are present. It would be very difficult; unless, of course, I gave up the London stage. That thought has crossed my mind. Perhaps . . ."

Ken waited for her to go on, but she left her words dangling.

After a long pause, he took a deep breath and said, "I'm glad you're so favorably disposed toward the gospel. It makes what I have to say so much easier." His heart pounded as he continued on. "When you appeared on the stage this evening, I suddenly realized that . . ." He gulped. "That I love you."

Nell took a deep breath and slowly exhaled. "I know you do. I saw it in your eyes when we met tonight backstage. But hearing it from you leaves me speechless. I don't know what to say. I know how much you loved Karen. I didn't suppose . . . I mean I thought . . . that is . . . I think I love you, too."

"You do?"

"I do. I don't know when friendship turned to love, but ever since the day you knocked on the door of the shooting lodge in Scotland, I've felt—how can I put it—an affinity with you. I guess you could say it was 'friendship at first sight.' But, of course, I never admitted that it could ever be more than that. Not even to myself."

"When did you realize that it could be more than friendship?"

She thought for a moment before answering. "I guess it was when we parted in San Francisco. I didn't want to see you leave my life, but I had promised my husband on his deathbed to marry Lionel, and I felt I must conceal my feelings for you. I felt very torn." She paused. "Surely you must have known something in San Francisco. I must have let something of my feelings show."

Ken shook his head. "No. You really are a very good actress. When I left you in San Francisco to return to Utah, I felt completely desolate. I guess my heart was telling me the truth, and my mind was denying it. Nevertheless, I'm glad we did the right thing and went our separate ways for a time. Now we can be together without regret." Ken smiled. "Although I was oblivious to your feelings for me, others were not."

"Others?"

He nodded. "Especially Karen."

Her mouth fell open. "Oh, no. I tried my very hardest to make sure that our friendship would not be misinterpreted, especially by Karen. Strange, but I also had a strong feeling of affinity with her. I wouldn't for the world have wanted to worry her in any way."

Ken shook his head. "She wasn't worried, only a little jealous." Ken thought of Karen's hint that Nell would make a good wife and mother. He wondered if now was the appropriate time to share this, but he decided against it—at least for the present.

He slipped his arm around her shoulder, and for a long time they basked in the glow of the feelings they now knew were shared. They talked on into the night, recalling the history that had led them to this bench by the Victoria Harbor. Suddenly, the moon slid behind the clouds, plunging the harbor into darkness. Nell leaned into Ken's shoulder, and he knew he was resolved to love and protect her always. At length, Ken reluctantly suggested that the time was late and that he should get her home.

"Where are you lodging?" he asked.

Nell smiled. "I wasn't joking about having a key to the castle—Craigdarroch Castle."

"That's right. Sara mentioned that you were staying in a castle. I was surprised to hear that there is a castle in Victoria."

"It's a new one. Just before he died, a Mr. Dunsmuir, who made a fortune on coal, built it for his wife. I met Mrs. Dunsmuir last year when she and her daughters were in England—Oh, I think I already mentioned them to you at the lake."

Ken nodded. "I remember. I'm surprised they invited you to stay with them on such a short acquaintance."

"Well, Mr. De Cosmos had something to do with it. I mentioned to him that I'd met the Dunsmuirs, and the next thing I know a carriage shows up at my hotel to take me to the castle." She smiled. "Craigdarroch is rather small as castles go, but with four and a half stories and thirty-nine rooms, I'm hardly in the way."

"I can't wait to see it."

"It's such a pleasure to reside—even for a short while—in a *new* castle after the years I've spent in old, drafty castles and manor houses in England. Mr. Dunsmuir spared no expense. Craigdarroch Castle has all the modern conveniences, such as central heating, and is decorated with lovely paneling, stained glass windows, and luxurious drapes and furnishings. Several of the fireplaces have stained glass windows above the mantels."

"Where the chimney is? How can that be?"

Nell smiled. "I asked the same question. Apparently, the concealed flues are bent out and go up either side of the window. Also, it has speaking tubes in the walls, so you can talk with people on the floors above or below you. They even have a telephone. It's truly a modern castle—the best of both worlds." Nell rose. "Come, let me show it to you."

Ken took her outstretched, gloved hand, and the two of them, filled with the warmth of requited love, strolled along the esplanade. As they rounded a corner, Ken stopped, listening to the darkness. Nell clutched his hand a little tighter, but after a moment, Ken shook his head, and they continued walking. Suddenly, a dark figure leapt from the shadows and blocked their way. Nell screamed and clung to Ken.

"Gandy!" Ken exclaimed.

"The very same," Jacob Gandy said, his scarred face twisted with mirthless glee. "M'guv's got unfinished business w' ye."

Gandy smiled as he made a quick motion. "'Ave at 'em, mates," he growled.

Before Ken and Nell knew what was happening, they were attacked from behind. Excruciating pain shot into Ken's skull from a crushing blow to the back of this neck. Nell's scream was the last thing he heard before he descended into blackness.

Sometime later Ken awoke in a darkened room. The pain in his head instantly reminded him of the attack. The room seemed to rock, and at first he thought it was due to his injury, but he soon realized that he was in the hold or cabin of a boat. Except for a gentle scraping noise, all was silent. As his eyes became accustomed to the semidarkness, he glanced around. Nell was lying a few feet from him. He moved to go to her, but his hands and feet were tied with rope. Crablike, he crawled over to her. A strong medicinal smell exuded from her.

"Chloroform," he said out loud. "Nell, Nell! Wake up." He pushed her with his shoulder, but she remained unconscious. "Gandy!" he yelled.

Gandy didn't answer. Ken finally sat back, dizzy from the raging pain in his neck. After about half an hour, voices above brought him alert.

"Sanderson too!" an exultant voice from above exclaimed. "Brilliant, Gandy. You'll get a bonus for this. Let's get under way."

Although it had been five years, Ken recognized the voice.

"Langton!" Ken yelled.

There was no reply, and soon the sound of the steam engine drowned out his cries. After a long time on the water, the noise ceased, and Ken assumed they had reached their destination. Nell still had not awakened from her chloroform-induced sleep.

"Bring her up first," Ken heard Langton say. "I'll take her ashore in the dinghy and come back for you and Sanderson."

Jacob Gandy lurched down the stairs, and, without a word, he grabbed Nell and threw her over his shoulder.

"Get your filthy hands off her," Ken cried.

Ignoring Ken, Gandy carried Nell up the stairs. In throbbing pain and full of apprehension for Nell's safety, Ken lay helplessly waiting for Langton to return. After twenty minutes he returned and ordered Gandy to bring Ken up to the deck.

"Right," Gandy said, as he drew a knife from a sheath at his belt and cut the rope binding Ken's ankles. "On yer feet. M'guv's lookin' forrard t' seein' ye again."

Gandy roughly pulled Ken to his feet and pushed him up the companionway. In the moonlight, Ken recognized Peregrine Island.

Chapter 27

A loud disturbance caused Laird Mackenzie to look up from the paperwork on his desk. He sighed. *What is it now?* Wearily, he got up and went into the outer office. Sergeant Yates was trying unsuccessfully to calm down a clearly distraught woman.

"He's murdered! He's murdered! M'lodger's murdered," the woman wailed over and over.

Taking the woman firmly by the arm, Laird directed her to a chair in his office and sat her down. "Get her a cup of tea," he said over his shoulder to the sergeant. "Now, ma'am, tell me your name and who's been murdered."

It took a while, but Laird finally learned that the woman was Mrs. Mary Connelly and her lodger was one Ward Peek, a small-time actor who had been knifed to death. The killing took place in the landlady's boardinghouse on the shadier side of Victoria.

"Did you get a good look at the perpetrator—the murderer?" Laird asked.

"Aye, later I did," the woman said. "At first a slouch hat an' 'is collar pulled up 'id 'is ugly mug, but in the fight wi' Wardy 'is 'at comes off and 'is collar comes down. But 'e covers up when 'e sees me. But I gets a look at 'im—a 'ulking, big brute w' scar from eye t' chin."

"Had you ever seen him before?"

"Never."

Laird considered this for a moment before asking, "Have you any idea why this man would kill your . . . your lodger?"

The woman hesitated, averted her eyes, took a sip from her teacup, and said, "None."

Laird pursed his lips and said, "Do you want us to find the perpetrator?" he asked.

She looked at him through narrowed eyes. "Course I does. That's why I'm 'ere, ain't it?"

"Well, if you want us to find the murderer, you'd do well to tell the truth. Now, I ask you again, "Do you know why Mr. Peek and the scarred man fought?"

Mary Connelly heaved a heavy sigh. "Well, I guess it ain't no odds tellin' ye now 'at Wardy's gone. The big brute tol' Wardy 'e'd get no more money from 'is guv an' it was worth 'is life if 'e went to the police."

"I don't understand. Was Mr. Peek trying to blackmail someone? Maybe you'd better start from the beginning. What hold had Mr. Peek on the murderer's governor? And who was his governor?"

The woman's knowledge of the affair was somewhat sketchy, but over the next few minutes, Laird learned that an unidentified man had hired Ward Peek to pose as his agent. Peek had been paid a good sum of money to perform the acting job and had promised Mrs. Connelly that he'd pay his back rent. The lodger, however, gambled the money away. When Mrs. Connelly threatened to call the police and have Peek evicted, the latter said he would get the rent money. He said that there was something "fishy" about the man who'd hired him and that he would press him for more money on threat of going to the police.

"Hold it," Laird said at this point. "How did Mr. Peek communicate with the man he was trying to blackmail?"

"Don't know," the woman said. "Alls I know is Wardy says there was more money from where the first money come from, and 'e was goin' t' get it and pay 'is back rent."

Laird considered this for a moment. "And the scarred man showed up in response to the blackmail attempt?"

"Aye. When 'e comes t' the door, Wardy shoves me into a back room and tells me to shut m' mouth. But I peeps out and sees him, 'is face all covered up. I stays 'id and 'ears the big brute tell Wardy there'll be no more money. Then I 'ears Wardy say, 'Git out or I'll slit t' other side o' your face. Then I 'ears fightin'. That's when I looked out and sees the big man stab Wardy w' 'is own knife."

"With Mr. Peek's knife?"

"Aye."

"Was Mr. Peek wont to carry a knife?"

"Aye. An' 'e knowed how t' use it. 'E'd've made short work o' 'im if the murderer 'adn't been such a big brute."

"Did the perpetrator—the scarred man—see you?"

"Aye. After 'e murders Wardy. 'E sees me peepin' out. That's when I sees 'is ugly mug. 'E comes after me, but I slams the door in 'is face. 'E tried t' break it down, 'e did. But I screamed bloody murder an' scares 'im off. Been frightened fer my life ever since."

Laird thought for a minute before saying, "And you're sure Mr. Peek said he'd slit the other side of the man's face before the hat came off and the collar up?"

"Aye."

"So apparently Mr. Peek must have seen the man's face before— probably he's the one who hired Mr. Peek, and Peek saw through the disguise."

A knock sounded at the door, and Sergeant Yates stuck his head in. "Mr. De Cosmos is here to see you, sir."

Frustration filled Laird's face. "Not now, Yates," he said. "Politely tell him I'm busy."

The sergeant persisted. "He says it's very important, sir. I think this time he really means it."

Laird sighed. "All right, show him in."

De Cosmos marched into the office, acknowledged the woman with a curt nod, and said, "Inspector Mackenzie, Miss Keene is missing. She did not return to her lodgings last night and did not show up at the theater for rehearsals this morning. This is altogether too much. You must do something forthwith. Being kidnapped in San Francisco is understandable, but being kidnapped in Victoria is intolerable."

Laird was about to correct Mr. De Cosmos by explaining that Nell hadn't actually been kidnapped in San Francisco, but he thought better of it.

"Don't worry, sir," Laird said. "Miss Keene is in good hands. She was with Mr. Sanderson after the theater performance last night. Mr.

Sanderson has been staying at our home. When he didn't come home last night, Mrs. Mackenzie and I speculated that perhaps he and Miss Keene eloped. This morning Sergeant Yates suggested that they might have done so on the *Serenity*. He saw them at the dock late last night. The ship sailed for Honolulu with the tide early this morning. I'm sure we'll get word from them eventually."

"Eloped?" Mr. De Cosmos said, his bushy brows arching. "What is this world coming to? Have propriety and responsibility gone out the window?" He shook his head and added, "If Miss Keene communicates with you, I want to be informed immediately. And let her know in no uncertain terms that I am extremely cross with her. Good day, sir."

Laird breathed a relieved sigh and glanced at the woman, who had remained quietly sipping her tea during the whole exchange.

"Where were we?" Laird asked.

The woman shrugged her shoulders. "Don't know. But I wants t'know who's gonna pay Wardy's back rent."

Suddenly, Laird had an inspiration. "What did Ward Peek look like?" he asked.

"Look like?"

"Yes. Was he tall, short, skinny, fat?"

"Well, Wardy weren't tall and 'e weren't skinny."

"So he was short and fat. Did he have much hair?"

"Not much."

"So he was bald. Do the names Selwyn Langley or Cecil Hardy mean anything to you?"

The woman dropped her eyes to her teacup. "Can't say they does."

"Can't say or won't say?"

"Well, I may've 'eard of 'Ardy afore."

"Thank you, Mrs. Connelly. Leave your address at the desk, and we'll be in touch."

"Who's gonna pay—?"

Laird hustled the woman out of his office. "Yates," he yelled, "send Simpson to get the *Prince Albert* ready to sail and then take down this woman's complaint about back rent."

Chapter 28

A groan brought Ken out of a half-sleep.

"Nell," he whispered in the darkness. "Nell."

"Where are we?" she said groggily. A clanking noise told Ken she'd found that her wrist was anchored to an upright joist. "What's this?"

Ken yanked at his chain. "We're chained in the cellar of Langton's house on Pergrine Island. Do you remember I told you about coming here before I saw you at the Hawkinses' place?"

"I remember. So you were right all along."

"I'm afraid so. Langton must have hired the short, bald man to impersonate the agent of the fictitious Selwyn Langley—"

Ken stopped speaking as the trapdoor above them squeaked open, and someone started down the stairs carrying a lantern.

"So, Nell," Stephen Langton said, "you're awake." The shadow cast by the lantern in his hand accentuated the dark circles beneath his eyes and gave him an even more sinister appearance. His lips formed a twisted grin. "I was beginning to think Gandy and his hirelings gave you a mite too much chloroform."

"Release us this instant," Nell cried. "You must be mad to think you'll get away with such an outrage."

"Oh, I'll get away with it," Langton said casually. "I had five long years in Newgate to think out the whole thing. I was still in prison when I heard about your American tour. I guess I should thank you because you motivated me even more to get out. Once out, I came here and began building this place just for you two. I originally had planned to snatch you in San Francisco after the dinner at the British embassy and bring you here."

Langton walked to where Nell was chained and reached out a hand to stroke her cheek, but she violently pulled away. His smile broadened, and he continued. "With your stage run over, no one would miss you. I even planned to have your personal things removed from your hotel room and your maid shipped back to England. Everybody would have thought you'd gone to Australia." Langton turned his vengeful eyes on Ken. "I planned to use Nell as bait to trap you, Sanderson. It's amazing what one can do with money. It was a perfect plan, except you recognized me at the dinner."

"Anybody connected with the theater would have spotted that false beard," Nell said scornfully.

Langton scowled. "When you disappeared after I saw you at the ferry and no one seemed to know where you'd gone, I returned to my new home to rethink my plans—"

"And where is that?" Ken asked. "Your new home?"

Langton ignored Ken's question and turned back to Nell.

"When I learned you were in Victoria," he said, "I could hardly believe my good fortune. And then, when Gandy snatched both of you, I knew the fates were on my side."

"We know who's on your side, Langton, and it isn't the fates," Ken said with disgust. "Enough of this. Release us and have an end to this charade."

"Release you?" Langton sneered. "You don't understand, Sanderson. You're in my power, and here you'll stay. You two made me rot in jail for five long years, and now you must suffer the consequences. I swore you'd pay for your treachery. And pay you shall."

"You built this place solely to incarcerate us," Ken said, shaking his head. "You are completely demented."

Langton's lips twisted into a grimace. "After you've been chained down here and survived on bread and water for five years, we'll see who's demented. Gandy—or should I say Mr. Godfrey, Mr. Selwyn Langley's caretaker—will be your jailer. In the meantime, I'll be off to my new home in . . . well, it's not for you to know, but I can assure you the climate is much pleasanter than Peregrine

Island, especially in the winter." He pulled out his pocket watch and glanced at it. "It'll be light in an hour, at which time I'll be on my way." His evil eyes surveyed the room and rested first on Nell and then on Ken, shackled to separate upright pillars. "Revenge truly is sweet," he said.

"Maybe for the moment," Ken said. "But your lust for revenge will land you back in jail where you belong."

"'Revenge is its own executioner,'" Nell echoed.

"I'll not trade words with you any longer, Sanderson," Langton said, ignoring Nell. "Except to say I'll never go back to jail. Depend on it. They won't take me alive."

"He *is* mad," Ken said after Langton had gone upstairs. "If he thinks he can conceal us here for five years, he's completely deranged. Don't worry, Nell. My friend, Chief Inspector Mackenzie, won't rest until he finds us."

With his free hand, Ken reached over to take Nell's hand, but his shackles prevented him from doing so. Nell tried the same and also fell short.

"Ironic, isn't it," she said. "We've found one another again only to be kept apart."

"We'll be together soon," Ken said. "I don't know how, but we will." He paused for a moment and smiled wryly. "'Revenge is its own executioner.' Where did that come from?"

Nell shook her head. "I've no idea. It must be a line from one of the plays I've been in. Or maybe it's from one of the numerous books Lord Darnley had me read when he was grooming me for society and for better acting parts. I must have read—"

An angry yell from above interrupted Nell's words.

"You think she saw your face?" Langton screamed. "You idiot! I told you to cover up that scar."

Ken and Nell couldn't make out the rest of the angry exchange between Langton and Gandy, but it was clear that the conspirators had had a falling out.

"It sounds like Gandy has displeased his master," Nell said after the argument had stopped. "I wonder what Langton meant by, 'She saw your face?'"

Ken didn't answer right away.

"Maybe somebody saw Gandy's scarred face, and Langton's afraid the authorities will trace him through Gandy the same way they did in London. As a matter of fact, I believe I told Inspector Mackenzie—"

The creak of the trapdoor opening interrupted Ken. This time it was Gandy who came down the stairs with a lantern. He placed the lantern on the floor. For a long moment, he stood staring at Nell.

"What do you want, Gandy?" Ken demanded.

Gandy turned to Ken and looked at him for a moment before saying, "M'guv wants her aboard the boat."

Nell gasped.

"Why?" Ken demanded. "I thought he was going to keep us here for five years."

Gandy shook his head. "Things 'ave changed."

"What do you mean, 'things have changed'?" Ken asked.

Gandy didn't answer, and Nell said, "Why do you let Langton bully you the way he does?"

Gandy stared at her. "Fer the brass, don't ye know?"

"Well, if it's money you want," Nell said, "I have buckets of money." Desperation filled her eyes, and she pleaded, "Send Langton packing, free us, and you can have all the money you want."

Gandy's eyes flickered with interest. Then the light died. "It's too late," he said. "I murdered a man t'other day. I've thrashed many a man, but I've nivver murdered one afore. If I don't do Langton's biddin' 'e'll see me swing fer it. He's no man to cross, is Mr. Langton."

"Did you kill the man on Langton's orders?" Ken asked.

Gandy shook his head. "I was on'y to scare 'im, but 'e came at me w' a gully. I murdered 'im w' it."

"It sounds to me like self-defense, Gandy," Ken said. "Miss Keene and I have powerful friends in Victoria. Free us, and we'll stand up for you."

Gandy's eyes again showed interest, and for a moment, no one spoke. The silence was broken by the squeak of the trapdoor.

"What's keeping you, Gandy?" Langton yelled. "Steam's up. Get her up here now!"

At the sound of his master's voice, the light in Gandy's eyes died once again.

"Right, guv," he said loudly, and under his breath he whispered,

"Sorry, miss. Ye 'ave t' come w' me." He withdrew his knife from its sheath. "Will ye come peaceable like, or do I 'ave t' slit 'is throat?" he asked ominously, gesturing with the knife toward Ken.

Nell glanced at Ken. "I love you," she mouthed, and she didn't protest as Gandy removed her shackles and pushed her ahead of him up the stairs.

In only a few minutes, Gandy was back in the cellar. Without saying a word, he drew his knife and walked toward Ken, who backed up as far as his chain would let him.

"Roll up yer sleeve," Gandy demanded in a lowered voice.

"Why?"

"Cause I'll slit yer throat if ye don't."

Considering the alternative, Ken obeyed, rolling up his sleeve with his free hand. Gandy grabbed Ken's shackled wrist, twisted it to reveal the fleshy part of his forearm, and sliced into it with his knife.

"Ow!" Ken cried. "Why did you do that?"

Gandy ignored the question. As the blood oozed from the wound, he wiped it with a rag. When it was soaked though, he put it and his knife on the floor.

"Gotta han'kerchief?" Gandy asked.

Ken withdrew his handkerchief from his pocket. Gandy took it brusquely and bound up the wound.

"All right," Gandy said. After picking up the bloodstained rag and knife from the floor, he started toward the stairs.

"Wait, why . . . why did you cut me?" Ken called, finding his voice.

"The guv says t' slit yer throat," Gandy said over his shoulder as he began to climb the stairs. "'E'll need proof, won't 'e?"

It dawned on Ken that Gandy had done him a good turn and that Langton's cat's-paw was not as loyal to Langton as he appeared.

"Thank you," Ken said, then added, "Please take care of Miss Keene."

Gandy didn't answer.

Chapter 29

A chill swept through Ken as he heard the launch chug away from the dock. In the ensuing silence, he prayed for Nell's safety and his own. He studied the manacle shackling him to the post and yanked the chain in frustration. It held fast, and he sank to the dirt floor, exhausted from lack of sleep and loss of blood. The bleeding from the cut in his arm had slowed to a trickle, but he felt dizzy and weak. All day long he numbly lay on the cold floor, worrying about Nell and praying for her safety. The throbbing pains in his neck and arm were nothing compared to the pain in his heart.

The prison was filling with shadows when the sound of a steam engine wakened him from a troubled slumber. Had Langton realized he was still alive? Had he returned to finish the job?

Ken remained quiet, but his heart beat against his ribcage at the sound of footsteps coming up the graveled walk. The front door creaked open, and a familiar voice said, "Anyone here?"

"Chief Inspector!" Ken yelled. "Is that you?"

"It is indeed!" Laird Mackenzie responded. "Where are you?"

"Down here—through the trapdoor."

"That looks bad," Laird said, nodding at Ken's bloody arm when he saw it. "How'd it happen?"

"Gandy—the London thug I told you about—cut it. But that's not important. Please, get this thing off me."

"Where's Miss Keene?" Laird asked as he studied the shackle around Ken's left wrist.

"She was taken by Langton, as a hostage I think. We must go after her."

Ken watched impatiently as Laird removed a penknife from his pocket and inserted the smaller of the two blades into the keyhole. In seconds, the manacle opened with a metallic click.

"There. You're free. Let's get to the boat."

Ken leapt to his feet and instantly crumbled. Laird caught him before he hit the floor.

"Steady on, old chap," Laird advised him. "You've lost a lot of blood. Constable Simpson's upstairs. I'll bring him down to help."

With Simpson's aid, Laird helped Ken up the narrow stairs and out to the dinghy.

"Any idea which way Langton was heading?" Laird asked as the constable rowed them to the boat.

Ken shook his head and took a deep breath of the sea air. "His plan was to keep Miss Keene and I locked up here for five years with Gandy as our jailer. But suddenly the plan changed. It had something to do with a woman seeing Gandy's face."

"Mrs. Connelly," Laird said. "It's fortunate for you she did see his face. It helped me solve the riddle of Selwyn Langley and Cecil Hardy—both aliases invented by Stephen Langton. Cecil Hardy was the alias used by a two-bit actor, Ward Peek."

Laird went on to tell Ken what he had learned from Mrs. Connelly.

"I figured as much," Ken said. "When we got to Peregrine Island, I put two and two together. I guess Langton at first tried to do everything through the mail, but he found it impossible and had to hire Peek."

"That's how I figure it," Laird said.

At last they were aboard the police boat. Ken, pale and haggard, accepted a clean towel to wrap his bloody arm, but he refused to go below or have his wound bandaged until they were under way, opting to sit on a life-jacket storage bench outside the wheelhouse. Laird, chart in hand, came and sat beside him.

"We're right about here," Laird said, stabbing a spot on the map with his forefinger. "As you can see, finding Langton among all these islands will be like finding a needle in a haystack. He probably went north, since we came from the south and didn't see him, but he could have doubled back or hidden in any one of a dozen coves. Are you sure he didn't give you any hint as to where he was going?"

Ken racked his fuzzy brain. "Like I said, he planned to leave Miss Keene and me incarcerated while he went off to a new hideout." Ken paused, then said, "He did let slip that the weather would be much warmer than Peregrine Island in the winter."

Laird thought on this for a moment. "That could be several places, perhaps Southern California or Mexico. But if I had all his money and wanted to go to a warm climate, I'd choose Hawaii." He tapped the chart with his finger for a moment before saying, "Let's say he is heading for Hawaii. Since he probably went north, he'd have to take the inside passage, round the north end of Vancouver Island, and head southwest. Is his boat big enough for the open sea?"

Ken shrugged. "I don't know. I know I wouldn't want to sail the open sea in it. I doubt he'd have enough fuel to take him all the way to Hawaii."

Laird considered this. "Of course, with all his money he may have chartered a seagoing vessel. He may be heading off to meet it now. If he is taking the inside passage, he'll have to go through the Seymour Narrows. We might be able to catch up with him there. His launch is no doubt much faster than this boat, but we have three things going for us. First, he doesn't know we've found him out; second, he probably won't travel at night; and third, the narrows will slow him down." Laird turned to the steersman. "We'll take the inside passage, Simpson."

"Aye, aye, sir," Simpson replied.

Turning back to Ken, Laird said, "Now, let me bandage that arm properly before you bleed to death."

As Laird worked on Ken's arm, Ken asked, "Can we travel by moonlight?"

Laird nodded. "Simpson could pilot these waters blindfolded."

Ken leaned over and studied the chart on the bench beside him. His eyes focused on the narrow body of water between Vancouver Island and Quadra Island. "Why would these narrows slow Langton up?" he asked. "They look broad enough for ships to go through."

"Oh, they're broad enough all right, but the tides there are treacherous. In fact, Captain George Vancouver called it one of the vilest stretches of water in the world. The tidal stream narrows into a two-mile-long by half-a-mile-wide stretch, creating a tidal flow of up to sixteen knots an hour. This fast-flowing current passes over giant mountain peaks below the surface, Ripple Rock, creating wicked whirlpools and eddies. Not only that, but during slack water, a ship has to contend with the twin peaks of Ripple Rock just under the surface. Old Rip has plowed the keel of many a ship and sent many sailors to Davy Jones's locker."

"If it's so dangerous," Ken asked, "why would anyone sail there?"

"Going through the narrows cuts the voyage to the north end of the island considerably. It's mostly dangerous for those who don't know what they're doing. A knowledgeable seaman will only go through the narrows during slack water and will take care to avoid Ripple Rock. The alternate route is around huge Quadra Island."

"How far are the Narrows from here?" Ken asked, feeling impatient.

"A fair bit. It will take us all night getting there. The chances are slim that we'll catch up with Langton—if we've even guessed correctly where he's headed. But since Miss Keene's aboard, we'll give it all we've got."

After a short rest in the cabin below, Ken was back up on the deck. Ignoring the throbbing in his arm and the weakness from loss of blood, he clung to the pointed railing, which mimicked the carved figurehead attached to the bow of old sailing ships. Scrutinizing every rocky cove and inlet, he kept his vigil for the rest of the day and well into the night.

Several times he thought he saw Langton's boat, but it was only the moonlight and exhaustion playing tricks on his weary eyes. Near midnight, Laird convinced him to go below to get some sleep. For a long time, he lay awake and finally drifted off, only to be awakened by what sounded like Nell's voice calling over the noise of the boat. He leapt out of bed, dashing up the companionway and onto the deck. He stared out into the night but could see nothing except the black bulk of an island passing on the starboard side. He went into the wheelhouse.

"Did you hear someone calling us?" he asked Constable Simpson loudly over the chug of the steam engine.

"No, sir," the constable said. "Heard nothing out of the ordinary."

Ken returned to his bunk, and, after a while, exhaustion overcame him and he slept. The light creeping through the porthole awakened him next. He went up on deck to find Laird at the wheel.

"How's the arm?"

"Throbbing like the devil."

"Have some coffee . . . oh, wait, you don't drink coffee," Laird said. "Have some milk and biscuits then."

"No thanks," Ken said. "I couldn't eat a thing. Where are we?"

"That's Campbell River flowing into Discovery Passage to port, and Quadra Island to starboard. We're about nine miles from the narrows. If you're up to it, keep a weather eye out for Langton. If we don't catch up with him by the time we get to Maud Island, a small island off Quadra, we're out of luck. Maud marks the start of the narrows."

As the minutes ticked by, Ken's confidence in finding Langton waned. Suddenly, the laboring noise of the engine pulled his eyes from the water, which had begun to roil. He entered the wheelhouse for an explanation.

"The tidal flow's against us," Laird said, anticipating Ken's question. "We'll have to go about at Maud. I'm sorry."

Ken returned to his post for one last look, just as Maud Island came in view. Suddenly his heart leapt as a sleek launch darted around a rocky headland and made for the narrows.

"It's Langton!" Ken yelled, dashing into the wheelhouse. "He's making a run for it."

"I see him," Laird said. "Looks like he's going to try and run the narrows at high tide." He shook his head, incredulous. "He must be out of his mind."

"He said he'd never be taken alive," Ken said.

Constable Simpson joined Ken and Laird at the bridge, and the three watched helplessly as the turbulent waters tossed Langton's launch around like a toy.

"I can't see Nell or Gandy," Ken said breathlessly. "They must be below." Transfixed by the scene before them, neither Laird nor the constable responded. "The dinghy's gone," Ken added.

"He cut it loose to give him more speed most likely." Constable Simpson said.

By this time, the police boat had come to a standstill, the thrust of the engines matching the tidal flow. Langton's powerful boat continued to fight its way against the force of the tide.

"He'll blow his boiler for sure," Constable Simpson said gravely. "To still be moving north, he must have the pressure at maximum. If he pushes it any more, it'll blow."

Ken's heart was in his mouth. The constable's words echoed in his head. With the police boat unable to move forward, they would not be able to save Nell from the narrows, even if she survived an explosion. His eyes focused on a gargantuan whirlpool near the rocky cliffs to the left of Langton's boat, and his heart sank.

Suddenly, before his eyes a column of white steam and smoke tinged with orange and blue flame shot skyward, and Langton's launch literally flew apart. The sound of the explosion reached him a split second later. When the steam and smoke cleared, all Ken could see was splintered wood and other floating debris being slammed against rocks and sucked into whirlpools. There was no sign of Langton, Gandy, or Nell. The three men on the bridge of the *Prince Albert* stared in horror at the flotsam. Ken felt a sickening knot clench in his stomach as he spotted Nell's cloak, tartan side out, become caught in the outer circle of the vortex and spiral around, closer and closer to the concaved center. Then it simply disappeared, swallowed up by the angry waters.

Bile rising in his throat, Ken leaned over the rail and retched. Laird put a comforting hand on his shoulder.

"I'm sorry, lad," he said. After a moment, he added, "We'll wait for slack tide and comb the area, but steel yourself. I doubt we'll find anyone alive."

Laird went into the wheelhouse to speak to Constable Simpson, leaving Ken to his grief.

How could this happen? Ken thought. *How could all the obstacles between Nell and me disappear, only for things to end like this?*

He refused to believe she was dead. For a long time, he clung to the railing, his eyes combing the narrows, hoping against hope that somehow the turbulent waters would give her back to him.

"The tide's turning," Laird said, coming up behind Ken. "Time to start looking . . ." He let the sentence dangle and for a moment was silent. As he went back to the wheelhouse, he muttered bitterly, "At least the narrows have saved the crown the expense of a hanging."

During slack tide, the police boat scoured every cove and inlet of the Narrows, but nothing was found of Langton's boat or its occupants.

As the tidal flow began again, Laird apologetically told Ken that it was time for them to return to Victoria. Except for a brief stop at Nanaimo to take on coal, they would sail nonstop to the capital. Ken nodded numbly. He felt weak in body and spirit.

"Why don't you go below, warm up, and get some sleep," Laird said. "You hardly slept last night."

Ken nodded and obeyed.

Wrapping himself in a gray, wool blanket, he knelt down in the cabin and poured his soul out to his Heavenly Father. He spoke his heart, telling God that losing Karen and Nell a scarce seven months apart was more than he could bear. In abject sorrow, he thought of his motherless children and bemoaned the fact that they, too, would suffer because of Langton's lust for vengeance. He tried to formulate the words that would convince God to give Nell back to him, but the words would not come. The minutes ticked by as he dumbly knelt in silence. Finally, he ended his prayer pleading for the strength to go on.

He climbed into the bunk and waited for the solace of sleep. But sleep wouldn't come. How could this happen to him, to his children? Why had Karen been prompted to hint that Nell would make a good wife and mother when Nell was to join her in death? How could he have had such a positive personal confirmation that Nell and he should marry and then lose her so quickly? He had no answers. Mercifully, his battered body subdued his anguished mind, and a blessed sleep overcame him.

Chapter 30

Ken awoke with a start, unsure at first of where he was. Then the rhythmic churning of the steam engine told him he was still aboard the police boat, and the stark reality that Nell was dead filled his being with blackness. He felt completely abandoned, even by God. As his eyes surveyed the small cabin, they fell on a dozen or so books secured on a shelf attached to the bulkhead. One of them he recognized as the Bible. Climbing out of the bunk, he retrieved it and got back into bed.

Thumbing through the book, he found Isaiah, chapter fifty-four, which Priscilla Reynolds had told him about—the verses that had helped her through the anguish of losing her husband. As Ken read the chapter, involuntary tears clouded his sight. He wiped his eyes with the handkerchief Laird had given him to replace his own, then read the chapter again, focusing on verses seven through thirteen:

> *For a small moment have I forsaken thee; but with*
> *great mercies will I gather thee. In a little wrath I hid*
> *my face from thee for a moment; but with everlasting*
> *kindness will I have mercy on thee, saith the Lord thy*
> *Redeemer . . . O thou afflicted, tossed with tempest, and*
> *not comforted, behold, I will lay thy stones with fair*
> *colours, and lay thy foundations with sapphires . . . And*
> *all thy children shall be taught of the Lord; and great*
> *shall be the peace of thy children.*

These last words brought a fresh surge of tears as Ken recalled Karen's sorrow that she would not be able to raise her children and her plea that the children be raised in the gospel by a kindhearted woman. He had found that kindhearted woman, and now she was gone too.

Tears streamed unabated from his eyes, and although he had faith that everything he was going through would ultimately be counted to him as a blessing, he wondered how he could go on. He quickly wiped his eyes when he heard someone coming down the companionway.

"Will you have a bite to eat, son?" Laird asked.

"No thanks," Ken said dolefully. "How much further to Victoria?"

"A couple of hours. We should be docking in the early evening. Anything I can do for you, lad?"

Ken shook his head. "No. I'll manage. I'll be up in a while."

Ken eventually dragged himself to the deck and spent the next two hours watching the green island shores go by. When the boat rounded Ogden Point and entered the inner harbor, the setting sun had turned the western sky a brilliant orange. The beauty of the scene mocked his mood. As the boat neared the government wharf, Ken could see someone waiting alone on the dock. It looked like a woman. Supposing it to be the wife of one of the crew, he felt even more aware of his bereft state. Turning away, he went aft, where he stared absently at the boat's white wake ribboning the blue-green water.

"Mr. Sanderson, Mr. Sanderson!" Laird exclaimed excitedly. "Come quickly!"

The excitement in Laird's voice caused a surge of hope in Ken's breast. He bounded to the bow, took the proffered telescope from Laird's hand, and trained it on the government dock where Laird was pointing. With shaking hands, he adjusted the focus. His heart leapt. It was Nell, joyfully waving at the boat. Ken grabbed the taffrail for support as overwhelming gratitude surged through his body.

The boat had barely docked when Ken leapt ashore. With unspeakable joy, they ran to one another.

Ken's cut arm ached with Nell's fervent embrace, but it was a small thing compared to the joy in his heart.

"How can this be?" he asked her. "When I saw Langton's boat explode and your tartan-lined cape sucked into the whirlpool, I thought I'd lost you forever."

"And I can't believe you're alive!" she said. "When Gandy came back to the boat with a bloody knife and rag and told Langton he'd slit your throat, I went into a frenzy. While Gandy held me, Langton subdued me with chloroform."

Ken looked at her, still unsure the woman before him was real. Standing on the wharf under a flaming orange sunset, the two clung to each other, thankful at being spared the vengeful wrath of Stephen Langton.

"Let's go inside," Laird called, pointing to a small building with the words "Government Wharf Office" prominently displayed. "There's a direct telephone line to the police station. I'll have Yates send someone to get us."

Inside, Laird made the call and joined Ken and Nell, who were sitting together on a wooden bench. Laird pulled up a chair and also sat down.

"You had this man worried sick," Laird said to Nell, who still clung to Ken, careful to avoid his left arm. "All of us, in fact. Tell us how you extracted yourself from the clutches of Mr. Langton."

"I will, gladly," she said. "Mr. Sanderson has told me all that happened from the time we were separated to the explosion of Langton's boat."

"The explosion was quite a sight," Laird said. "Thankfully, you weren't on the boat."

"And now it's your turn, Nell," Ken said. "How did you escape from Langton?"

"We have to thank Jacob Gandy for that," she said. "If it hadn't been for him, we both would have died in the explosion."

"Gandy?" Ken said. "He's alive?"

Nell nodded.

"Where is he now?" Laird asked.

"At the infirmary. Langton shot him in the upper arm in the struggle, but according to the doctor, the bullet went right through, so there's a good chance he'll recover fully. He's being guarded by a policeman Sergeant Yates posted."

"Good," Laird said. "Please go on."

"Well," she said, "I was tied up below deck in Langton's boat. When Gandy came down to check on me, I asked him to loosen the rope around my wrists, as they were chafing me. He refused. But I remembered that back on Peregrine Island I had had an inkling that Gandy was not as fierce as he looked, so I decided to see if I could charm him. I asked him about his life in London, and it turned out that he actually knew my father when they both worked on the Thames's docks. Once I'd softened him up, I again asked him to loosen the rope, and he did so. Then I pled with him to help me escape from Langton."

Ken took Nell's hand. She smiled at him and continued. "I was making good headway when Langton called him to the deck. The next thing I knew, they were engaged in an awful row. Gandy demanded that I be put ashore, and Langton would have none of it. Then a fight broke out. I managed to wriggle out of my loosened restraints and quietly climb the companionway. When I got to the head of the stairs, I cautiously peeked out and saw Gandy's knife lying on the deck. Langton was holding a gun on Gandy, who had his back to the railing. 'Jump, Gandy,' Langton commanded. 'Your imbecility has run its course.'"

Ken suppressed a smile at Nell's delivery of Langton's words. *Ever the actress,* he thought.

Nell went on. "Gandy refused to budge. Suddenly, he noticed me, and his glance gave me away. Langton turned toward me, giving Gandy the chance to lunge at him. While they wrestled for the gun, I darted onto the deck, picked up the knife, ran to the stern, and leapt into the dinghy. I quickly cut the painter and rowed for all I was worth until I got a rocky headland between the launch and me. I had no sooner done so than the sound of a shot echoed across the water, followed closely by a loud splash.

"All this time, the launch had been drifting toward the headland. I heard the engine engaging, and I supposed that whoever was at the helm, Langton or Gandy, was moving the boat to deeper water. I rowed back around the headland and saw the launch steaming up the channel. Gandy was in the water surrounded by a slick of blood and, amazingly, still afloat. I rowed over to him. His bloody left arm was useless, but with his good arm he clung to the boat until I could beach it. We spent a miserably cold night on what I later learned is Denman Island."

"You've obviously rowed before, Miss Keene," Laird said admiringly.

Nell smiled at Ken. "I have," she said. "As a girl, I rowed for my father on the Thames. I even gave Mr. Sanderson a lesson when we were on Loch Lomond. When I towed Gandy ashore, it took me back to the days when my father and I would tow corpses to land."

Laird looked a bit taken aback but nodded.

"Tell me," Ken said, directing the conversation back to Nell's escape. "Did you see or hear a boat passing by last night?"

"I did. I screamed my lungs out, but it just chugged on past."

"So I wasn't imagining it," Ken said. "I scrambled up on deck and could see the black outline of an island but could hear nothing above the noise of the engine. The noise must have also drowned out the sound for Constable Simpson, who was at the helm."

"How did you get to Victoria ahead of us?" Laird asked.

"A fisherman picked us up early this morning and brought us directly here. I managed to get Gandy to the infirmary and then went straight to the police station, where I told Sergeant Yates everything."

"Our transportation is here," Laird said as a carriage pulled up.

Ken and Nell were alone in the carriage as Laird sat with the driver. Ken held fast to Nell's hand, unwilling to let go even for a moment. Nell said, "It's hard to believe that Langton's new boat would blow up. How could that happen?"

"According to Constable Simpson, Langton pushed the pressure to the breaking point in an attempt to fight his way through the strong tidal current of the Seymour Narrows. He could have surrendered to the police, but as we know, he said he'd die before going back to prison."

"I guess it's all over," Nell said and leaned back in relief. "I tried not to think about Stephen Langton over the years, but his threats against you, Karen, and me never really left the back of my mind. When I heard he escaped from prison, of course my concern heightened. But I thought I was safe in America. I'm so glad it's finally over." She paused. "But I do have one great regret."

"What is that?"

Nell's hazel eyes twinkled. "I really did like that tartan-lined cape."

Ken smiled. "When I saw it disappear into the whirlpool, I thought you were gone."

She tenderly touched his sleeve and smiled. "You needn't have worried. As I told Marian before we parted, I always land on my feet."

Ken smiled and hugged her to him. "I'll buy you a dozen tartan-lined capes," he said.

Nell lay her head on his shoulder. "One will do."

Chapter 31

"When will you marry?" Marjorie Mackenzie asked Ken and Nell at supper in the Mackenzie home two days later.

Nell let Ken answer. "After Nell is baptized a member of my church, we'll be able to marry in the temple," Ken said.

"Ah, yes," Laird said. "Your father told me that both must be members of your church in good standing before you can enter the temple. But aren't you still working on the temple in Salt Lake City?"

"We are," Ken said. "But there are three other temples in operation."

Laird nodded. "We wish you the very best. Will you be going directly to Salt Lake City after the Ward Peek inquest?"

"Soon after," Nell said. "I just have two more performances in Victoria, and then my understudy will take over and complete the run."

"How does Mr. De Cosmos feel about that?" Mrs. Mackenzie asked with a smile.

"He's acquiesced," Nell said. "He's actually not a bad sort and, as you no doubt know, his bark's worse than his bite."

The next morning at ten, the inquest over the death of Ward Peek commenced. Coroner Erastus O. Carmichael, a long-faced, gaunt old man, presided. Mrs. Connelly and Jacob Gandy were the only witnesses, and Ken, Nell, and Laird the only spectators.

"Please tell us all you know of this unfortunate incident," the coroner asked Mrs. Connelly.

The landlady adjusted her flowered Sunday hat and took a deep breath before launching into her story, the same one she'd told the chief inspector—except for a few time-grown embellishments.

"Is the man who stabbed Mr. Peek in this room?" the coroner asked when the landlady had finished her testimony.

"Aye," she said, pointing at Jacob Gandy. "That big brute w' the bad shoulder."

The judge scowled at the witness. "Temper your language, if you please, madam," he said. "You say that this man, Jacob Gandy, threatened Mr. Peek when the latter demanded money."

"Aye, sir."

"Then Mr. Peek pulled out a knife and threatened to cut Mr. Gandy's face, and the two men commenced fighting?"

"Aye, yer honor, Wardy was a wee, fat man, but he knew how to defend hisself."

"Obviously not well enough," the coroner muttered under his breath, and then in a louder voice he said, "Thank you, Mrs. Connelly, you may step down. Mr. Jacob Gandy to the stand."

Gandy's testimony paralleled that of Mrs. Connelly. When he had finished, the coroner took only a few minutes to come to a conclusion. "It appears that Mr. Jacob Gandy did indeed act in self-defense. However, there is still the matter of his other crimes, which are beyond the jurisdiction of this inquest. I assume that Mr. Gandy will be bound over to face these charges."

The coroner looked to Laird to confirm this.

"Yes, sir," Laird said. "However, Miss Keene and Mr. Sanderson have spoken on Mr. Gandy's behalf, and the crown prosecutor will stay these charges in light of Mr. Gandy's involvement in helping Miss Keene and Mr. Sanderson escape from Stephen Langton." Laird turned to glare at Gandy. "However, if Mr. Gandy is involved in any further infractions, the whole weight of the law will descend upon him."

"Thank you, Chief Inspector Mackenzie," the coroner said. "My final judgment in this case, then, is death by misadventure. The Ward Peek inquest is at an end."

"Thank you for what you did, Gandy," Ken said later when the coroner and Mrs. Connelly had left the room.

Gandy, his right hand clasping his left shoulder, winced as he twisted his body to face Ken and Nell. With his eyes down, he said, "And thanks to ye as well. If Miss Keene hadn't come fer me, I'd be fish food for sure."

"What will you do now, Mr. Gandy?" Nell asked

"Don't know," Gandy said. "'Aven't got two brass farthin's. Get work on the docks, I s'pose, when m'wing 'eals."

"You'll need money to get you by until then," Nell said. "I promised you money if you helped Mr. Sanderson and me. You fulfilled your end of the bargain, and I will fulfill mine."

Gandy shook his head. "'Twouldn't be right, miss," he said. "If it 'adn't been fer ye, I'd be a goner. 'Twas me wot stole ye and Mr. Sanderson off the dock. 'Twouln't be right. Not after ye saved me miserable hide."

"Be that as it may," Nell said. "You'll need money for food and lodging, and we wouldn't want you breaking the law to get it. Here's twenty pounds. Consider it a loan. You can pay me back when you get working."

At the mention of money, Mrs. Connelly appeared out of nowhere and eased back into the room.

"Speaking of working," Laird said, "how would you like to use your . . . ah . . . talents on the right side of the law?" Gandy's face showed interest, and Laird went on. "We're in need of a . . . special constable to patrol the docks at night and keep drunken sailors in check. Are you interested?"

Gandy grinned. "Aye, guv," he said. "I'm yer man."

"Good," Laird said. "Come to my office when you're feeling better, and we'll work out the details—but remember, the charges of causing grievous bodily injury and kidnapping are still hanging over you. As you heard, Miss Keene and Mr. Sanderson have generously arranged for these charges to be stayed, and the crown prosecutor has agreed. But one misstep and you'll be locked away for good."

"Aye, guv," Gandy said, his head bowed and a penitent look on his scarred face. Then he looked up and grinned. "Just think. I've been dodgin' crushers all m'life an' now I'm gonna be one. Who'd ave thought?"

"A word afore ye go, Mr. Gandy, sir," Mrs. Connelly chimed in, sidling up to him from the shadows. "Now 'at ye 'ave a promise o'work, you'll be wantin' lodgin'?"

Ken, Nell, and Laird exchanged smiles that the "big brute" had suddenly become "Mr. Gandy, sir."

"Aye, I will, that," Gandy said.

"Then come w' me, sir," the landlady said, taking Gandy's good arm, "an' I'll show ye m'first class 'stablishment."

Laird smiled as the landlady and her potential lodger exited the room. "I've no doubt Gandy'll be able to handle drunken sailors," he said wryly, "but will he be able to handle Mrs. Connelly?"

* * *

"I guess you were right after all," Nell said to Ken as they took their seats on the train heading for Salt Lake City.

"About what, love?" Ken asked.

"About patiently waiting for God's blessings. When we parted in San Francisco, I thought I'd never see you again. But here we are, betrothed and soon to be married."

He took her hand in his and said, "Except for how I felt when Karen died, I don't think I've ever felt so lost as I did that day. Even though I knew I was doing the right thing in returning home, it was a bitter pill. The night before I left, I contemplated trying to stop you from going to Australia and marrying Sir Lionel. But you'd given your promise to Lord Darnley, and I didn't feel it my place to interfere. I'm glad I left things in your hands and God's. Besides, I was in no condition to make a commitment to you. I was still numb from Karen's death."

Nell nodded sympathetically. She said, "When a theatrical agent approached me to go on the stage in Sydney, I was thrilled at the offer. I even went out to see an estate with the intention of renting it. But when I knelt down and prayed about it, I had second thoughts. Then, when I found Mr. De Cosmos's letter of invitation in the Book of Mormon you gave me, I knew exactly what to do." Nell snuggled closer against Ken on the railroad carriage seat and sighed. "How will your mother and all the rest receive me, do you think? They all loved Karen so much."

"We'll soon see. When I wired them, I told them what train we'd be on. But I have no doubts about their reception; they'll love you as I do. And as Karen did."

"As Karen did?"

Ken smiled. "I guess it wouldn't hurt to tell you now about a conversation I had with Karen before she died. Although she didn't come right out and say it, she hinted that you would make a wonderful wife and mother."

"Me? Really? Did she say why?"

"In a way. She praised you to the skies and couldn't say enough about how well you got along with Ainsley and Gage. Karen's greatest regret was not being able to raise her children. She hinted that you would raise them properly."

Nell was silent for a moment. Then she turned to look into Ken's eyes.

"I hope I'll be a good mother, but the prospect both delights and scares me. Nevertheless, I will devote myself to raising your children . . . and *our* children if we're so blessed." She looked thoughtful before adding, "Poverty drove me onto the stage, and abundance has released me from it."

"That sounds like a line from one of your plays."

She shook her head and smiled. "No. I thought of it all by myself."

"You'll make a wonderful mother. Ainsley said she likes you, so that's a good start."

Nell squeezed Ken's hand. "Why didn't you tell me before about your conversation with Karen? It would have relieved my guilt in having feelings for you. Even though you were a widower, I still felt guilty . . . that somehow I was betraying Karen."

Ken shrugged and leaned forward to tenderly kiss his future bride's forehead.

"I guess I didn't want to influence you unduly. If I'd told you that Karen hinted that we should be together, it would have put pressure on you. I knew that you would have to receive your own inspiration. I'm telling you now because I don't want you ever to have doubts about the propriety of our marrying. I've heard that when a widow or widower remarries, the memory of the late spouse sometimes comes between the new couple. I want you to know that Karen approves of our union, so you can rest easy on that score."

"Thank you. It does help. And I want you to know that for my part, Karen's memory will never come between us."

For a while they enjoyed a companionable silence as the train chugged its way to Zion.

"I'm glad you want to have children," Ken said. "I recall you telling me of that desire—I think it was at the end of our journey from Scotland to London—and I remember sincerely hoping that your desire would be fulfilled. Ironically, we may fulfill it together. Do you think you'll miss acting and the applause that goes with it?"

"Maybe a little, but no matter," Nell replied. "Perhaps when the children are all grown, I'll return to the stage—maybe play some meaty roles, like Lady Macbeth."

Ken laughed. "I can't see you as the 'fiend-like queen.' But a queen you are, and I'll ever be grateful to Heavenly Father rescuing for you from Langton and reuniting us."

Nell smiled and laid her head on his shoulder. "Who needs applause when I have you?"

* * *

"Surprise!" many voices exclaimed as Ken and Nell stepped off the train at Ogden. Tears sprang to Nell's eyes, and her apprehension about being accepted dissipated like frost before the warmth of the sun. She dabbed her eyes, moved to see so many smiling faces: Ainsley and Gage, Gren and Elisabeth with baby Karen in their arms, Maggie and Jack, and Jonathan, Doris, and their children. All these and a host of other relatives and friends surrounded the couple.

Nell's heart was full to overflowing, especially when Ainsley and Gage rushed into her outstretched arms.

Nell Keene, the girl who had grown up in poverty in the slums of London, whose talent and beauty had thrust her to the apex of fame and fortune, had finally found a home in the mountains of Utah—and a love that she knew would last through eternity.

Author's Note

The Vancouver Island setting of this book came about from a casual question from one of my friends: "Why don't you write about where you live?" So I did. Considering my praise for the Vancouver Island scenery, I trust readers won't think that the Vancouver Island tourist board has paid me to drum up business.

Incidentally, the twin peaks of Ripple Rock mentioned in the story were removed in 1958 in the largest peacetime, nonnuclear explosion. The racing tides of the Seymour Narrows, however, are still a menace to unskilled boaters.

If I were to ask readers, "Which one of the characters in this novel is a real historical figure?" they most likely would not choose Amor De Cosmos. Nevertheless, De Cosmos was a real person, and I have tried to depict him as accurately as possible. All the facts in the story about him (his name, his stays in Salt Lake City and California, etc.) are historically accurate. As hinted in the text, he finally did cross the line into insanity and had to be institutionalized for the last two years of his life. All other characters are fictional.

Like Karen Sanderson in the story, my first wife, Betsy, died young, leaving me with five of our six children still at home. And like Ainsley, my youngest daughter, Janae, was four years old. Several months after her mother's death, we were on our way to the babysitter's when Janae said for the first time, "I miss Mommy," and dissolved in tears. Although it seems strange that it would take her so long to admit this, that's the way it happened.

Sweet Lavender, written by the popular English playwright Sir Arthur Wing Pinero, was first staged in London in 1888. It was a smash hit and for many years was presented all over the world and made into at least two movies.

About the Author

Tom Roulstone was born in Donegal, Ireland, and lived for a time in Glasgow, Scotland. With his parents and two brothers, he immigrated to Canada, landing at Halifax on his thirteenth birthday. He joined The Church of Jesus Christ of Latter-day Saints in Toronto when he was eighteen and served a mission in Western Canada. He has a BA in history from Brigham Young University and an MA in history from Utah State University. After teaching college for almost a quarter of a century, Tom took early retirement to pursue a writing career. This is his fifth LDS novel and third in the *Passage of Promise* series. He and his late wife, Betsy, have six children and eight grandchildren. In 2005, Tom married Serenity Borrowman in the Salt Lake Temple. They currently live in a home overlooking Long Lake on Vancouver Island, British Columbia.